# THE FOURTH VICTIM

## JOHN MEAD

The Book Guild Ltd

First published in Great Britain in 2018 by
The Book Guild Ltd
9 Priory Business Park
Wistow Road, Kibworth
Leicestershire, LE8 0RX
Freephone: 0800 999 2982
www.bookguild.co.uk
Email: info@bookguild.co.uk
Twitter: @bookguild

Typeset in Adobe Garamond Pro

Printed and bound in Great Britain by CPI Group (UK) Ltd, Croydon, CR0 4YY


ISBN 978 1912575 367


British Library Cataloguing in Publication Data.
A catalogue record for this book is available from the British Library.

*Dedicated to my colleagues, family and friends,*
*for all their support and advice.*

*'victim: noun \ 'vik-təm\ 1. The moment you tell everyone you have a mental disorder, in order to excuse your behaviour.'*

*– Shannon L. Alder*

# 1

The shopping trolley, filled with her week's shopping, was heavy and Essey missed Solomon's help. She missed his company, his laughter; life was lonelier and smaller since he had passed away a year ago. Returning from the shops through the park always brought back memories of her dead husband. It was not a warm day and Essey wore her old, navy-blue overcoat tightly buttoned, even so walking into the shadow of a stand of trees still caused her to shiver and brought her back to the present from the memories of happier days. Automatically she glanced around her, taking stock of where she was, surprised she had reached the crossroads of the paths that criss-crossed the small park.

Strange, she thought, someone was lying amongst the trees. Essey's first instinct was to keep moving as occasionally there were drunks, rough sleepers she had learned they were called these days, who used the park as a toilet and resting place. However, this was a young woman wearing tight, clean looking running clothes, laid on her back and staring up at the sky, eyes un-blinking. The stillness of the supine figure drew Essey forward, dragging her trolley off the path to look more closely. 'Are you alright, dear?' she began, but she could see something was wrong, the unblinking eyes told her so.

Joanne Hensley sat on the sofa in her small front room, hunched over and intently peering down at her mobile phone which she held cupped in both hands. She desperately did not want to text her daughter, Lynsey, again. She had once already, without forethought, only half an hour ago. What would her daughter think? Lynsey was nearly eighteen and preparing to live away from home to go to university, what would she think of her mother not coping with her being barely an hour late back from her usual run.

The first text had been an involuntary reflex, she had noticed the time, realised her daughter was overdue and had text, 'Hi, where are you? Dinner as normal?' Then she had started preparing their meal, peeling and cutting vegetables to sit in plastic boxes waiting to be cooked when her daughter returned home. However the lack of any response, so unlike her daughter whose phone seemed an extension of her body, began to gnaw away at her.

A half hour passed. Perhaps her daughter had bumped into a friend and stopped for a chat and a coffee, just like the young woman she had become, independent and social, so unlike her earlier teenage years of misery and isolation. Eventually, increasingly worried at the uncharacteristic lack of response, Joanne had picked up her phone and sat down. Although she did not know what she could say without sounding the overly anxious parent, so for more than ten minutes she had sat rejecting each phrase she came up with. Now she just sat, telepathically willing her daughter to take the initiative and phone. Then the door bell rang.

She jumped, dropping the phone and swearing at her own stupidity, realising how life was going to torment her when Lynsey finally left home, and went to the door knowing her daughter would see through her hurriedly assumed composure. Only as she opened the door did she wonder why her daughter had rung the bell when she had a key, but it was two other young women on the doorstep and not Lynsey. It took Joanne a moment or two to register that the women wore police uniforms: the bulky blue vests, trousers, white shirts, hats and equipment belts. Her mind resisting the implications of what the uniforms might suggest.

'Yes?' was all she could think to say, her tone suggesting she resented their presence although she was acutely aware that she had no reason to feel this.

'Mrs Joanne Hensley?' the slightly older looking police officer, an asian woman, asked. Her companion was fiddling with her phone, exactly like Lynsey, she couldn't even put it down while she was on duty. The phone even looked like the one Lynsey owned, even had the same case.

'Yes,' Joanne's mind had lost the ability to communicate as she focused on the phone in the second officer's hand. Why was the phone sealed in a clear plastic bag? Why did the young constable, a pretty blonde just like Lynsey, scan her face then nod to her companion?

'You have a daughter, Lynsey Hensley?' the first officer asked, barely waiting for Joanne to nod her head in acknowledgment before continuing, 'I am Sergeant Mehta and this is Constable Porter. May we come in?' The sergeant glanced behind her as she spoke causing Joanne to look in that direction and, for the first time, she noticed the tall, slightly overweight man in a suit and tie standing at the gate intently watching the scene play out.

'Who are you?' Joanne asked, annoyed at the man's intrusion.

'Detective Inspector Merry,' the man informed her, his voice calm though authoritative. 'We should go inside.'

The two female officers got her indoors and sat down, with well practised ease. Scanning the room as they entered, checking out the various photos of Lynsey that were dotted around: memories of school, holidays and selfies often taken with a friend or her mother. Any residual doubt in the inspector's mind was banished by those captured memories. The sergeant took a seat beside Joanne on the small sofa while the constable stood at her side and the inspector remained standing, shifting uneasily, in front of the three of them.

'What is it you want?' Joanne demanded, she could understand two uniformed officers coming to tell her that Lynsey was injured in a fall or they had found her phone and were returning it but why send a detective inspector? Then it struck her she didn't want to know what she had known from the moment she had seen the uniforms, the officers, blank faces and concerned eyes. All Joanne really wanted was for everything to go back, for the day to restart again so she didn't have to face what was about to come.

'I am sorry to have to tell you,' Inspector Merry began, noticing the mother's face already starting to crumble and the tears forming in her eyes, 'that a body of a young woman has been found in Swedenborg Gardens. From the details we have taken from her phone we believe this to be your daughter, Lynsey.'

'No, she is out jogging,' her words did not sound right, slurred and masked by her dry throat, her body trembling, her mind fixated on the phone in the police woman's hands. The phone which looked exactly like her daughter's.

'She was wearing a grey top with a zipper front, with a white stripe down each arm, plain black jogging pants reaching to above the ankle and bright orange trainers?' Joanne nodded unable to speak, tears starting to flow, as the sergeant reeled off the description of what her daughter had been wearing, 'Jogger's waist bag, with her keys, student oyster card and five pounds in change, her phone in an arm carrier with earphones.' Joanne tried once again to speak but words would not form, though she nodded in confirmation.

It was then that it came out, the grief erupting from deep inside her. She slipped forward, collapsing onto her knees, tears pouring down her face, her body heaving from the racking sobs. The officers continued to assist her in their well-ordered and distant manner, their own emotions being kept at bay behind their wall of professionalism, but she was not aware of them. She could only focus on the well of swirling black misery that her world had become.

In many respects the day had started well for Inspector Matthew Merry, a promising day he thought as he was determined to remain optimistic, despite what logic seemed to dictate. He'd had a couple of days off, which he'd been able to spend with his wife, Kathy, and his two daughters, starting to make the tree house he had promised his eldest, Becky. The call for a meeting with Chief Superintendent Jackson was no surprise, Matthew hardly set the world alight in the Met's Murder Investigation Team East and a recent bad showing in court, which had nearly undermined a case, hadn't helped. The meeting had been arranged for after lunch and, as the chief superintendent took the concept of agile working to heart, they had met on the balcony of the South Bank Centre. The weather, cold for the time of year, kept the meeting brief which suited Jackson as she was on her way to a roundtable on knife crime at the mayor's office.

Jackson had been cheery and upbeat, she had read the police manuals on people management and ensured she ticked all the boxes so that the inspector would not see her offer of reassignment as anything other than a positive move. He had readily accepted the offer, which threw Jackson off her planned course as she had expected more resistance or at least a counter suggestion. However, Matthew Merry was a realist and had come to terms with the fact that his career had stalled and he was probably more suited to a desk job; as he was, after all, really quite good at logistics and systems. It also had the added benefit of regular office hours and more time with his family. He had made up his mind on the spot but the chief superintendent had decided before the meeting he would need time to consider his options, so they parted and he had taken a stroll down to the Tate feeling like a schoolboy given an unexpected half-day off.

The call from his govenor, DCI Malcolm Swift, telling him to head for Whitechapel to deal with a suspicious death was not entirely welcome but he mentally shrugged and took the opportunity to tell his govenor he was taking the chief superintendent's offer. The pause in the conversation as Swift tried to think of something positive to say pretty well said it all, he wasn't that bothered about keeping Merry in the team but probably thought Matthew should have pushed for something more.

'OK, we'll talk,' was all Swift could think to say, his Welsh accent still detectable despite his years in London, it always reminded Matthew of Tom Jones – he even thought Swift looked a bit like the singer; if the singer had been a six foot three inch black man of Jamaican descent. Merry sent a text to his wife saying he had good news but, despite his expectations, was likely to be home late and then he headed for Mansion House tube station.

Detective Sergeant Julie Lukula arrived at the crime scene within fifteen minutes of being informed by Swift; it was just her luck to have been at Bow Street nick making her the nearest officer in his team available. Seven years in the army, three as a red cap, had taught her that chaos was the normal state of affairs and bringing order to that chaos was the first priority of a professional soldier and was just the same for a police officer. The financial crisis and public sector budget cuts, however, were on the side of chaos and she was not happy to hear that local units had only just beaten her to the scene minutes beforehand.

'The two that called it in, the old lady and the youth, are over there,' the asian uniformed sergeant told her, nodding towards the pair standing with a female officer. 'Constable Porter is taking their details. The paramedic who attended has gone but he and the lad did their best to divert people away from the scene.' As they spoke Julie noticed that uniformed officers were sealing the park entrances and moving people on their way. 'The police surgeon is on her way, the photographer and a forensics team have started work.'

'How long before you arrived?' Lukula wanted to know as she turned to watch two SOCOs erecting a small tent, to retain evidential integrity as much as to conceal the corpse, while another did an initial sweep to safeguard lines of access to the body and the photographer was digitally preserving every aspect of the scene.

'The paramedic was here within five minutes, our first car was forty minutes later,' Sergeant Mehta's expression was resigned. 'You were lucky, we had a suspicious death wait for four hours the other day as it wasn't considered a priority. I take it you will be taking charge now?'

Swift had told Lukula that Merry was his only option at the moment but once an assessment had been made he would reallocate, unless it was a short and simple case. Lukula didn't dislike Merry, he seemed OK, it was just that he gave off a lacklustre vibe and she much preferred the go-getting Swift. Although, to be fair, she and the DCI shared more in common. Swift had been born in the wrong part of Cardiff and, after completing his A levels, had been uninterested in what university could offer so he'd joined the army and done a brief stint with the paras, until being injured. He had subsequently joined the police, quickly rising through the ranks. Lukula, when first appointed to MIT East, had found herself with a slight case of hero worship, fortunately he was male otherwise she might have been starry-eyed with love.

'We'll need officers to canvass the area and someone to collate CCTV,' Julie stated in response to Mehta's question.

'You'll have to speak with my boss,' Mehta informed her, still with the same resigned stare, used to if not liking the fact that her team had a dozen highly important and urgent things to do but with only the manpower to do one. 'Once the scene is secure I really need to be off, we are way past our shift change.'

'We won't hold you up longer than needed, if you can see that forensics have all the support they need,' Lukula saw no reason to berate the sergeant, budget cuts were not her fault, and knew that no one would would actually leave until the replacements had arrived. 'I'll speak to the pair that found her.'

'You won't be leaving her there any longer, will you?' Essey demanded, her voice concerned and worried. 'Someone is missing her, her phone ringing and all. The poor thing has been left there all this time, it isn't decent.'

'Mrs Rawlinson, Mr Kingsley,' Lukula ignored the elderly woman's indignation, 'I'm Detective Sergeant Julie Lukula. I've been told you both found the young woman.'

'I saw her lying in the trees as I was coming back from the shops,' the elderly woman related, she ached from standing for so long and the chill from the breeze wasn't helping her sciatica. 'It was lucky I saw her, I was thinking of how I used to walk through here with my Solomon…'

'I could see that Mrs Rawlinson was in distress,' the young black man at her side gently interrupted. 'She lives on the same floor as my mum and dad in the flats,' he nodded at one of the sixties's high-rise buildings that towered over the small park. 'When I came over I saw the girl. I know first aid and checked to see if she was alright as Mrs Rawlinson phoned for an ambulance.'

'Did you touch or move the body?'

'No, only to check for a pulse,' an almost imperceptible shiver ran through his body at the thought of coming so close to the dead, 'but there wasn't one.'

'You were coming from the flats?' Mr Kingsley confirmed the sergeant's supposition with a nod. 'Did you see anyone else around, as you came in?'

'Only a muslim woman, she was at the entrance, but I couldn't tell if she was going in or coming out. I think she was lost, she seemed to dither then went in before me but turned left to follow the other path out, at least I think she did, I wasn't taking much notice.'

'What did she look like?' Lukula asked making brief notes on her pad, she had learned long ago not to trust to memory.

'Small, wearing a headscarf, one of those hijab things. I didn't take much notice, I'm afraid. Being big and black I tend to find some muslim and white women turn away from me,' he smiled and shrugged, giving Lukula that conspiratorial *hey, we both know how being black works* look but Julie being part French, part Congolese and part Mancunian made no response to show affinity.

'Mrs Rawlinson, I believe you came in from the opposite end, did you see anyone?'

'I wasn't paying much attention, I'm sorry, but I don't remember seeing anyone. It's quiet this time of day, no kids, no drunks, just the odd mum with a pram,' Essey stated, sorrowful that she could not be of more help.

'Sorry to interrupt, but we have an ID,' Sergeant Mehta, walking up, informed Lukula. 'One of the SOCOs got the girl's phone working.' The police surgeon had arrived and, having confirmed life was extinct, was examining the dead girl and had assisted one of the forensic officers to access the girl's phone. The witnesses were escorted home by two constables, where they would take their statements and Mrs Rawlinson, who looked increasingly frail and tired by her experience, could rest and have a cup of tea in the comfort of her own home.

'The phone was in an arm case and, after he checked for prints, the SOCO used the girl's finger to activate the phone. Constable Porter has her name, address, next of kin and life story.' Mehta and Lukula exchanged smiles, both thankful at how technology was a boon to policing; everyone wanting privacy until they were the victim of a crime.

Julie arranged for the sergeant, who was now resigned to working even later and the plans she had for the evening were defunct, to pick up DI Merry from Aldgate East tube and then take him to the dead girl's home. 'You'll recognise him easily enough,' she informed her colleague, 'he's big and looks like he works in an undertakers.' Then she got on the phone to ensure the CCTV from around the area was collected and then back onto

Swift, he could tackle the locals to get more manpower for the house to house.

'Blunt force trauma to the rear of her head,' the surgeon, a calm, cheerful looking, middle-aged woman informed Lukula, as she pulled off her protective clothing. 'You'll have to wait for the PM report for an official time but death was very recent, I'd go as far as to say only minutes before she was found. From the wound to her head I would think it unlikely she survived very long after the blow was struck. There would not have been much blood, just some splatter from the blow, but whoever moved her is likely to have picked up some on their clothing.'

The surgeon held on to the sergeant's arm as she pulled the slip-on covers from her expensive looking shoes, 'Oh, and one other thing, though I'm not certain how relevant this is, she has some old scars on her arms, looks like self-harm to me but it will be in her medical notes.' Lukula nodded, then added her thanks, making a note to contact the coroner about the post mortem.

'I'll put everything I have observed in my report for the pathologist. I'll see it's done today, especially as it is for the rather sexy Swift. Though it all looks straightforward to me,' the surgeon stated, winking. She knew that the younger officers were always somewhat taken aback by the flirtatious nature of what they initially assumed would be a rather staid and matronly middle-aged woman, it was her way of countering ageism.

'Thank you, I'll pass on your good wishes to the govenor,' Lukula told her, keeping her face deadpan in order to call the surgeon's bluff, only causing the older woman to smile.

'Too bloody young,' the surgeon stated, nodding back at the body as she hefted her bag ready to leave. 'What is it about teenagers that so many of them get killed?' She shook her head, not expecting an answer and not receiving one.

# 2

'The mother is in a bit of a state, understandably,' Merry informed Lukula, as he pulled on the protective overshoes and gloves she'd handed him. 'They don't live far, one of the houses over by the canal a few streets away, less than a twenty minute walk. I've arranged for a family liaison officer but for now I've left uniformed with her and said we'd go back later.'

'Lucky you got them to stay,' Julie muttered without sarcasm. 'The surgeon and SOCOs are happy for the body to be moved but I thought you'd want to look first.' Merry nodded but didn't feel that viewing the body helped much. A young, slim, fit looking woman with short blonde hair and a pretty face, the tightness of her running apparel would have attracted glances but now simply emphasised her vulnerability, making her look more like a child than an adult.

'The surgeon believes it was a blow to the back of the head that killed her,' the lead SOCO, pulling down the mask covering his mouth, summarised what had been initially discovered. 'Obviously cause of death is still to be confirmed but the rear of her head is smashed in by a single blow. There is blood on the path and it looks like she was attacked there, the force of the blow is likely to have killed her outright. The drag marks and some more blood suggest she was then pulled into the cover of the trees,' he stated pointing to the marks on the grass as he spoke. 'No obvious signs of sexual assault, although it can't be ruled out at present. We've also found a supermarket bag with blood on it, at a guess I'd say the murder weapon was wrapped in it then discarded after the attack. But no sign of a weapon, as yet.'

The forensic officer paused briefly, waiting for any questions or observations but getting neither went on in his clinical manner. 'If it's OK with you we can get her moved for the post mortem as the coroner's men are here. Although you'll want to know that initial indications are she died only a few minutes before it was called in and the force of the blow suggests she would not have survived more than a couple of minutes if that.' The man's tone and expression was neutral, just another day at the office, his focus was on collecting evidence, the waste of yet another young life was something that only troubled him when he slept.

'We'll need the eastern end of the park throughly searched, and the surrounding streets, looking for the murder weapon. Chances are it's been dumped,' Merry stated, looking round to take in the size of the operation, 'I'll get more officers to assist.' He smiled and nodded his thanks to the SOCO then turned back to Lukula, her hard face studying him, 'What more do you have?' he asked. Rather like DCI Swift the sergeant somewhat unnerved him, she was fit and agile looking, seemingly always ready to take on whatever was thrown at her. She was the opposite of Merry whose first reaction was always to hesitate, to consider options, he was not one to be decisive.

'Not very much I'm afraid, though the surgeon also mentioned some old scarring, self-harm she thought,' Julie, checked her notes as she spoke, ensuring she kept to the facts. 'An old woman and a young man, both live locally in the flats over there, found her. I doubt if the woman could lift a weapon let alone strike someone. She's been arrested a couple of times, some years ago, for drunkenness and public affray, basically fighting with her husband in the street. Nothing on record about the young man, the paramedic who attended first and the uniforms who followed said he was a bit rattled but helpful. The pair are giving statements as we speak. The male witness did mention a muslim woman by the entrance, up the steps over there, but apart from that neither saw anything or anyone else. Oh, and the scene wasn't secure for the first forty five minutes.'

'What do you think, mugging gone wrong?' Merry was watching the small crowd in the distance huddled behind the police tape at the edge of the park and rubber-necking the scene despite the police trying to move them on. 'It won't be long before the press is here.'

'A group of youngsters have been snapping away on their phones since arriving so I wouldn't be surprised if the story isn't already the latest headline,' Lukula pointed out, she would have preferred to have completely shut the small park and portions of the approach roads from the start but they hadn't had sufficient manpower to make it happen until now. 'There is a petrol station with a supermarket just the other side of those trees, to the right, though there is a fence stopping direct access. The main entrance to the garden is just up those steps, where the muslim woman was seen, and on the other side of the trees, where the victim was dumped, is a small play area. As you can see the place is overlooked by two high-rise blocks and the park, especially the path from Wellclose Square leading across to Betts Street, is well used by local residents. The entrances all have CCTV coverage, as does the play area. Not a great place to mug someone and it seems odd they should hang around to move the body but didn't even take the phone off her arm.'

'Don't underestimate the stupidity of the average criminal,' Merry told her, though he agreed with her summation. 'You are getting CCTV and having uniforms canvas the area, I take it?'

Julie nodded, accepting he needed to ask even if they both

knew she had already seen to both things. 'Yes, sir, the govenor has pulled in support and is having an incident room set up at Leman Street nick, the station is half closed down so there's plenty of space. I also assumed you'd be wanting an appeal put out for further witnesses, so I asked for authorisation.'

'Good thinking, Julie,' praise where it is due, Merry thought, hoping he didn't sound patronising. The smile that quickly appeared and immediately faded from Lukula's face telling him he didn't. He was standing next to the markers showing the blood stain on the path, where the SOCOs thought the girl was first attacked, trying his best to envisage how the attack took place. 'It's not the sort of place you lie in wait to jump out on someone, the trees don't give enough cover. Makes you wonder why they bothered moving her at all.'

'Perhaps they hoped she'd be mistaken for a rough sleeper, people tend to give them a wide birth,' Julie suggested, wondering what was exercising Merry's mind.

'Something like that I expect. People won't step over a body but they might walk past one with a clear conscience, so it would give the attacker a few more minutes to get clear,' he agreed with a cynical appraisal of the human race. 'What's more the trees here screen the path from being seen by those high-rise blocks and, though it's only a few yards away, you can't easily see the entrance from here. At this time of day, when mothers are waiting outside the local schools, the playground is likely to be empty and is out of sight from here in any case. It's quiet and has four possible exit routes, more if you are able to climb out over a fence.'

'So a good spot for a mugging then?' Lukula was already starting to suspect the inspector was writing the case off to 'person or persons unknown'.

'Suppose so,' Merry couldn't quite square things in his mind. 'A good place to attack someone but not to hang around waiting to attack them but, if that's the case, it suggests it wasn't a random attack and our victim was targeted. Doesn't seem likely though, does it?' Matthew was almost talking to himself, his voice quiet and low so Julie had to strain to hear him over the rustling of the trees in the breeze and against the rumble of early rush hour cars from the road beyond the park, 'Come on, we need to speak with the mother, hopefully she will be up to it by now.'

The day had been a pleasant one, despite the chill breeze, so much better than the past few weeks of cold, grey, rainy skies. Leanne had been looking forward to cutting through the small park, green spaces were calming, and was disappointed that the park was closed off. Something had happened and the police were there. She hesitated for a moment, curious, but there was a small crowd and she didn't want to know if someone was hurt or ill, she needed her world to be calm and orderly. She clutched at her bag not trusting the youngsters that roamed around in the shifting crowd. People were captivated, like moths to a flame, by the unusual event in their otherwise uneventful neighbourhood.

Leanne resumed her finger exercises, her right thumb repetitively touching each finger tip. Her therapist had said it would help her keep focus, keep her calm and 'in touch' with herself thereby keeping the others at bay. She had kept her part-time job at the Berner Centre supermarket for a few months, which she thought a good sign, so perhaps the doctor coming back into her life was not a bad thing despite her initial concerns and worries. She smiled, happy in her isolation within the crowded city, where everyone diligently ignored each other, unaware she was being watched by a woman in a beige hijab and sunglasses.

Joanne Hensley had that dazed and bewildered look that Merry had seen too often in his work. Joanne's sister, an older, plumper version of her, sat next to her on the sofa holding her hands and making consoling, if ineffectual, noises mixed with the occasional hug.

'Mrs Hensley, I am sorry to intrude again,' Merry began, Lukula was outside being updated by Sergeant Mehta, who was going off duty. 'You remember me, Detective Inspector Merry? I am truly sorry for your loss but I am investigating your daughter's death and need to ask you some questions. I can come back another time if you don't feel up to it at present, it would be understandable, although it would be a great help if you could speak with me now.' Merry was trying to sound sympathetic but felt hypocritical in doing so, he couldn't begin to imagine how the shattered looking woman in front of him felt, and his only real concern was to move the investigation on; time he knew was of the essence before the case went cold.

'Yes, of course, though I don't know what I can say,' Joanne couldn't look directly at the inspector, he was too much a reminder that the events she was living through were real, and stared at a spot in front of his feet instead, 'she was out jogging, like always.'

'Did she jog every day? By the same route?' Matthew asked, seating himself in an armchair, the only other seat in the room.

'Yes, pretty much, though I'm not certain where she ran exactly, she normally went through the parks,' Joanne's face creased as she tried to focus, desperate to make certain she gave every detail she knew as clearly as she could. 'She always said she wanted fresh air not fumes, not easy for her around here of course, with so much traffic.'

'Was she at college or did she work at all?'

'She is just finishing sixth form, doing her A Level exams and is expecting to go to university…' Joanne caught her breath, struggling to hold in her grief as she realised her daughter no longer had a future, could not be referred to in the present tense but now just existed in the past, only a memory to be grieved.

Julie had taken rather a shine to Sergeant Mehta and her no-nonsense approach to the task in hand, mingling with the occasional snide remarks about budget cuts, under-staffing and the 'computer says' attitude of despatch. Julie beamed her best smile at the sergeant, looking for a hint, no matter how slight, of a positive reaction but saw nothing to encourage her. To make up for the disappointment Julie was rather profuse in her thanks for all the support the uniforms had given, and was working up to suggesting she owed Mehta a drink after work when she was cut short by the sergeant's radio sparking into life. Mehta turned around, moving away telling whoever had contacted her that her shift had ended over two hours ago and, having already racked up six hours overtime that week, she was heading back to the station regardless of the urgency of the call.

Joanne tried to be gracious to the detective sergeant as she introduced herself and offered her condolences, however, she struggled to control the sudden rage that unaccountably welled up inside her. It wasn't just Lukula's involuntary smile that had briefly lit up her pretty face, her dark skin and frizzy hair set her apart from Joanne's daughter, but the slim figure and self-assured air reminded her of how Lynsey had been recently. It was how Joanne expected her daughter to have been in ten years time, undaunted and unafraid of the world.

'Joanne, are you alright?' her sister's soft, cajoling tones insinuated themselves into her thoughts, mingling with the inspector's, 'Mrs Hensley?'.

'Yes, sorry,' Joanne looked away from the sergeant, whose face was shocked by the obvious, unlooked for affront she had somehow given the grieving mother. 'What was I saying... yes, her part-time job, just a few hours working in a shop up at the Berner Centre.'

'Any particular friends, a boyfriend perhaps?' Merry asked in his quiet, calm voice, glancing over at Julie who was trying to fade into the background, obviously concerned at the impact she had had.

'She wasn't much into boys, though there was one, Joey, but I think she was backing off,' Joanne paused, again desperate to order her thoughts which seemed all over the place, wondering why the sergeant's brief smile had so upset her.

'She was such an attractive girl,' the sister muttered, a hesitant smile on her lips at the memory, inwardly still giving thanks that it wasn't her own daughter.

'She was moving on,' Joanne went on, 'putting everything behind her. Going to university was going to be a new start for her, a bright future...'

'A "new start"?' Merry gently asked as the mother's voice trailed off. 'From what?'

'From here,' Joanne suddenly roused. 'She had been very young when her father left, only a baby. He didn't keep in contact, which eventually became a blessing and Lynsey seemed to grow up not missing him. She did well at school, had lots of friends, teachers all spoke highly of her, then the bullying started just after she turned thirteen. Nasty, unpleasant texts, comments on her Facebook, that sort of thing at first. I went to the school but they said to just ignore it, that it would pass. Then one day she came home beaten black and blue, blood on her uniform. I called the ambulance and police but she wouldn't say anything, just said she had fallen down and refused to name anyone. Your lot were concerned, said the bruising wasn't consistent with a fall, tried to get her to speak but in the end what could anyone do?'

Lukula slipped out of the room and was on her phone trying to dig up what was on record about the event.

'She retreated into herself,' the mother continued, a fleeting smile at her elder sister who now hugged her, the aunt's indignation and anger at what had happened to her niece all too evident on her face. 'She wouldn't go to school, wouldn't see her friends. I tried to get her into a different school but that didn't help. The attendance officers were very good, supportive but nothing worked. Then I realised she was hurting herself, cuts on her arms and legs,' the mother's tone had become monotone, relating a story she did not have the emotional strength to deal with. 'Our doctor referred her to the mental health people, truth was we were both on anti-depressants by then. Even that didn't seem to work at first, then they put her into some group under a specialist and suddenly Lynsey started to change. She had been having home tuition and they got her to visit the school as part of an art project, there was a new headteacher and the bullies were gone. She began to attend again at fifteen, part-time at first then they gave her extra tuition after school and suddenly it was like she had moved in. Her strength came back, she came back, she did well in her GCSEs. They expect her to get As and Bs for her A levels, a shoo-in for her university choices they said.' Then the tears returned.

Matthew suggested Julie and he make tea, leaving the sisters alone in their joint grief for a while. Lukula confirmed that there wasn't anything to add from the police file on the incident though there had been a link to a local gang. They left the tea and took the opportunity to look at Lynsey's room. SOCOs had already been through it, taken the laptop and iPad for analysis, completed a brief search and left again.

'There isn't much here to help,' Lukula commented, 'somewhat bland and impersonal.'

'Everything is neat and orderly,' Merry agreed, scowling slightly as he felt he was missing something.

'No passions,' Lukula stated, 'everything is in moderation, everything middle-of-the-road.'

'What?' Matthew asked, still wondering what it was he was missing in the room. It looked like the female version of his own teenage bedroom: neat rows of books, a few classics and school texts, a tidy desk, clothes folded in drawers and on hangers in the wardrobe, a couple of sci-fi posters though in Lynsey's case they were arty landscapes.

'No passion,' Lukula elaborated, going through the desk, 'no sign of teenage rebellion, no expressions of *self* or what she wanted to become. My room, when I was a teenager, was part *tart's bedroom* and part a shrine to Madonna and Kylie, both wearing as skimpy costumes as I could find.'

'Really, I had a poster showing Picard as a Borg,' Matthew smiled at the memory.

'Hmm, inserting things into older men turned you on did it?' Lukula stated before she had time to think through what she said, then quickly changed topic, 'This room is all about control and holding emotions at bay.'

'This is a map of her running routes, isn't it?' Matthew said, opening a folded map he had pulled from the bottom of a draw, ignoring Lukula's comment about his teenage years. He would miss Julie's direct, often insightful, in-your-face take on life.

'I would never have had you down as a Madonna fan,' he told her as they headed downstairs, hoping she realised he hadn't taken any offence at her comment.

'Desperately wanted to be like her,' Julie told him, remembering she had desperately wanted to screw Kylie, before saying, 'Then I joined the army and got into guns in a big way.' Both switching off their smiles as they walked back into the living room. They spent a little time getting a list of names and details of Lynsey's few friends, including the boyfriend, patiently listening to anecdotes of Lynsey's achievements.

'Have you already contacted her father?' Lukula asked, apparently forgiven for being the the attractive, self confident woman that Lynsey would now never be.

'I did,' the sister spoke up. 'I got his wife, his third now. At least she sounded upset, when he came on it was only to ask why I was still bothering him after all this time; the fucking shit. Excuse my language, but she was still his daughter whatever else has happened.'

'We didn't keep in touch and I gave up trying to get anything from him,' Joanne took up the story, her voice now tinged with anger. 'Child support were useless as well. His number two soon got wise and left him and he is now on number three. She has him by the balls, and he has her daughter and son to look after as well as a son of their own.' Although the father didn't sound as if he were a part of Lynsey's life Lukula made a mental note to get him checked out, nothing could be ruled out at this stage.

'Going back to the bullying incident,' Matthew judged the anger Mrs Hensley felt for her ex-husband might just carry her through the next few questions he had to ask. 'Have there been any subsequent incidents? Has Lynsey had any problems at school or work, any threats, anything like that?'

'No,' Joanne emphatically shook her head, she wasn't going to admit watching her daughter like a hawk for the slightest sign of anything untoward, but she was certain her daughter had been untroubled on that account. 'Everything was going fine, she was at peace with herself again. I'm certain if there had been anything she would have had the strength to say.'

'I have to ask this, Mrs Hensley, under the circumstances,' Matthew had left the worst to last so they could leave if it was too much for the mother. 'She was a teenager after all, virtually an adult, but was she involved with drugs in anyway?'

'No she didn't do drugs, didn't drink either,' Mrs Hensley, could be relaxed on this point, more so than most parents as she knew what her daughter thought on these subjects, 'she was very anti-both. She had stayed in touch with the mental health people, it was why she wanted to study psychology. She organised various things at the school, to educate the younger ones for a healthier lifestyle.'

'Did any of this bring her into contact with any of the local gangs, some of their members perhaps?' Lukula wondered. 'Had she argued with anyone, any jealousies?'

'I doubt it, she was happy and looking forward to her future,' Joanne sighed, feeling drained and without energy to continue, she wanted to help but her mind was blank.

# 3

'There isn't much to go on, is there?' Merry wondered out loud, contemplating their next steps as Lukula drove him to Whitechapel tube. 'What are your thoughts?'

'We need to visit the school, run down any connections with this bullying incident. It's also possible her anti-drugs thing may have brought her in contact with some of those involved in selling them,' Julie summarised.

'Or others with even worse inclinations for violence,' Matthew commented, resignedly adding, 'There are almost too many permutations at the moment but following up at the school seems sensible.'

'You will be glad to hear that Ray has been allocated as office manager and is setting up the incident room, though it won't be fully functioning until tomorrow,' Lukula informed him as the car idled in a queue waiting for the lights. DS Raymond Rosen was a dour man in his late forties, he'd regularly worked with Merry and the inspector considered him the best operations manager in the Met despite Ray's chequered past. 'We should get a prelim on the PM and CCTV tomorrow. The govenor text me to say he had leaned on them, I think he's hoping for a quick result on this one,' Julie stated without thought, yawning as she did.

'Understandable,' Matthew said, ignoring the *understandable* fact that his govenor had text Julie rather than himself with the information, after all she would be the one remaining on the case, 'what with having two people off on long term sick. And, to add to his woes I've put in for a transfer. I doubt I'll see this case out, unless it is a random mugging and quickly goes nowhere.'

Julie bit her tongue, not wanting to say she knew Matthew's transfer wasn't exactly at his request, settling for, 'I'm sorry to hear that.'

'Crap,' Matthew laughed, somehow telling Julie made it all real and he could now acknowledge to himself the relief he felt at going – a new start indeed. 'The govenor will be desperate for a new DI and I would think you are a shoo-in for that. You deserve it and you'll be a damn sight better at it than me, you just need to ensure you complete the training.' Julie gave him an embarrassed smile, but couldn't help herself at being pleased by the thought. 'How about a quick pint before you drop me, a double celebration on me?' Matthew suggested.

Kathy Merry could smell the beer on her husband's breath but she didn't begrudge him a drink, he needed some downtime when coming home from a case, some space between home and work life. They talked about their daughters over a late dinner and she mentioned the need for a babysitter if he was going to be late tomorrow, as she had a parents meeting. Somehow this got them onto the topic of bullying and drugs in schools, both of which were things she was passionate about, being the deputy head for pastoral matters in a large, popular local secondary school.

'Reality is I doubt if either can be completely kept out of any school,' she admitted as they sat in bed, sipping their special herbal tea, which helped them both relax and get the sleep they needed to cope with the stress of their respective jobs. 'Though staying vigilant and not being complacent, never thinking you are the one school in the country that is a no-go area for bullies or drugs, and, with luck you'll keep it to a minimum.' However, she was speaking to herself as Matthew had started to snore. She smiled, looking down at the man she loved, he was dependable and hardworking, he lived his life for his family and she hoped, prayed, that was enough for him. Occasionally though, despite all he said about wanting a quiet, regular life, she wondered if he needed more. Truth was she had not married him for being quiet and dependable.

Malcom Swift was at home working at his desk, going through emails on his laptop before tackling the pile of papers he'd brought home in his case. He had eaten with his current partner, a barrister at one of the Temple chambers, but given that she was as busy as he was they had agreed she wouldn't stay the night. He already had a number of cases on the go: ranging from the straightforward, such as a domestic that had gotten out of hand and resulted in the wife being strangled, to the much more complex, in particular one involving a series of gang related knifings. The chief superintendent was coordinating the latter cases but in reality Swift was acting as second-in-command and, given that his team was carrying two officers on long term sick, manpower was tight.

It wasn't the workload that worried Malcolm. Matthew was competent enough to head the inquiry team on the Lynsey Hensley case, especially with the help of Julie and Ray. What was playing on his mind was the Jody Grahame case. Inspector Paul Baynard, before he had fallen off a ladder cleaning his gutters and gone long-term sick, had already arrested a drug pusher for the murder. However, apart from a confession there was little evidence to tie the man to the crime and they had initially delayed bringing charges and held the suspect for nearly the full four days before deciding how to act. In the end other charges had been brought and the murder case had shifted to a lower profile. Given the obvious, if superficial, links to the Hensley case, a young blonde woman with head injuries attacked in a park, Swift was all too aware he should already have raised this with Matthew.

However, it wasn't that straightforward and Malcolm had decided to speak with his boss before passing the file to Matthew. It was a sensible, cautious approach justified by not wanting to distract Matthew at such an early stage. Though Swift could not escape the self-recrimination that he was playing politics and covering his back, not wanting to jeopardise the 'upward trajectory' of his career. Small step by small step he felt himself becoming one of those senior officers he had once so despised, officers who put their career before good policing.

Julie looked at herself in the full length mirror, assessing whether at thirty-two her body had peaked. She had exercised and showered, as was her usual morning routine. She also ran five kilometres twice a week, spent an hour at the gym once a week and now stood contemplating the results of her efforts. She was finding it harder to motivate herself to maintain her rigorous exercise routine, of course the annual fitness test at work helped, but the increasing workload she faced got in the way, eating up her spare time. However, on reflection, she rather liked her slim, toned body and over the years had enhanced it with a number of tattoos, a couple to cover scars but on the whole she went for tasteful black ink designs.

She had inherited her looks and creativity from her French mother and grandmother, her temper and aggression from her Congolese maternal grandfather (an ex-Légion Étrangère) and her, now faded, Mancunian accent and an inability to commit to any serious relationship from her long absent father. 'Not a bad package,' she thought to herself, a little on the short side for her liking, but at five foot seven, on the whole, still desirable. She wondered what Sergeant Mehta would say if she were in the room now, would she admire or ignore her in her naked glory? Thinking about Mehta was a mistake, she was already running a little late but had no intention of going to work horny, so she opted to spend five minutes, well ten in reality, with one of her vibrators.

'We have spent the morning speaking to the friends and the boyfriend,' Merry explained to Swift and the team, as they sat in the musty briefing room at the Leman Street police station. Now largely disused and soon to be sold off to help fill the hole in the police budget, the old sixties station had ample, if frowsty, spare office space for the incident room and team briefing. 'The mother gave us a list and it pretty well tallied with what was on Facebook and the victim's phone. It's a relatively small number of people all much the same age, but they seemed to spend a lot of time together, they are all into anti-drugs and healthy life choices campaigns. Unfortunately it didn't give us very much.'

'Any hint she had stepped on any toes as a result of her campaigning?' Swift asked, showing he was listening even if he was preoccupied with texting as Merry spoke.

'No, doesn't seem so. The campaigns are national ones, Lynsey and her friends simply volunteered to help out: fundraising, events at local schools, that type of thing. Everyone said she was liked, that she worked hard but didn't offend anyone, they were all pretty cut up about her death. The boyfriend wasn't happy she had broken up with him but admitted it was a pretty lacklustre relationship and, with them expecting to go to different universities, he admitted the end was inevitable. He was also at some family do all day yesterday, had stacks of photos on his phone, we're getting the locals to check it out but I don't think he is involved as he seemed genuinely upset at her death.'

'OK, what else?' Swift asked, wanting the briefing to move on as he had a number of urgent things to chase up on the recent spate of stabbings the rest of the team were dealing with.

'Prelim PM report has arrived, doesn't add much to what we already know,' Lukula had it open on her iPad but hardly needed to refer to it as Merry had asked her to lead on it and she had virtually memorised it in preparation. 'It confirmed no evidence of recent sexual activity. No other wounds on the body other than the blow to the head. The skull fracture corresponds to a single blow from a hammer, they have given dimensions and forensics are preparing a 3D image for reference. The blow, struck directly from behind, is likely to have come from an assailant between five foot four to five foot eight. The blow was delivered with some force, to do the damage it did, but the use of a hammer means it could have been done by either a male or female. What's more a reasonably fit woman could have dragged the body the few feet into the bushes. The apparent posing of the body, with the arms folded across the chest, could have been accidental. Time of death is confirmed as being within five minutes of it being called in at three twenty in the afternoon. We are currently working on a time frame of between three and three fifteen when she was attacked, with the key period being three to three thirty overall.

'Old scarring on her lower arms and thighs, most likely to be the result of self-harming, ties in with what the mother has told us. Toxicology is still being worked on but the preliminary report should be ready late tomorrow. Although, given her lifestyle, I can't see her taking drugs and, apart from the pill, her mother said she wasn't on any medication. On the plus side forensics have lifted a number of prints from the plastic Tesco bag they think the hammer was in and at the moment they are trying to work out if these came from more than one person. Unfortunately, none of the prints are in the system and, given the number of people who could have handled the bag, none of them may be the attacker's. The blood on the bag has been matched to the victim. SOCOs also recovered some trace fibres from under her arms, where she was lifted, which might help if we get a suspect. Likelihood of DNA is a bit more fraught but it's early days.'

'Nothing was taken?' Swift turned back to Merry.

'Not that we can find, the mother confirmed all her belongings were still on her,' Matthew paused, knowing Swift didn't like uncertainty.

'I sense a but coming,' Swift said, already guessing what the cautious DI was about to say.

'We can't rule out a robbery gone wrong. The place where she was killed is quiet and not overlooked although anyone hanging around would be spotted and likely to be reported, especially with the play area nearby.'

'So, someone seizing an opportunity, bungles it and suddenly it's murder,' Swift summed up, sensing this was going to be the unsatisfactory outcome they would be left with in the end. 'Which brings us to CCTV.'

'Ehh, yes, again only a prelim,' Julie tapped at her iPad, she'd had less time to study this so wanted the summary in front of her. 'As yet nothing obvious jumps out. They have cameras at the entrances, the petrol station and around the front of the high-rises but not where the walls back onto the park and coverage is much less around the eastern end. The two DCs seconded from the local CID have been working on the tapes with tech support. Not one hundred per cent coverage but, for the half hour leading up to the attack, everyone seen going into the gardens also comes out within an acceptable time frame, apart that is from our two witnesses and Lynsey. The timelines on both witnesses pan out and, as yet, there is no other connection between them and Lynsey, so I think they are ruled out.' Swift and Merry both nodded in agreement. 'We'll continue checking further back on the tapes, up to an hour before Lynsey was attacked, but at present there's nothing suspicious showing up. There are no other witnesses coming forward, the local uniforms canvassing the area haven't come up with any leads and the press statement put out appealing for help hasn't produced much either, just some reports about youths hanging around the playground last week and drunks spotted in the area.'

'What about the woman in the headscarf or hijab the young male witness mentions in his statement?' Rosen asked, looking up from the copious notes he was taking. It was exactly the detail Swift expected Rosen to notice and he also took in Merry's nod of approval at the question.

'The only sign of her is a shadow at the corner of the main gate, other than that she doesn't seem to have gone in or out. There is deep shadow from the trees and bushes along that side of the short approach road so she could have walked up to the entrance then turned back without showing up on the cameras. And, there are cars parked near the gate so alternatively she could have gotten into one of them,' Lukula shrugged. 'So far there's no sign of her going in from any other entrance which suggests she wasn't leaving. But, we still can't work out exactly what she was doing.'

'Statistically, muslim females committing violent crimes is a very low number,' Swift commented, signalling that it wasn't an issue of any consequence and they should move on. Lukula nodded, Rosen scowled and Merry simply looked on, his expression neutral, though he wondered if they were missing out on a witness, perhaps one dithering at the gate and not wanting to be involved. 'OK, so what is next?'

'We are off to her school to see if we can track down anything on the prior history of bullying. It was a few years ago but currently we can't find any reason why someone would want her dead,' Merry stated, not sounding overly enthusiastic about their chances.

'Why should there be?' Swift scowled, he would like to have pointed them to another option but they seemed to be doing a thorough job. 'A young girl like that, you need to have lived longer to put hatred into another person's heart. Ray, anything to add? Your team up and running?'

'Yes, sir, we've been allocated a constable from the local team, she is a probationer but was at the crime scene yesterday,' Rosen stated matter-of-factly, though still obviously annoyed that his comment on the missing witness in the headscarf had been too quickly dismissed. 'I've sent her to help with the CCTV evidence.

I hope that was OK?' Merry and Swift nodded in response, 'The DI from the local CID is co-ordinating the house to house canvassing, given how little of the area is actually overlooked he was wondering how much of the tower blocks we want done.'

'Anything that overlooks the streets approaching any of the park entrances, so both tower blocks, surrounding houses and shops,' Merry stated, not deferring to Swift, he could correct him if he wanted more. 'And, have officers at the gates questioning people who use the park, anyone stopping to ask questions or acting suspiciously. We also have officers following up on what information we are getting from the public appeal, but could do with a couple more if they can be spared. I know it's a lot, but we have so little to go on any lead could help.'

'Right, well done so far,' Swift meant it but they all knew the case was fast petering out, 'keep me informed. Matthew,' – he'd never learned to call him Mat – 'can I have a word?' The others took their cue and left the briefing room, giving Lukula a chance to map the route to Lynsey's school, so as to take in a sandwich stop at some point, as Rosen muttered something to her about headscarves as he passed her.

'I am going to have to keep you on the case for a few days,' Swift dove straight in with the bad news, it wasn't that awful that it needed sugar-coating. 'I've checked with the chief and she is happy for a delay in your reassignment.'

'Sure,' Matthew gave a half-hearted smile, it didn't bother him one way or the other. 'Though in all fairness to Julie she hardly needs me to hold her hand.'

'If I were you I wouldn't try,' Swift gave a broad grin, which faded under Merry's unresponsive stare, 'but your recommendation is understood. Although I'm more than aware of her abilities but, what with the local press coverage and everything else that is going on, we don't want it to look as if this death is low priority, so you are leading the inquiry.'

'No problem, sir,' Merry got up to leave, then thought he

should add, 'I hope you don't think I don't like it here, I've learnt a great deal from the team and you.'

'Good of you to say, we'll expect a drink you know,' Swift smiled, already out the door and glad to be out of the musty room. 'Though it's understandable that you need to use your talents where they will have the best effect.'

# 4

Leanne didn't know what else to say, other than to apologise for being late, as far as she could tell she had lost the entire morning but had phoned in as soon as she was able. She had explained her medical condition when interviewed and although the branch manager had been part of that, he had seemingly forgotten all about it.

'I have no control over it,' she said, once again, as he berated her tardiness.

'Then you should take medicine or see your doctor,' the young man, of Chinese descent, told her in no uncertain terms, his normally impeccable diction slipping as he got angrier, revealing his East End origins.

'My condition can't be medicated for, not as such, and I regularly see a specialist…' she tried not to plead, she thought she had been doing so well, things had been relatively settled for the last few months.

'You've been warned before,' he interrupted, despite what HR said he knew the important thing for a manager was the 'bottom line', his uncle always went on about this and the need for him to show the workers he was the boss, 'I should sack you now but I give you one more chance, only one and a written warning.' Leanne seemed to have collapsed in on herself, her head having fallen onto her chest, her body trembled slightly. 'It's no use crying,' he told her sharply. 'It's actions I want to see, your tears carry no weight with me, next time you're late you are…'

'What?' Leanne suddenly sat up, then leaned back, taking a deep breath and fixing her manager with a defiant stare. 'You'll what? What will you fucking do the next time I'm late?' The manager's mouth opened then shut, Leanne's stare as much as her words, so unexpected and harshly spoken in a Scottish accent, completely threw him. 'Well?' the normally meek Leanne demanded, shifting herself forward in the chair. 'I'll tell you what you'll do is nothing. Understand, shit for brains, you'll do nothing.'

'You get out now or I'll…' the manager quickly got over his shock and decided enough was enough.

'Shut the fuck up,' Leanne laughed, sitting back, 'or I'll call your boss, ever heard of discrimination, shit face. Then there's bullying, harassment and with my illness you are going to look a bigger idiot than you are. It won't be me that'll get kicked out.'

'I… That is…' the manager was lost for words, staring, goggle-eyed at the transformed shelf-filler sat before him.

'You'll do nothing, except be supportive of my condition,' Leanne stood, still grinning and leaned over the desk, to hiss, 'and, if you don't I'll be back to kick the shit outa, yer. So leave us alone.'

It was a very confused and uncertain young manager that emerged from his office a few minutes later to look for the unexpectedly aggressive Leanne.

'I'll get the delivery out on the shelves, shall I, sir?' Leanne asked him, her eyes wide and innocent, her voice once again soft and her accent evocative of the estuary, 'I'm really sorry I was late but I promise to make it up.' She smiled her usual meek, ingratiating smile.

Thinking she was mocking him he drew in his breath ready to shout at her, to order her off the site, when he noticed a customer approaching and glancing back at Leanne her innocent stare unnerved him. 'Yes, do that,' he agreed, his voice uncertain, thoughts of what HR might say starting to override his anger, 'however, you must be on time in future.' Leanne nodded as if that was a given and turned away, leaving him to deal with the customer.

The headmistress' office was suitably imposing: large desk with family photos, framed certificates showing her academic and teaching qualifications, pictures of her at school events with local dignitaries, coffee maker in the corner with cups and biscuits, two grey filing cabinets and, dominating the room, a conference table for the many meetings she conducted throughout the day. Merry and Lukula had received a well rehearsed speech as they followed the headmistress from reception up to her room, giving them a brief history of the school under her headship: its successes to date and an outline of how she intended to keep the momentum of improvement and growing success rates going. It reminded Merry of his wife when she was in 'Ofsted mode', no doubt headteachers couldn't afford to turn it off. Lukula had quickly tuned out and peeked suspiciously into each classroom they passed. School was something she had fought against and found the rooms full of eager youngsters, happily and purposefully working, somewhat at odds with her own memories.

Matthew had expected the school to be more cautious about helping the police with their inquiries, especially about the previous bullying, but they turned out to be very helpful. The current form teacher was present, full of praise for Lynsey Hensley and how she had been expected to do brilliantly in her A level exams, one such exam she should have been sitting that day.

'Such a waste,' the head muttered, seemingly genuinely upset. 'She had made such strides forward in such a short time, such potential gone.'

'Yes, though it wasn't always like that,' Lukula pointed out, hearing about the dead girl's academic prowess and how well liked she had been wasn't really why they were here, 'she had problems in the past, traumatic bullying, had any of that carried over to the present? Is there any suggestion of her still having problems?'

'It was never officially bullying,' her former tutor, from when Lynsey had stopped attending, spoke up for the first time. She was a rather mousey looking woman in her late fifties but the strength and determination in her voice surprised the two police officers. 'I visited her a number of times and never once would she say what had happened to her was anything other than an accident. Although I knew it was those girls, I'm certain of it.'

'Girls?' Merry asked, he'd assumed the bullies to be boys.

The teacher glanced at the head before continuing, 'I have no proof of course, but there was a group of three girls and five boys who pretty well ran the place before Mrs Chillcott was appointed, she couldn't undo what was done but she did act decisively in rooting out the bad apples from day one.'

'My appointment was as headteacher of the newly constituted academy school,' Mrs Chillcott elaborated, smiling in acknowledgment at the form teacher's praise, though she was not certain about the analogy of rooting for apples, which rather cast her in the role of a pig. 'As such I was able to act without the interference of the Local Authority. The five boys continued to break the school rules and were quickly expelled. Unfortunately the three girls were a little more astute in outwardly complying, though in the end they were also expelled.'

'What were the grounds for expelling them?' Merry wanted to know.

'For the boys it was straightforward enough, it was the weight of evidence rather than the gravity of the offences that was sufficient,' the head explained, the expulsions had won her a lot of support amongst staff, parents and governors; a new broom they could all agree with. 'For the girls it was actually more serious: harassment and bullying through the misuse of social media. Some of it was aimed at staff, myself included, as well as pupils.'

'That must have been difficult to prove,' Lukula commented, well aware of the invidiousness of trolling.

'At first we were suspicious but had little evidence, as they used various accounts, but our local police liaison officer was very helpful, unfortuately he has been moved on since and has yet to be replaced,' she looked pointedly at Merry, as if he controlled police staffing allocations. 'Then our IT technician discovered they had used school equipment to send some of the messages and things quickly fell into place.'

'They were quite bright girls,' the former tutor stated, 'for the boys it was simply a case of proving themselves as "alpha dogs", to push others around, but for the girls it was something more nasty. I think they just liked hurting people, some staff even left the school because of them.'

'What happened to them? The girls, are they still in the area?' Merry asked, wondering how things could get to the point where children could exert such power, but then many gang members are fourteen to sixteen or younger.

'They would have gone to the local behaviour unit,' the head explained, offering more coffee as she did, 'I didn't follow up as there was no chance of their returning here. However, I can let you have their details if you require them. Although I have to be clear we have absolutely no proof,' she glanced at the mousey looking teacher, who clamped her mouth closed in a smile, 'to believe them involved in bullying or attacking Lynsey, either previously or now.'

'Well, any luck?' Matthew asked Julie, as he placed ham and cheese sandwiches and mugs of tea from the tray onto the table in front of her.

'Was this all they had?' Lukula asked, she had wanted a tuna baguette, barely glancing up from her phone but getting no response from Merry who had simply ordered two of what he'd wanted. 'My contact in Gangs, has some background on a few of them, including two of the girls, and the office has checked out their records.'

'And?' Merry asked with a mouthful of ham and cheese.

'Of the five boys, two have dropped off the radar, though one of them is thought to be working at a garage in Essex, the other moved north. The other three are known to be members of the Towers Crew. What?' Lukula looked up certain Merry had muttered an obscenity. She noticed he chewed with his mouth open, his manners were rather crass when he was off his guard and it made her wonder about his upbringing; her own mother would certainly not have approved. But Merry shook his head, drinking his tea to wash another mouthful of ham and cheese down. 'Of the girls one is off the radar,' Lukula continued, scowling at her phone, 'the other two are both subjects of interest.'

'What does that mean?' Merry demanded, ceasing to chew.

'Ongoing investigation,' Lukula smiled, her friend, a rather tall brunette with whom she had flirted once or twice, was rather prone to using phrases from American cop shows, 'into extortion and assault.'

'Sounds a possible lead,' Merry was trying not to put two and two together at this early stage but it was tempting.

'Yes, but we can't go blundering in on another investigation, we will need to go through channels first,' nor did Lukula want to upset her friend as she still had hopes the flirtation might become something more.

'That doesn't stop us from speaking with the three lads first, does it,' Merry stated getting up. Then, noticing that Julie had yet to touch her sandwich and tea, added, 'Get those to go, you know the govenor always eats on the run, if you want to get into his good books you'll need to get with the programme.' Lukula was too busy collecting her lunch to decide whether the normally humourless inspector was joking and refrained from making any response.

Key's Gym is located in a back street off the Commercial Road and the owner, Donald Key, being an old friend of Ricky Towers, tolerated gang members hanging out there. However, any dealing was done at the Albion pub on the corner, although most drugs were simply pushed on the estates and street corners near schools.

'Hello Donald,' Merry was almost cheery in his greeting as he walked into the small office next to the entrance, 'long time.'

The huge man behind the desk looked up from the paper he was laboriously reading, slowly smiled and in a deep, bass voice, replied, 'Sergeant Merry, you've put on weight.'

'It's inspector now,' Merry laughed, glancing down at his waistline, he had to admit he was getting a bit portly. 'You still have the same trim figure I see. This is Detective Sergeant Lukula.'

Donald stood, still broadly grinning, and offered his hand to the sergeant, 'Donald Key, owner and proprietor of this establishment, Sergeant Lulu.'

'Lukula,' Julie corrected, stunned by the size of the man, he would have to stoop and turn sideways to get through a normal doorway, her hand was like a small child's in his.

'We are here to talk to a couple of your patrons,' Merry informed him.

'There ain't nothing new in that,' Donald responded, slowly edging his way from behind the desk, like an adult carefully negotiating his way around play furniture. 'Who is it this time?'

'They go by the street names of PeeWee, Dabs and Tobes,' Lukula stated, taking her cue from Merry's glance.

'Dumb nicknames kids have these days,' Donald informed her, suggesting such a polite young woman as she wouldn't be aware of such things.

'I know,' she smiled, still mesmerised by the size of the man, much of his bulk was muscle, 'I've a step-brother, nearly forty and an estate agent, and his mates still call him Whizzy because he liked cheese whizz when he was a kid.'

'At least it isn't after Sooty,' Donald pointed out half seriously, as his visitors backed out of the office so he could follow them out. 'Do you remember the TV puppet show, Sooty and Sweep? Izzy, wizzy, lets get busy?'

'Used to sit on my Gran's knee and watch it when I was little,' Lukula, for all of the giant's pleasant manner, noticed Merry's mild amusement at the exchange and wondered if she wasn't having her leg pulled, but she smiled in any case as the owner was readily cooperating.

'That's the three you want, working out on the weights in the corner, Tobes is the one on the bench, he's who you should talk to,' Donald pointed to three muscular and tattooed youngsters, one of whom was bench pressing as the other two stood at either end of the barbell watching. It was a scene that reminded Lukula of her army days, the young men bare chested, egging each other on to 'go one more lift', two of them even wore light, baggy camouflage trousers, while the third wore tight gym shorts, emphasising muscular legs and buttocks. Such scenes always made Lukula wonder how much male rebellion and violence originated from suppressed homoerotic tendencies.

'I am DI Merry and this is DS Lukula,' Merry began, his tone quiet and polite, 'we need to ask you about this girl, do you recognise her?' The three young men barely glanced at the photo the inspector held out, shaking their heads in automatic denial. Although the one in the shorts flexed his chest muscles and grinned lewdly at Lukula, all three were taken off-guard by Merry's direct and polite approach.

'Are you certain?' Merry calmly persisted. 'You all went to school with her.'

'I'd remember that cute face,' Tobes, sitting up on the press bench, having put the bar on its stand, and looking Lukula up and down, stated. 'Though I prefer an older woman myself.' Lukula continued to stare into the middle distance, unperturbed, not only could she bench press ten kilos more than was currently on the bar but sweaty, muscular bodies were also her biggest turn off.

'She's probably changed a bit since you last saw her, more than four years ago,' Merry continued in the same tone, aware that Donald was still over by the entrance, intently listening and watching, 'just before you were expelled from school.' The third member of the trio maintained his silence but sucked his teeth in response, his face disapproving and angry, though as he and the one wearing shorts continually glanced at their seated companion Merry took it that Tobes was the leader of the three.

'I didn't get expelled because of her, I can tell you that,' Tobes handed the picture back, still puzzled as to what the pair confronting him thought he knew.

'Her picture has been in the news as she's been killed,' Merry noticed the immediate change in the young men, switching from being relaxed and on their home ground to defensive and wary. 'A few people seem to think you have been in touch with her recently. We were wondering what that might be about?'

Lukula's passive stare was obviously starting to get to the guy in the shorts, his grin having turned to a snarl and his head dropping ready to strike out.

'That's wrong,' Tobes replied, trying to sound relaxed but standing so as to put himself between his two companions and the officers. He was also aware of Donald watching the proceedings, not entirely certain why the big man was taking such an interest. The Towers crew might coincidently bear the name of Ricky Towers but his connection with the gang was through a long line of intermediaries and his only interest in them was that they were one of a large number of outlets for his product, and drugs were only a small part of his empire. Donald was known to be an old, if now distant, friend of Ricky's; not that the big man needed to call on Ricky's protection as he could bench press more than Tobes' bodyweight.

'We don't know her, so piss off,' Lukula's passive stare was finally too challenging for the shorts wearing youth and he now felt a need to exert his dominance.

'OK, well thank you for your help,' Merry's sudden backdown surprised them all, including Lukula. 'You understand we have to follow up on every lead in cases of murder. Of course, we will have to speak with you again, search your homes, places you have been recently. You'll have alibis and we'll have to check those out, put your friends and associates under the spotlight but I'm sure they will understand. Murder isn't like other crimes, there is no letting up.'

# 5

Lukula's smile had returned but was no longer benign, picking up on the Merry's lead, it was now clearly meant to show how much she was going to enjoy taking the three young men's lives apart. There was more to her boss than she had given him credit for.

'You'll be wasting your time,' the trio's leader, told them, 'but I can't help if I don't know her, can I?' If his two companions hadn't understood Merry's threat the look Tobes gave the pair clearly told them to keep their mouths shut unless they wanted to lose a few teeth.

'From what we have been told,' Merry started to spell out exactly what he wanted from the trio, 'the three of you beat her up, quite badly, when she was thirteen because she told on one of your girlfriends and got her in trouble at school. You would have been about fifteen yourselves, which is not so long ago, so I don't believe you can't remember that. Your girlfriend's name was Michaela.'

Topes' deepening, puzzled frown suddenly gave way to one of insight. 'That fucking black bitch, we had nothing to do with that. I'm sorry, nothing meant,' he almost added 'Miss' as he turned in sincere apology to Lukula, 'I ain't no racist but that cow and her mate are real nasty bitches.'

42

'Although you still hang around with them?' Julie decided a change of tone would now press home the breakthrough Merry had achieved.

'They like to hang around, buy a little of this and that to sell on, wind some of the guys up to see if they can start a fight,' he turned to look at the young man wearing shorts, who looked suitably sheepish. 'Every so often they might like a change of pace by adding a bloke into the mix, for a bit of variety, but as a rule they are so close they share sweat.'

'The other girl is Karen Swarsky, the white girl?' Lukula asked, receiving a nod as confirmation. 'You are saying they beat up Lynsey for grassing on Michaela, when you were all in school?'

'Yeah, mad fucking bitches.'

'What about their other friend?' Merry interrupted. 'We were told there were three girls involved, another black girl called Teresa?'

'Tessy, yeah, she was in on it as well. The three of them did for your dead girl real good, didn't see nothing of her after that. We ain't seen Tessy since getting kicked out of school, she moved away to some fancy place in Essex called Ongar.'

'Has Michaela or Karen mentioned anything about Lynsey since?'

'Not to me,' both his companions shook their heads as well, happy now they thought they had deflected the police suspicions onto the girls. 'The only other girl they ever speak about is Tessy. They all party at Tessy's place, she has a little studio set up so they can sell their get togethers live on line. Ask PeeWee here, he has a subscription.' PeeWee who had maintained, his hard man silence throughout suddenly erupted into a series of expletives, his voice sufficiently high pitched to suggest the origin of his nickname being a once well known American TV comic.

The three continued to swap insults as Merry, without much concern, told them they might be needed to give statements at some stage, as unlikely as he thought it to be. His and Lukula's going was barely noticed except by the owner, who still loomed, mountain like, by the entrance.

'Get everything you need, *Inspector* Merry,' Donald asked, taking care to emphasis Matthew's rank.

'Yes, thank you Donald, it's been a help,' Merry smiled back. 'Seen anything of Ricky lately?'

'Not as such,' Donald replied with a shrug. 'He's too high and mighty these days.'

'Oh well, pass on my love,' Merry said over his shoulder as he went out of the door, followed by Donald's deep, rumbling laugh and Lukula's surprised and puzzled countenance. This was a side to her boss she hadn't seen before and hadn't expected, out on the job he was starting to give glimpses of the possibility that he actually enjoyed the work.

Merry told her, 'Get in touch with your friend in Gangs and say I'd like to meet with her boss, as we need to formally interview the two girls. A chance meeting between them and Lynsey in the park could have resulted in her murder. It's a stretch about using a hammer but it's a good alternative to carrying a knife and less risky than acid.'

Lukula nodded as she started the car and was thinking of asking Merry how he had come across Key and Towers when his phone rang. Matthew could barely hear Mrs Hensley, even though he had turned to one side to face away from Julie as she started to speak on the handsfree set. The mother's voice was faint and he had to apologise that the line was bad so could she speak up.

'I'm sorry, I said I have been to see Lynsey,' Joanne's hollow voice still barely carried to his ear. 'I don't know what too say to anyone.'

'That must have been traumatic for you,' it was a bloody stupid comment to make to a grieving mother who had just been to view her deceased daughter's body, but it was all Merry could think to say. Then guessing at what her second comment referred to, he added, 'You don't have to talk to anyone about it, unless you want to, especially not the press. It's not for me to say but personally I'd wait until I knew what to say.' There was a long pause, only her breathing telling him she was still on the line.

'People call, telling me how sorry they are to hear Lynsey is gone. So many people, I didn't expect that. Staff from the school and the clinic, where she still helped out, people whose names I don't recognise.'

'Has the family liaison officer contacted you?' he could hear the confusion and her inability to cope in the mother's voice, 'They can help and advise you about all this.'

'So many people in her life that I didn't know about.'

Merry thought he should tell her he was following up on some leads, still working hard to find whoever had done this, but the line went dead and he didn't have the courage to phone her back.

Julie had caught enough of the conversation to leave him to his silence for the remainder of their journey. Merry's sullen mood deepening as the DI from the Gangs Unit gave them the bad news that the two girls they suspected of being involved in Lynsey's murder had an alibi.

'I'm sorry, but they were in court all day,' the inspector from Gangs looked as fed up as Merry, 'the case isn't going too well and they spent the day looking smug.'

'What exactly have they been up to?' Lukula asked, as much to extend the time with her friend, the brunette sergeant, who was casting admiring glances in her direction, as from professional curiosity.

'Extortion and sexual assault, they came on our radar because of their links with the Towers Crew but they seem to be working on their own on this. Basically they pick up young women, get them drunk or high, then film them having sex with one or both of them,' the Gangs inspector paused to stretch himself, his neck muscles taut with stress were protesting at his recounting the case. 'Then when it's over, they take the girl somewhere quiet and beat her up, tell her they will do it again and put the film out on the internet if she doesn't give them something. A couple of the victims have had the strength to inform the police. However, all but one have withdrawn their statements after more threats and beatings, though nothing we can prove. Our last hope is a woman in her mid-twenties, an LGBTI activist, but the case is weak as it's her word against theirs and they have a tape where she *consents* to a bit of rough sex. On top of that the physical evidence isn't that great. The hold they have over their victims, what with the photos and videos they have and the threats of violence, is hard to break,' the inspector twisted his neck as the muscles tightened like vices squeezing at the frustration he felt about the case that was slipping away from him. 'We've gone back over all the reports made about the pair since they were both sixteen, but we can't find where they keep the videos. No doubt they're securely stashed in some *cloud* or other we can't find a link to.'

'What about Teresa, their old school friend who moved out of the area? She's into the internet and that sort of thing,' Merry asked, listening but still distracted by the mother's phone call, now knowing he had to tell her they had no viable leads. 'We've been told they all still keep in touch.'

'I owe you a drink,' Lukula told the brunette, as the Gangs inspector, suddenly animated by the information Lukula and Merry supplied about Teresa, made a number of phone calls and Merry stared distractedly out of the window.

'Actually, from the sound of things I owe you a meal, it's the best lead we have had for a while,' the brunette smiled, bringing a warm, welcoming look of expectation to her face.

'Well, I don't have anything on tonight,' Lukula's stomach flipped with anticipation.

'Let's skip the meal then,' the brunette's smile widened, she saw no reason not to be direct as Lukula's eyes completely gave away what was going through her mind.

'I can't help feeling I've missed something,' Merry told his wife, as they sat sipping wine having put the girls to bed. Kathy had been telling him about her parent meeting but had stopped as he obviously wasn't listening. 'It all points to some random attack, a mugging gone wrong, but it doesn't feel right. Perhaps I'm over thinking it, that's what Malcolm would say.'

The silence between the pair lengthened, then Kathy stood up, picking up the half-empty glasses. 'You know your trouble is your gut tells you one thing and your head another, you need to decide which is in charge and go with that.'

'Well at least I know who's in charge in this house,' Matthew muttered as he got up to follow her, as they were obviously having an early night.

Leanne had been as good as her word and had stayed late at the supermarket to make up time, not that the manager had seemed appreciative, giving her nothing but black looks. Once home she had begun cleaning, as she always did when she suspected one of the others, apart from the children, had been about. She could never be completely certain who had been there so she took all precautions: scrubbing the small shower and toilet with bleach, stripping the bed, hoovering, dusting, clearing the fridge of anything open, cleaning the kitchen and washing all the crockery and cutlery. She had long ago given up throwing out clothes she didn't recognise, unless they were soiled in some way, it was too expensive no matter how disgusted she was at the thought of wearing someone else's clothes. Instead she put out to wash anything that looked as if it had been worn. By the early hours, she was exhausted and sat at her kitchen table eating a cheese sandwich with a glass of milk and working on her diary.

The cover of the diary, a thick, ruled notebook, had the title

'Leanne Solbury – age 32' on it, she had a dozen others like it and had been keeping them reasonably consistently since her therapist, Doctor Alima Hassan, had recommend doing so. She hadn't always trusted the doctor and had left her care for a number of years, only recently meeting with her again. However, in all fairness, much that the therapist had advised her to do had been beneficial. Keeping the diary helped her with the gaps in her life and what caused them, on occasions she could even make a good guess as to who had taken over control of her life. Although she knew not to dwell on this as it brought about the stress she worked to avoid.

The irony of her life was the more that she understood her condition the greater the chance she would lose hold, the first time she had realised this had caused her to leave therapy. She was particularly terrified by a nagging dread that constantly hung over her, that one personality in particular might take complete control thereby banishing her to some dark recess of her own mind. She could only comprehend that as some form of death.

The last thing she could remember from the previous night was watching TV, a talent show, then turning it off to avoid the news, another potential stressor. Then nothing until after lunch time today, some three hours after the start of her shift. From the clothes strewn in the bedroom and the general state of the place she guessed it had been the one she labelled 'The Slut', refusing to acknowledge her name helped make her seem less real. Not that it mattered, what worried Leanne was why this had happened now after what had been a few incident free weeks of calm; apart from the children who tended to emerge when she was at home, the feeling of safety luring them out.

She knew her condition would never go away, knew these episodes would happen throughout her life but the aim was to keep them to a minimum. She was also pretty certain that she had had a mini-episode during the interview with her manager, his reaction and her inability to remember the end of the meeting suggested this was the case. She could even guess who was the most likely candidate for that as well. But she got no further. Exhausted she fell asleep on her arm, the half eaten sandwich and untouched milk beside her. Her diary, her lifeline, still open in front of her.

Julie Lukula was pissed off. Sex with the brunette sergeant from the Gangs Unit had been great but barely before she had gotten her breath back the woman was getting dressed and saying she had to go.

'Can't be too late back,' she had stated with a smug smile, 'my partner might get suspicious.'

It wasn't that Julie was a prude about such things and in all likelihood would have bedded the brunette even knowing she was in a relationship. It was the not being told beforehand, not being given a choice in the matter that annoyed her. She was left alone, angry at being used, a quick lay who wasn't trusted to say yes if told the truth. The anger flared inside her, sending her out of the bed and into jogging bottoms, top, trainers and out the door. It was late and the recently rain-washed streets were nearly deserted. At first she had run hard to burn off the adrenaline, so she would be able to sleep, but after a while her pace slowed and her running took on a rhythm so that she hardly noticed the exertion.

On one street she slowly overtook another runner, a man of about her own age, who glanced over his shoulder on hearing her footfalls and slowed his pace so she caught him up.

'Hi,' he smiled, hardly any sign that he laboured for his breath. 'Nice night for it.'

She nodded back, there had never been a time when she had preferred men over women, boys over girls, she had never been in the closet. Although she had, once or twice, given thought to having sex with a man and she could appreciate a well toned male body, like the one jogging along beside her, but she had never gone beyond speculation as the thought seemed unnatural to her. She could rationalise why women might be attracted to men but, beyond the occasional fantasy, could not contemplate it as a reality.

'You OK running on your own, at this time of night?' the man asked trying to sound gallant and without ulterior motive.

'Yes, thanks,' she replied, without looking at him and increasing her speed, glad to hear his footfalls receding. That briefest of flirtations had cheered her up and she turned for home, reflecting on how shallow she could be. She enjoyed being a woman and felt at ease in her body and she was amused by receiving admiring glances from the opposite sex, providing it went no further. Although she was under no illusion about her own sex: women, as the brunette had proven, could be arseholes as well as men. In that there was more equality between the sexes then most people appreciated.

Joanne Hensley lay sleepless, her mind numb from going over all the 'what ifs'. As if any of them could change things, could change the reality she didn't want. Her emotions rasped to nothing, her tears drained, she lay now existing only in the ticking of the seconds of the endless night.

As Malcolm Swift pulled into the Leman Street nick he reflected on the changing nature of the ground he worked. Gentrification of London was sweeping, north and east, affordable housing was disappearing to the extent that most Met officers now lived outside the M25. The glass high-rise in Canter Way opposite the police station gave views, from the top half, of the Thames and the Tower of London. Whilst not far from the bottom of Leman Street was the oldest theatre in London, a renovated music hall, a time capsule half buried in modern, upscale apartments; just round the corner from Swedenborg Gardens where Lynsey Hensley had been unlawfully killed. For some reason it passed through his mind how the mother could afford to own a small terraced house by the canal but then realised it had probably been bought years ago when she was married, before house prices in the area soared. Of course gentrification didn't stop crime: wealthy youngsters were targeted by muggers, demand for recreational drugs increased and gangs could commute in and out of the area on the excellent transport links. Such was life.

Swift was pleased at slipping into the incident room unnoticed, it was a hive of activity, Ray had done a good job in staffing the place and he and Matthew seemed engrossed in mulling over some notes and files. There was no sign of Julie nor either of the two CID constables, even the probationer constable was absent, making tea he hoped.

'If you are here for an update I'm afraid it isn't good,' Merry informed his govenor, he'd been aware of Swift's arrival but had finished listening to Ray, before turning and launching into an update without being asked. 'The bullying the victim sustained in the past doesn't seem to have carried over to the present, the leads we were running down on that score have come to nothing. The postmortem report has revealed nothing new and toxicology hasn't found anything in her blood, not even traces of the pill as her mother thought. The prints that forensics found on the plastic bag aren't in the system, there's trace evidence on the victim but we have nothing to match it against. We are also having problems tracking people in and out of the eastern end of the park. Fortunately it seems to have been a quiet time of day and so far we only have the one oddity.'

'Oddity?' Swift asked, pulling up a seat and wondering if he dared ask for a drink, there seemed to be a scattering of Costa to go cups across various desks and piled in bins but no sign of any on-site facility, the problem with using a semi-defunct station, he thought.

'Apart from the two witnesses and the victim, there is only one person we can find who seems to have been nearby at the time of the attack. Of course, as I've said, surveillance isn't one hundred per cent and the wider the time frame the harder it is to track ins and outs but for the key period fifteen minutes either side of when the victim was found then the only person unaccounted for is the woman in the headscarf.' Swift looked as if he was about to say something but Merry went on before he could speak. 'Ray thinks she might have seen something and been too scared to come forward, hence her dithering at the east entrance. He's had Gillian Porter, the probationer from the local team, print off an image, it is only a hazy beige and grey smudge on a black background but it's the best she could pull off, even with enhancement. I've sent her out to do some specific canvassing in the area just to see what we can get but it's a long shot.'

'Where's Julie?'

'Out with the local CID officers looking up the usual suspects and informants to see if they can pick up on anything,' Merry explained, wondering if he should ask one of the administrative staff to get Swift a drink, but dismissing the idea as somewhat feudal given that Malcolm hadn't mentioned it.

'So you are focused on a mugging gone wrong?' Swift asked, feeling even more guilty about holding on to the file he was about to pass on.

'It's all we have at the moment,' Merry acknowledged the inevitable, sensing the dead end fast approaching.

'It can't be ruled out, so don't lose sight of that line of inquiry,' Swift drew breath, not wanting any hint of the uncertainty he felt to come through in his voice, 'but you should look through this case. There's more detail in the system but this gives a good outline. There are some obvious links with the Hensley killing, although they are somewhat circumstantial and given that an arrest had already been made it didn't initially seem relevant. However, I now think you should give it some consideration, look at it with fresh eyes, so to speak.'

Rosen and Merry shared more than an eye for detail, they were both able to keep a deadpan expression on their face as their govenor admitted a mistake. The fact that Rosen had been telling Merry about the case they had just been handed before Swift's arrival helped them keep any hint of surprise well hidden.

# 6

'It's a Hawksmoor, you know, the church,' Merry stated as he and Julie entered St George's Gardens.

'Oh,' Lukula sounded unimpressed, glancing up at the ornately designed but plainly rendered building, she had noticed and wondered about the name – St George's in the East Church – on the gate as they parked.

'He worked with Wren and his churches are considered some of the finest in London,' Matthew went on, leading them past the church and into the gardens, which had once been the original cemetery.

'Who's Wren?' Lukula asked, straight-faced.

'You are joking, aren't you?' Merry glanced at Julie, it might have been his wife's influence but every family outing contained a number of learning points, and he rather enjoyed history, wishing he had studied it at university instead of economics.

'Isn't he the guy who built the Gherkin?' she asked, grinning, she was starting to see subtler shades to what she had once thought of as his monotone personality.

'He'd have probably approved the design,' Merry smiled, recognising he was having his leg pulled. 'My point is that this is something of a tourist attraction. Admittedly not the most popular in London, not another St Paul's, but a steady stream of visitors. Plus there is a pub in the north east corner of the park, a swimming pool in the south east and a playground halfway between the two. Add to that the through traffic, all the usual dog walkers, people out for a stroll and it's a relatively busy place, just ten minutes walk or so from where Lynsey Hensley was killed.'

'Why did the govenor hold back on telling you about this case? Given the proximity and the links you should have been informed sooner,' Lukula cut across the thread of the conversation, Swift was an officer she looked up to, respected, his apparent playing politics with their case rankled her.

'She was attacked at this spot,' Merry said taking a seat on a metal and wood bench, it was cooler in the shadows of a tree and he pulled his suit jacket closer, wondering if he should have brought his coat from the car, 'three and a half weeks ago. There was blood splatter on the ground and the end of the bench there. She was small and could have been easily lifted, picked up and dumped in the bushes behind us.' Lukula followed her boss's retelling of the events as she stood a few steps to one side in the warmth of the spring sun, visualising the scene as he described it. 'Her body was found by a retired couple out walking their dog, the normally placid animal flipped and dragged them over.'

'Must have been a shock,' Julie observed, looking around and noticing how quiet the spot was despite a steady stream of visitors to the church and people walking in the distance.

'Blunt force trauma to the rear of her head possibly from a hammer, though not ruling out other blunt instruments. Her phone was missing, but otherwise no signs of it being a mugging. She had quite a record and was easily identified as Jody Grahame. No family, she'd lived rough on and off since she was thirteen. She was into drugs, prostitution, theft, had been in and out of foster homes since she was five and was finally given a short custodial sentence at seventeen. She had only just turned eighteen and was in supported accommodation for young offenders. Apparently she was doing well, despite mental health problems, until two days prior to her attack when she went missing.'

'As I understand it,' Julie hoped to speed up the account, taking a seat on the bench next to Merry, 'Paul made an arrest the following day, some small-time pusher.'

'They found his fingerprints on a packet of drugs, opioids, in her pocket. CCTV had shown him as being in the area, although mainly over by the swimming pool. At first he denied everything, but on being cautioned and having spoken to his solicitor he gave a statement, confessing to selling her drugs, then getting into an argument with her and pushing her over. She hits her head on the bench, he checks her pulse, realises she's dead, so dumps her body and runs.'

'Checks her pulse?' Lukula's tone could not be more disbelieving.

'Paul was equally suspicious so didn't charge him straight off but got an extension and left him to stew a couple of days. Apart from the fingerprint and his confession there was nothing to tie the pusher, forgive the pun,' – Merry looked sheepish if pleased at his quip on the word pusher – 'to Jody's killing. She had undoubtedly bought the drugs from him and toxicology showed she had taken some a couple of hours previous. And, although there was blood splatter on the bench, nothing suggested the blow she received had happened as the pusher described.'

'So what?' Julie was starting to wonder if Merry was going to answer her question about their govenor.

'Paul Baynard did some digging into the guy's background, it wasn't difficult as he was known to local CID, and it turns out he was in debt to some loan shark by the name of Trotsky,' Merry explained, then paused, sitting back and taking in a lungful of the pleasant, cool, green air. He loved London for its architecture, history, frantic pace and peaceful pubs. Whilst its innumerable green spaces, large and small, added a much needed element of tranquility and the deception of clean air.

'Trotsky?'

'Apparently his real name and a very nasty piece of work. To cut a long story short, Paul eventually got the pusher, name of Nowak, to agree to testify against Trotsky in return for protection. In celebration Paul goes home, cleans his gutters and falls off the ladder, landing him in a hip cast. Working with CPS and local CID, the govenor publicly announces the pusher's arrest but blurs what the actual charge is. Insinuating it is related to the manslaughter of Jody Grahame, as a cover story for holding him in protective custody, as no one wants Trotsky alerted to what is going on. At the same time he asks Ray to *quietly* reopen the Grahame case.'

'So, why not inform us straight away, given the similarities between the cases?'

'What can I tell you?' Merry got up, intending to saunter around the gardens, 'It was his call to make. This Trotsky guy is a real shit. He charges ten per cent per day, a hundred quid or so to tide you over until the end of the month quickly grows and each month it's harder to pay off. You sell your car, TV, other valuables to get out from under, or he takes them off you at a greatly knocked down price. Miss a payment and it's your wife or kids who take the beating, if the debt gets too big he will expect your wife or daughter to pay it off in kind. Basically, you end up selling your soul. The pusher, Nowak, used more of his product than he sold and had a gambling habit, his debt was pretty big and with no assets or family to pay it off he knew what was coming.'

'A few brief minutes with a sledgehammer or acid that would put him in a care home for the rest of his life,' Julie assumed. 'I can see the appeal of prison.'

'Getting Trotsky off the streets counted for more than finding the killer of a family-less, drug user,' Merry shrugged at Lukula's scowl, thinking she should know how these things worked. 'Ray had drawn a blank and, at the govenor's instigation, compared the two cases. The govenor may have dragged his feet more than he should but he's really busy what with the stabbings,' Lukula looked as if she was about to say something but Merry pushed on, 'and with knife crime and terrorism overlapping that's a whole world of shit to be involved in. Plus he would need to consult with CPS and those investigating Trotsky before acting. Ray had already started to brief me when the govenor passed it on. Now we are being proactive on the case inevitably the whole situation will get out and Trotsky will work out what is going on, time is not on the govenor's side.'

They continued to walk along, in silent contemplation, taking in the air much as others were doing as they passed round the other side of the church and returned to the car.

'It is what it is,' Lukula philosophically commented as she opened the driver's side door, 'and I have too much respect for the govenor to say he should have done things differently, but do you think it has made a difference, put us behind in some way?'

'You know, I'm told you are the *real deal*. You were in the army in Helmand, line of fire and all,' Merry obtusely responded.

'I know,' Julie snorted, knowing she had more experience of life than many her age and shouldn't be so naive, but she had naturally high expectations and still hoped for perfection in a world built on chaos, ' "What ifs" count for nothing, it's only the "what is" that's important.'

Swift had asked for a full briefing after lunch and Merry, with Rosen's help, had gotten the incident room ready. Rosen's team remained at their desks, Lukula had appropriated one of the few remaining ones while Gillian Porter sat at the other spare, as she had been working on reviewing CCTV footage all morning. The two DCs from local CID sat on chairs at the back of the room with DC Patricia Hayden, who had worked with Baynard and

Rosen on the Grahame killing and was now also part of the core inquiry team. Swift walked in, with another smaller but burly man, just as Merry considered himself ready.

'Afternoon everyone,' Swift, after a nod at Merry, started the briefing. 'This is Chief Inspector Consgrave, from the local CID. I've invited him to observe this briefing as he is in charge of a case that runs parallel to our investigation and, as we are also drawing on local resources for assistance, I thought it useful for him to be present.' It was as much of an introduction to the team as Consgrave was going to get, no doubt Swift had already summarised things for him before they entered.

'As you are all aware,' Merry began confidently enough, he had a mental script prepared but was already wondering if he should have written some points down to stop himself wandering off topic. It was a trait that didn't normally bother him but with an observer present he didn't want to sound muddled, 'we are now dealing with two cases. First we have Jody Grahame,' he paused to point at the pictures of the young woman, four shots taken by the photographer from the scene, two face shots, a full body and one of the head wound. 'Eighteen years old, mid-length blonde hair, though with coloured streaks, small build, she hardly looks her age. Attacked and killed in St George's Gardens three and a half weeks ago, single blow blunt force injury to the rear of the head. Paul Baynard investigated and, from fingerprint evidence, arrested Joseph Nowak, small-time drug dealer.

'Although Nowak confessed to manslaughter, subsequent investigation by Inspector Baynard, who's now on longterm sick leave,' – Merry and most of the team distinctly heard Swift hiss 'Stupid arse fell off a ladder, I've always said DIY is too dangerous and should be left to the professionals,' causing a cough covered laugh from Consgrave and smiles from others on the team – 'and Sergeant Rosen assisted by Constable Hayden, has shown the confession to be false. Although Nowak, is now helping with other significant inquiries that DCI Consgrave leads on.

'Lynsey Hensley, now our potential second victim,' again he pointed to the pictures he had pinned up earlier, 'was attacked the day before yesterday in Swedenborg Gardens, less than a fifteen minute walk from where Jody had been found. Lynsey was seventeen years old, looked older, was taller and fit, with short blonde hair. Again blunt force trauma to the head. With Jody it was a sideways swipe,' Merry explained, demonstrating the action as he spoke, 'possibly using a hammer though other weapons can't be ruled out. Lynsey's head wound came from a downward motion, almost certainly from a hammer, a standard size that can be bought in any DIY shop. Both blows were delivered with considerable force, both from behind, which suggests that someone was able to come up behind them unseen, remember Lynsey was out jogging at the time, or had managed to stop them and hit them as the girls moved away. Both victims were then dragged a few feet and dumped off the pathway, in Jody's case more effectively in amongst some bushes, perhaps giving the attacker a slight advantage in getting away.'

'Does the force of the blows or moving the victim rule out a female attacker,' Hayden's no-nonsense, smoker's voice cut into Merry's exposition. She was a long serving, experienced officer whom her colleagues described as 'formidable and unswerving' in her sense of duty but was not without her idiosyncrasies. She always introduced herself simply as Hayden as she hated being called by her first name: Patricia, after her abusive grandfather, Patrick.

'No, they don't. The swinging blow with the weight of the hammer, would have done most of the work but even so it suggests a very violent intent, perhaps an intention to kill rather than accidentally doing so. Moving them also suggests a degree of calmness and possible premeditation, as does the choice of where the attacks took place.'

'How's that?' Consgrave asked, forgetting he was there to observe.

'Both attacks took place at quiet times of day, at points that are sheltered and not overlooked. If you wanted to catch someone in a public place which isn't very public, these are good choices. It also suggests that the attacker knows the area and these parks well. Lynsey regularly jogged through both parks, the two crime scenes, and along with Wapping Woods, are constants on the different routes she takes. At least, that is what her running route plans we found seem to show.'

'Jody frequented St George's, at least during the dry weather, a number of people recognised her when the area was canvassed and she was picked up on CCTV,' Rosen informed them. 'She may have gone there to buy drugs. Nowak has confirmed that he had sold to her a couple of times previous to their last encounter, which was a few hours before she was killed.'

'I can't see that Jody could be mistaken for Lynsey,' Merry continued, 'so we can rule out the first attack being a mistake but there could be other links between them rather than their being random victims. Both had mental illness issues and attended the same local clinic, I'll be following up on that after the briefing. Jody was a drug user and had a number of arrests for possession, and toxicology showed she had recently taken fentanyl, of the China Girl variety. Whilst Lynsey volunteered on anti-drugs projects, so their paths could have crossed though on different sides of the fence. Julie, I'd like you and Gillian to look into that, plus follow up on our missing headscarf-wearing witness.'

Porter, who had sat up at the mention of her name, half raised her hand to indicate she had something to say, which added to her earnest youthfulness and made Merry feel like a lecturer in a classroom. 'I think I've identified her passing by Shearsmith House on the northern side of the gardens, though nothing of her actually entering the park, which seems odd, as she is next seen by the witness and CCTV at the eastern exit. It looks like she was leaving, as shortly after, CCTV also shows a woman in a beige headscarf, wearing a dark top and trousers leaving the area of the community centre just further east of the gardens. I can't trace her very far before or after these sightings but she was certainly in the immediate vicinity of the park fifteen minutes before and after the attack.'

'Anything of her face?' Swift asked.

'No, sir,' the constable was apologetic despite it not being her fault, as she started to pass out photos she had taken from CCTV, 'she seems to walk looking down, perhaps not uncommon for a muslim female to help preserve her modesty, but there is more than a passing resemblance about her figure in each shot that makes me think it is the same woman.'

'Not much use for identification purposes,' Merry stated, peering at the blurry photos of side and rear shots, 'but I see what you mean. It's good work though, well done,' causing Porter to smile, a slight blush on her cheeks. 'Perhaps we could put out a fresh appeal for witnesses and include a mention of this person.'

Swift was quick onto his feet at this point, 'Yes, both myself and Chief Inspector Consgrave are talking with the press office on this and we want to be careful about the message we send out. We all understand that two killings, whilst disturbing, may not amount to very much else but given the associations the Whitechapel area has, we don't want any "Ripper" headlines. We want the message to be more on the lines of: extra police vigilance around the area's green spaces, wise precautions for females out alone, that sort of thing. We'll include a fresh appeal for witnesses and further canvassing and patrols around local parks but at the moment I want to keep the two deaths separate in people's minds as it might also help ward off the more fanciful tips we get back.'

'Talking of tip-offs,' Rosen spoke up as Swift regained his seat, 'Gillian isn't the only one with news.' He nodded to the two CID constables sitting at the rear.

'Yes,' the younger of the pair, Barry Youlden, taking his cue and, following Swift's example, getting to his feet. 'We have had a number of calls about a black youth lurking around the high-rise blocks on the north side of Swedenborg Gardens, Stockholm Towers in particular. One witness said he saw a young black man climb over a wall into the gardens, given there is a gate not far off it seems an odd thing to do. And, this was just before Lynsey Hensley was attacked. The bad news is we can't find anything of him leaving the gardens, but we have picked him up earlier, getting out of a car, passenger side, near Stockholm Towers and we have the car registration.'

'You've got the driver's name?' Merry asked, alert to the possibilities of a breakthrough.

'Just come through,' Youlden smiled at the stir his news had caused amongst the others.

'Good, immediately after this you and Hayden go and question the driver, bring them in if they don't cooperate. Otherwise get your wall climber picked up and brought in for questioning. Get what you can out of him but hold him until I'm back from the mental health clinic. Ray and his team are going to review both cases and each victim's background to see if there are any further possible ties between them. Forensics are looking at the trace that was recovered at both scenes to see if they are linked, no bloody plastic bag was found at Jody's attack and in neither case do we have much physical evidence. Nor do we have any motive as neither appears to have been robbed, although Jody's phone is missing but that could have been picked up by anyone. Neither girl was sexually assaulted, so what did the attacker get out of this?'

'The thrill,' Lukula piped up, Merry had meant it as a rhetorical question but it seemed an obvious answer to her.

'How so?' it was Swift who asked, his face both puzzled and concerned as he half-guessed what Julie meant.

'The growing excitement over planning it,' Lukula explained, her army experience giving her an insight to a world of conflict and violence the others could only guess at, 'checking out the different localities, the best place to strike from, going over and over it in their head, perhaps practising with the hammer. Then the adrenaline pumping wait, followed by the explosion and high of adrenaline during the execution. It would be hours before they started to come down off that high. Then the realisation they had gotten away with it and could start the whole process over again.'

'Fuck,' Swift muttered to himself but clear enough for the others to hear, his own army career had ended after breaking an ankle on a final training jump and he'd never seen action but he recognised what Lukula was describing.

'OK,' Merry stated, taking up the reins again, 'it's all good thinking but let's not get ahead of ourselves. Although Julie is right about escalation,' Merry hesitated for a moment as he decided on how best to allocate the next task he wanted done. 'David can you work with our analyst and check back over the last twelve months for any attacks using a hammer or similar weapon? Start with assaults on young women and then widen it out to anyone, there may have been some practise runs leading up to the murders and his methods could have evolved.' David Anderson, who had worked solidly in the local CID for eight years nodded, wondering if this would be his moment to shine and break out of his otherwise plodding career.

'OK, anything else?' Merry paused, but seeing a chorus of shaking heads finished by saying, 'On one other note, I know there's no canteen on site and the drinks machine is plugged into the sewerage pipe but can we do our best to keep the office clean of Costa cups and takeaway boxes. If you bring it in then take your rubbish out, as apparently the cleaners don't do these rooms since the station was put on restricted opening hours. Briefing at ten tomorrow, that should give us all time to follow up on our assignments.'

# 7

Hayden phoned Merry as he arrived at the local Child and Adolescent Mental Health Service centre for his prearranged appointment with the manager. Her news wasn't good. The black youth seen climbing over the wall at the rear of Stockholm Tower was with the driver when Hayden and the young DC from CID called, it turned out the pair were cousins. The youth had gone to the high-rise to visit his girlfriend, but spotting the girlfriend's older brother, who disapproved of the relationship, he had jumped over the wall to hide. The girlfriend confirmed the event and had, with a salacious grin, alibied the youth for the time of the attack on Lynsey.

'Thanks,' Matthew told her, trying not to feel dispirited, he was usually more pessimistic about such leads but for once he had hoped for a breakthrough. 'Call it a day for now but first thing in the morning go over all the outstanding calls from the public, see if anything else is worth following up.'

'Their times with us do not overlap, I'm afraid, so there is no obvious connection,' the office manager, Liz, told him, she was a women in her mid-forties and she managed to look both cheerful and efficient whilst appearing tired. Her clothing reeked of tobacco smoke, which Matthew considered a pity as she had an attractive, neat figure and searching eyes that denoted intelligence. 'Lynsey Hensley finished with us as a patient nearly two years ago. Though she remained in touch and we are aware of the work she has been doing in local schools. Occasionally she gave talks about her experiences here. Such a bright girl, such a loss,' the manager sighed, before continuing. 'Jody only attended here fairly recently as part of her transition period. She received excellent treatment when she was in custody and came to us while waiting placement with adult services as she was turning eighteen.'

'Could they have met here, in passing say?' Merry tried a long shot though with little hope.

'I'll ask reception to check back over the visitor's log, everyone has to sign in.' Matthew waited as the manager had a tense conversation with the receptionist who obviously didn't think it part of his duties to check back through the archived logs. 'It will take a little while,' the woman smilingly explained, 'Lynsey's visits were also logged as part of a support programme we run, so it is only a matter of checking a few dates but, unfortunately, the old visitor's logs are stored in our archive.'

'Thank you, while we wait can you give me any details about who took over Jody Grahame's case,' Matthew asked, then waited while the manager tapped away on a computer.

'I can print off details of the doctor, support worker and case file worker for you, but to be honest they might not be much help,' the manager sounded both apologetic and resigned at the news. 'We keep notes on progress during the transition period to see that everything goes OK, which it did. However there's a note on file to say both the support worker, who was helping with her drug addiction, and the doctor, who treated her for depression, had contacted us for information as she had stopped attending their sessions. It is down to the case worker to ensure a client attends their sessions but at the end of the transition period her case worker moved away and in the period when a replacement was being found, Jody dropped off the adult services map.'

'How is that possible?' Merry asked, though guessing that budgets and poor resources would figure in the answer.

'Jody wasn't a high risk,' the manager stated, looking more tired and stressed than she had a few minutes ago, twirling a fidget spinner in the absence of a cigarette break, 'she hadn't self-harmed for sometime and, since her attempted suicide at fifteen, her biggest problem seemed to have been drugs; her depression and self-loathing was thought to stem from her drug use. Whilst the case workers do their utmost to keep patients attending sessions, if they refuse or, as in this case, simply don't push for help, then they tend to get dropped off the list. Unfortunately demand for these services greatly exceeds the NHS's ability to supply, so cases are prioritised and Jody wasn't a harm to others nor particularly herself. At least she wasn't that different from anyone else on the list in that respect.'

'I suppose I shouldn't be surprised,' Merry confided, 'a lot of people we deal with have mental health problems, either as victims or perpetrators of crime.' Then realising how pretentious he sounded, Matthew asked, 'Is there anything else on either file that can help us?'

'Nothing really,' the manager again was tapping on the computer keyboard, scanning files, 'Lynsey had a strong support network in her mother, aunt and school, which would have tipped the balance in her favour, Jody didn't. There's a note on each file that their details have been used in a clinical review, with the possibility of individual follow ups.'

'What does that mean?'

'A graduate student preparing a PhD dissertation on factors influencing recovery rates, it would have been fully vetted before approval and it was sponsored by a very well known researcher. Actually I know the sponsor, she has done some work with our team both on a consultancy basis as well as some free work in recognition of how well we operate,' the manager explained, a hint of pride entering her voice that the centre had such a link.

Any response Merry would have made was cut short by his phone ringing.

Porter had quickly retrieved a file containing all of Lynsey Hensley's volunteering work, which was on the girl's laptop taken from her bedroom. Most of the contact names in the file had already been spoken to but Lukula left Porter to phone the remaining ones and took the lists with her to visit Jody's mentor at her supported accommodation. Julie had little hope the information on the file would produce a link to Jody Grahame as nearly all the talks Lynsey and her friends gave were at junior schools and the content hardly looked as if it would engage an older, established user, like Jody. Her view was confirmed by Jody's mentor.

'Jody was alright,' the mentor, a university graduate who was trying to establish a career in the charity industry by working for a low wage at the accommodation project, informed the sergeant, 'not a problem as such. She was typical of the young, ex-offenders we house here but she did seem to be making a serious effort.'

'How was that?' Lukula asked, noticing the young man seemed a little in awe of talking to a police officer. Like the majority of the population, outside of traffic incidents, he had probably never had any contact with the police other than seeing them walk the streets.

'Nothing from her case worker for the last couple of months, which is a good sign,' he explained, feeling his work with ex-offenders gave him a connection to the rather attractive, if slightly older female officer, 'she also talked about regular meetings with her therapist. She seemed very positive about those, said they were helping a lot. The only setback she'd had was recently losing her part-time job at a supermarket, it was a blow but I was surprised when she went missing. We give them a day and a night then report them missing to the police or probation officer, often they are in custody already when we call.' The mentor smiled, knowingly, sharing a moment with a fellow professional, then quickly turning serious on seeing the sergeant's stony visage.

'Do you have any details of the therapist or the place she worked?' Lukula asked, thinking the graduate out of his depth amongst the streetwise ex-offenders he was supposed to be helping. Julie was of the view that life experience counted for more than academic learning, though she realised her own background biased her viewpoint.

'We have the case worker's details, who oversees that end of things, the workplace details will be on file. I'll get them for you.'

'Hi, sir,' Julie phoned her boss the moment she got back to her car, pleased at the link she had found, 'I've got details of Jody's case worker for her mental health support and where she had worked part-time, and guess what?'

'She didn't have one,' Merry was quick to throw cold water on Julie's findings.

'What?' Lukula was taken aback at the unexpected response.

'She hasn't got a case worker and hasn't been attending therapy or drug support,' Merry explained, smiling at the manager as he spoke on the mobile. 'The very helpful manager at CAMHS, has checked her records and phoned a contact she has at adult mental health services. Jody doesn't have a case worker and doesn't access the service anymore.'

'Bugger, her mentor thought she was doing well, seeing a therapist regularly,' Lukula shouldn't have been surprised, addicts tended to lie a lot to hide their addiction and Jody had obviously relapsed, but then remembered her other piece of information. 'However, she did have a part-time job, until recently, the same place Lynsey worked. It's up by the Berner Centre, I'm on my way there now.'

'I'm sorry we couldn't be of more help,' the manager stated politely, if without real conviction, she was walking Merry out and already had a pack of cigarettes in her hand ready for her smoker's break.

'That's fine,' Merry acknowledged, waving the file containing copies of the few details they had gleaned for him, none of which seemed of any use, but he would pass on to Rosen for entry onto HOLMES2 just in case an unseen or future connection was revealed. 'Every little helps,' he said over his shoulder leaving the manager to her coffin nails.

The young manager, of Chinese descent, who managed the supermarket was less than helpful and bridled at Sergeant Lukula's deepening scowl of frustration.

'I already said that I've told your other officers that Jody Grahame used to work here but was sacked six or seven weeks ago because of very poor timekeeping. Lynsey Hensley worked weekends, she reduced her hours to Saturday mornings while she studied for her A level exams. She's a very good worker and it's a pity she cut her hours but qualifications are important,' he stated, somewhat pompously, glancing at his own certificates in Business and Management Studies gained from a local college, adorning his office walls. 'Jody Grahame only worked part-time, weekday mornings usually, and was not a good worker, no qualifications.'

'Did they ever meet each other? Who were their friends here? Did either of them ever get into arguments with staff or customers?' Lukula patiently asked, trying to keep her frustration at the manager's attitude in check.

'No, the staff are here to work not socialise,' the manager stated with a shrug, wondering why the police were wasting time with such things. Shouldn't they be out looking for the killer of these two girls? He had taken rather a shine to the pretty, polite and shy Lynsey, so sad she had been killed, but as for Jody, she was a waste of space and wouldn't be missed.

'OK, we will need details of all the staff that have worked here since both girls started,' Lukula didn't bother to be polite about her request. 'While you are doing that I will speak to the staff that are here.'

Leanne didn't like the assertive police sergeant or her questions, she found it upsetting to be told that two of the staff who had worked at the supermarket had died recently. She had explained that she knew Jody, a little, but didn't really talk to her that much.

'I keep myself to myself and don't say much,' Leanne explained to Lukula, she found that the women working at the store chatted a good deal during breaks but also bickered and talked about each other. She found it less stressful to keep out of such things and often spent her breaks locked in the toilet, 'Jody used to talk more with Miah, the woman on the till. I don't know any of the people who work at the weekends.'

Lukula left the supermarket much less happy than when she arrived, the manager had been less than helpful, Leanne Solbury, one of the shelf-fillers, obviously had some sort of learning difficulty and Miah Hussein, who worked on the till, suffered from verbal diarrhoea. Lukula had had to listen to the woman's lengthy and detailed retelling of every conversation she had ever had with Jody, all of them centring on Miah's desire to have a baby and the ins and outs of a number of TV soap operas and reality shows. However, at least the till operator had worked on some weekends, money being very tight at home, and knew Lynsey – such a tragic loss – not that the girl ever said very much and was probably a bit stuck-up. Julie checked the notes she had made of the various conversations, realising another dead-end loomed. She and Gillian Porter would speak with all the remaining staff on the list in the morning but, so far, the only link they had found between the two girls was not proving very useful.

It was after ten at night when Malcolm Swift decided to phone Matthew, he knew the hour was late but he wanted an update and to make it clear that if he had delayed telling Matthew about the

Jody Grahame case it was not down to a lack of trust in him or his inquiry team.

'It was your call to make,' Merry said, doing his best to stifle a yawn and avoid his wife's look of annoyance as he spoke with Swift. 'Anyone taking up the investigation was bound to start taking a proactive look at things and Nowak's cover story would be blown, alerting Trotsky and his mates.'

'Yes, that's understood,' Swift stated, not entirely certain that Merry's calm acceptance of events didn't mask some degree of annoyance, in Merry's shoes Swift would have been pissed off. Swift couldn't decide if Matthew's attitude was a good or a bad thing, 'but I don't want you or anyone on the team thinking it was down to a lack of professional trust on my part.'

'If anyone raises it, sir, I'll make the situation clear to them,' Merry tried to sound reassuring, wondering why Swift was so bothered as they had more important things on their plate than such a storm in a teacup. 'On the plus side you'll be glad to hear that Julie has discovered both girls worked at the same supermarket, though they seem to have worked different shifts, she's started talking to the staff but will finish up in the morning. As for the mental health links and Lynsey's anti-drug volunteering neither are going anywhere. Despite the superficial similarities between the girls it would seem that their worlds didn't actually overlap.'

Merry paused, thinking Swift was about to say something as his boss drew a deep breath, but then went on as he realised he was mistaken. Though in truth Swift had been about to speak, then bit his tongue, keeping to himself his concern over their lack of progress, understandable though it was, and Julie's words in the briefing about the attacker seeking thrills played on his mind. Malcolm thought Julie was right and the logic of that thought meant there would be another death in the near future, a death he really wanted to see avoided and the whole shit show put to bed.

'Hayden's also drawn a blank,' Merry continued, cutting into

Swift's melancholy thoughts, 'the black youth seen climbing over the back wall has an alibi, some farce involving his girlfriend. David Anderson phoned a while ago, nothing in the records involving recent attacks in the local area with a hammer or other blunt instrument, apart from a road rage and a pub fight but they used a chair and a car jack. Still he used his initiative and asked the analyst to do a wider search tomorrow first thing.' Again Merry paused and again Swift made no comment, so he continued, 'We've all got some follow-up to do but unless Ray has come up with something we have missed then we really need to spend the briefing brainstorming new ideas and leads. If we could find that hijab wearing witness or glean some idea of a motive we might have a better way forward.'

Merry stopped talking, his wife was listening to the conversation as they sat in bed and he could see reflected in her face what Swift was no doubt thinking and what he, himself, already knew: a motiveless killing by a stranger was going to be near impossible to solve.

'Perhaps we should chat just before the briefing,' the deep well of tiredness in the Swift's voice, echoing through the ether between their mobiles. 'Nine thirty at Leman Street, that OK?'

Matthew was the last to arrive at the scene, just before dawn, at the western side of Wapping Woods where the path joined up with the canal path. He could see the neon floodlights the forensics team had set up plus the small tent to shelter the body, and followed the police tape until he reached the officer taking details of those entering and leaving the scene. The photographer was still at work and forensic officers were combing the area around the tent, before circling inwards for a more detailed sweep. The surgeon, a uniformed sergeant, Swift and Hayden were huddled in a group well away from the body while Lukula, who had been the first of the team to arrive, stood slightly apart carefully surveying all that was going on. Despite their distance from the body they all wore protective overshoes and gloves.

'Another girl,' Swift informed him as he approached, 'Madeline Turner, we think, from the description the parents gave when they reported her missing at one ten this morning. Seems they were concerned, given the recent attacks, though they said she often stayed out with friends. White, sixteen years old and long blonde hair, with blunt force injuries to the rear of her head.'

'Looks like a hammer blow again,' the surgeon stated, 'very similar to the victim I examined in Swedenborg Gardens. Subject to the pathologist's findings but, as guidance, I would say the time of death is approximately midnight, no sign of any other injuries nor sexual assault. I can't be certain of the last point but her rather skimpy attire and her underwear was in place so, unless we have an unusually meticulous rapist, it isn't looking likely.'

'No obvious signs of robbery. Her purse, with phone, money and cards still in it, some cheap jewellery and watch are still on the body,' Swift resumed.

'Who found her?' Merry asked, watching the activity around the tent.

'Anonymous tip,' Hayden said, 'by phone at one twenty five, a male by the sounds of it. The phone number was withheld but I've asked providers to see if they can trace it back.'

'I've asked the sergeant,' Swift informed Merry, who recognised Sergeant Mehta from a few days ago, 'to get officers out canvassing and searching the park and canal as soon as it's light.' Mehta did her best not to look sceptical, her boss was likely to have a melt down at the amount of manpower it would take. 'As for now,' Swift told Merry, 'I'll stay here with Hayden to organise things, you and Julie can go and speak with the parents.'

# 8

'Did you see that new detective show on the TV?' Merry asked, breaking the silence on the short car ride to the Turners' flat. 'The lead detective has flashbacks, resulting from the murder of his wife and son by an unknown killer, so he can now talk to the recently departed who help him solve his cases.'

'Is he an alcoholic and, or a drug user?' Lukula asked, knowing how common such detectives were on TV, their angst fuelled lives driving them to be the 'number one' detective.

'No he's a DCI but his sergeant, who seems to spend a lot of time changing in and out of her clothes in front of him and has great boobs, is a black lesbian,' Merry informed her, checking his watch and regretting his interrupted sleep, 'so I feel a certain affinity with him.'

'Sod off,' Lukula laughed, 'I'm not an exhibitionist and you are not a DCI, not yet anyway.'

'Can't see that happening soon, not with the cuts,' in any case part of Merry's recent reassessment of his career had made him question whether he wanted the additional stress of another promotion and was having second thoughts about completing the required training to prepare for being a DCI.

'How do you know Ricky Towers?' Julie asked out of the blue

as the question popped back into her mind at the re-emergence of Merry's sense of humour.

'We were at school together with Donald Key,' Merry told her. 'Towers was always a bit of an evil git but a lot calmer when his old man was inside. When his dad got out it all changed and we ended up fighting.' Julie would have liked to have heard more but they pulled up at the tower blocks at the rear of Swedenborg Gardens, where the Turners lived.

'It's a repeat, you know,' Lukula told him, wondering why all lifts in high-rise blocks smelt of piss. 'The last episode ends with them in bed, like all TV lesbians she has a hankering for men.'

'Don't get your hopes up, I'm always too knackered to do more than sleep when I get near a bed.' They both composed themselves as they waited for the door to be answered, ensuring they showed no sign of any levity and were radiating an aura of solemnity and respect.

The parents huddled on the sofa, the mother sobbing, doing her best to hold back the tears but failing, the step-father looking befuddled and disbelieving. There was no doubt it was their daughter lying just off the end of the canal path in Wapping Woods, not only did the description match the one the parents had already given to the police, but the photo on the TV cabinet of their daughter and her step-brother matched the one SOCOs had pulled off the girl's phone.

'We are sorry for your loss and having to bring you this news,' Lukula pressed on, less patient than Merry who was giving the pair time to process the news of their daughter's death. 'Alan, isn't it, you're Madeline's step-father and it was you who reported her as being missing at one ten, is that correct?'

'Yes,' Alan Turner, a short, ordinary looking man in his mid-forties with thinning hair and a body going to fat explained. 'We'd seen the local news earlier, about the two girls being attacked and killed in the parks,' Maureen, the mother, gave a loud sob at this, still struggling to keep her grief in check thinking it wrong to allow outsiders to see her raw emotions. 'Maddy had promised to be back early, no later than half eleven, as she had work.'

'Where did she work?' Lukula asked, knowing her boss would take over when he was ready.

'At a hair and nail bar, in the arcade of shops over by the Berner Centre,' Alan explained.

'She was good at it,' Maureen, her voice deeper than normal from the tension, told them. 'She had done work experience there as part of her college course, Hair and Beauty,' her tension eased as she repeated her well practised boast of her daughter's success. 'They were so impressed that they offered her a part-time job, helping with the nails. She did mine,' the mother held out her hands to show the sergeant the pink, sparkly nails. 'Next term she will be doing my hair,' she smiled, then her face dissolved again as reality struck her.

'She had been there a few months now,' Alan said, to cover his wife's confusion. 'I used to take her and pick her up.'

'Before she started college what school did she go to?' Merry asked the pair.

'She knew that Lynsey Hensley, the girl on the news,' Maureen had taken a deep breath, pulling herself up, determined to see this through for her daughter's sake. 'Maddy told us she had heard her give an assembly about bullying and how it changed her, so she recognised her when she came into the nail bar. She did her nails a couple of times, said they chatted about the school and how Lynsey was hoping to go to university. Maddy wanted to save up and get her own salon when she finished her course next year. She had a practical head on her shoulders and wanted to earn money, not rack up a debt going off to study for a piece of paper.'

'Who was she going out with last night?' Merry asked, wondering how Jody Grahame fitted into this.

'Just a couple of her mates: Gillian, I think, and Amanda.'

'Sergeant Lukula will take a list of all her friends later, and we will need to go through her room, laptop, that sort of thing to get a complete picture of her social and work life,' Merry explained, as his mind worked out the order of the questions he wanted to ask. 'Does she have a boyfriend?'

'No, she went through boys like tissues,' Alan snorted then shut-up seeing his wife's exasperated look, not wanting her daughter's memory to be tarnished.

'She was young, no need for lengthy attachments with her whole...' Maureen started to justify her daughter's flirtations then realising what she was saying stopped, confused how to go on.

'Did she socialise with Lynsey Hensley?' Merry asked, deflecting the interview back to his next question.

'No,' the mother said, 'she spoke about her when we heard the news, but she only knew her to speak to from the shop.'

'What about Jody Grahame?' but the mother just shook her head, the thought of the three dead girls was too much for her. 'Did Madeline mention any arguments, problems at college or work?' Merry was ticking off his mental list.

'No, she got on with everyone,' her mother paused before adding, as an afterthought, 'Although she complained about one of the lecturers always being on her back, pushing her for assignments. I don't think it was anything more than the usual teacher stuff. Maddy got bored quickly and always spoke her mind so she didn't always get on with teachers.'

'Did she do any volunteering, anti-drug stuff, that sort of thing?'

'Not Maddy,' Alan stated, thinking himself on sufficiently safe ground to re-enter the conversation.

'She smoked a bit,' her mother conceded, 'just the occasional bit of pot, nothing more than anyone else. But she stayed away from that crowd, the ones who hang around the park.'

'No problems that would cause her to access mental health support?' Merry could tell from the shocked and perplexed looks he received from the parents at this unexpected question that their answer was going to be negative.

'No, why should you ask that?'

'It's just routine,' Merry explained, the doorbell rang and Lukula indicated she would answer it, 'there will be a lot of things we ask that might not seem reasonable or linked with your daughter but we have to ask them all the same. It's all part of the process to ensure we don't miss anything, it's important you understand how useful all your answers are.'

'Sir!' Lukula called from the hallway that divided the flat in two: bedrooms one side, kitchen and bathroom on the other with the living room at the far end, 'uniformed and forensics are here.' The Turners had looked slightly brighter at Merry's explanation but their faces fell again at Lukula's statement.

'One last question, then we need to examine your daughter's room and, if you are up to it, take down some details,' Merry explained, giving a little smile of reassurance to the bewildered pair. 'Do you know why Madeline should be on the canal path and in Wapping Woods so late at night?' Both shook their head in response.

'There's a club down on Wapping Lane she sometimes went to,' her mother explained, 'she might have been taking a short cut back but it doesn't make sense. She would have been with her mates, not alone. Where were her mates, why'd they leave her on her own?' Maureen's voice started to sound shrill.

'We'll look at her room now, which one is it? The two constables will take down some details...'

'David,' Maureen suddenly remembered their young son, still asleep and unaware of the tragedy that had overtaken the family, 'we should wake him,' she looked pleadingly at her husband, relying on his support, 'tell him what's happened. Dear God, he loved Maddy, they always got on not like some step-brothers and sisters.'

Merry explained what he wanted of the two uniformed

officers, both young men: lists of friends, work mates, where the parents were for all the murders. Telling the pair not to push too hard, given the sobs that could be heard coming from the step-brother's room.

'Message from your DCI,' the SOCO told them as he placed Madeline's laptop and iPad in plastic evidence bags. 'He said the briefing is being brought forward to eight thirty. You also need to know we have already found a few interesting things on her phone, sex texts, pictures of a few different men's junk, some revealing selfies, plus a few dating apps. Seems she was what you might call *outgoing*, although sixteen seems a bit young to me but these days who knows? We'll be going through her social media sites and emails. Hopefully we'll have something for your briefing.'

'Thanks,' Merry stated, watching Lukula as she ferreted around Madeline's room, 'anything that links her to the other two victims would obviously help but also anything that might link her with mental health support or drug issues.'

'Her stash was well hidden,' Julie quipped, having pulled a plastic zip-lock bag from the toe of a boot in the back of the wardrobe, 'hardly original but as the mother said, nothing more than you'd expect to find in eight out of ten households.'

'Not mine,' Merry muttered, knowing his wife's vigilance on such matters. 'What else?' he asked, surveying the room which, in line with most teenagers' bedrooms, looked as if a small tornado had passed through it.

'Birth control pills,' Lukula stated, working her way through a set of drawers. 'Sensible at her age though she doesn't seem to have been that rigorous in taking one each day. Also some condoms, different types, a vibrator, range of clothing, shoes, some magazines, no books apart from those for her college course. Given that she was nearly seventeen nothing to be too shocked about. Some of this underwear looks pricey, and this…' Lukula handed Merry a small photo album she had just found at the back of the undies draw.

The two uniformed constables were entertaining the confused and sleepy eight year old step-brother in the kitchen, on the pretence of making the British cure-all: a cup of tea. The lad might not fully comprehend what was going on but was not going to miss the opportunity of seeing what kit the two officers carried around with them, his mates were going to be as envious as hell.

'We found these photos in Madeline's room,' Merry explained, 'a dozen Polaroids, nine of which seem to be standard family pictures, shots of your son when he was younger sitting on Madeline's lap, a couple of yourselves and Madeline at Christmas or birthdays,' the inspector flipped through the album showing the pictures as he described them, the parents' faces growing stonier as he progressed. 'Then we get to these three, from the dates in pencil on the backs Madeline would have been about twelve or thirteen.'

'God, not this again, not now,' Maureen put her head in her hands, despairing, whilst Alan went quiet and pale. 'She swore blind they had all been destroyed, we burnt them all having shredded them first. It isn't what it looks like,' Maureen emphatically stated, raising her face to look the two scowling police officers in their eyes.

'How is that?' Lukula demanded. 'What do you think they look like? These three photos: two of you and Madeline and one of your husband and Madeline, the three of you naked and, how would you describe what you are doing?'

'Tickling, that's all, it's the only way to describe it,' Maureen tried not to sound defensive, she knew she had nothing to defend against but decided to have the whole thing out. 'We used to be naturists, that's how Alan and I met, through a magazine after my divorce. I didn't want Maddy to be afraid of her body, not to be embarrassed about it, to feel she could share any concerns with us. When I was small I was as thin as a rake as I got older I got fatter. Now look at me, five two in a size twenty dress – that's me. I don't care what I look like to others, I diet for my health not their approval. For Maddy it has been the reverse she was podgy as a child then during puberty it went to her hips and bust, but at twelve that wasn't obvious and I didn't want her obsessed with her body shape, not to have to go through what I did.'

'So these photos?' Merry asked, trying to understand what the mother was telling him.

'Taken on two different holidays, the ones with me are in our hotel room, the one with Alan is on the beach, look at the edges you can see the sand under the towel. He was just putting suncream on her that's all,' Maureen paused, glancing at her husband who was staring into the middle-distance as if he was some uninvolved bystander, while the two officers continued to watch her with the intensity of someone looking to detect a lie. 'Social services have already looked through everything and found nothing amiss.'

'Social services?' Lukula asked, pushing the mother to dig the hole deeper.

'We had a couple of bigger albums with photos, taken on one of those Polaroids, Maddy showed them to one of her friends about a year after we had taken them. Her friend told her mother who reported us to social services, didn't even think to ask us what it was all about first. It was three months of hell but in the end they concluded there was nothing to answer, the photos were returned and we were left to pick up the pieces. We shredded the photos and gave up on naturist holidays, it was like a witch hunt, guilty until proven innocent,' Maureen looked more angry than repentant, her tense body posture revealing the memory of the stress of those three months. 'It was years ago, past history, and was never taken up by the police. We still have a copy of the social services report if you want to see it.'

'That would be useful, though we will have to check with social services as well,' Merry stated trying not to sound suspicious, the photos probably had nothing to do with Madeline's death and he didn't want to stress the parents over something that had happened and been dealt with a couple of years previous.

'What do you think?' Lukula asked as they got in the car, the uniforms would stay a bit longer taking details before leaving the family to their grief until family liaison would call later in the morning. 'It may have been innocent tickling in the mother's eyes but the step-father's dick shows he was enjoying things more than he should have been.'

'Very observant of you, Sergeant,' Merry smiled. 'Though it was more the step-father's silence on the whole matter that caught my attention, rather than the size of his semi-erect penis.'

'Believe me I have no interest in men's junk, semi-erect or otherwise,' Lukula sardonically replied. 'Now how exactly did you get into a fight with the young Ricky Towers? And, has Donald Key always been that big?'

It wasn't worth going home only to come straight back, so the pair busied themselves, preparing and swapping ideas in readiness for the early briefing. Merry shared a text from Swift with Lukula which simply said 'Twitter shit hits fan', by which they assumed that social media sites had picked up on the killings. Lukula settled at a desk to go through various sites to see if she could see what was being said, as Matthew brought the others up to date as they arrived for duty. Swift and Hayden arrived last, laden down with trays of coffees and Danish enough for the whole team.

'Right,' Swift began, putting his muffin and coffee to oneside, 'we have something of a Twitter storm, with #WhitchapSmash, #WhitchapEdBanga and, my least favourite, #RipperHitsAgain. Why these fucking morons don't have better things to do with their lives defeats me but some shit has got to Madeline Turner's Tumblr account before we could get it shut down, so there are some nude pics of her she posted now going viral. There's also stuff starting to appear on Madeline's and Lynsey's Facebook accounts that the FLO's are monitoring. Fortunately Jody Grahame doesn't seem to have had much of an online presence. Although we are having the trolls traced, I have instructed family liaison to work with the families to get everything shut down and help them through this. They will also inform them about the press conference called for later today, it'll be led by the chief superintendent and myself. We will be confirming Madeline Turner as the third victim and appealing for witnesses but also asking for the privacy of the grieving families to be respected.' Swift paused for the team to take in what he'd said and ask any questions but getting none continued, 'You all need to be aware that the people you question might have picked up on this crap and have altered their perception of what they know or have seen.'

'Perhaps,' Lukula suggested, 'we should start a #whitchapcopssayfuckoffandletusdoourjobs?'

'I'll run it pass the press office,' Swift said joining in the laughter and allowing the tension in the room to dissipate before saying, 'Right Matthew, the floor is yours.'

# 9

Once again Inspector Merry found himself pointing at photos of a young, dead woman and reviewing a brief list of details about Madeline Turner, her death and her family. 'Hayden, I believe you interviewed the man who found the body?'

'That's right, sir, he didn't give a name or number at the time but the call was traced,' Hayden explained, 'Antoni Kowalczyk, has some priors but all traffic offences. Claims he was out for a late night stroll to help him sleep, saw the girl, panicked and phoned it in.' Hayden paused, to take a sip of coffee before continuing, 'When pushed he admitted the park is a place couples and singles go to pick up like minded individuals, or "dogging" in popular parlance. I brought him back to make a formal statement and he has alibis for the other two killings, claiming he was at work, I'll check that out immediately after this. He also said things were very quiet when he found the girl and he'd only gone down to the canal path to see if anything was happening, but didn't see anyone else around.'

'OK, let's list him as a witness for the moment,' Swift concluded, 'though check out the rest of his family.'

'He lives with his two brothers and an uncle,' Hayden said, she was an experienced DC and not inclined to leave stones unturned. 'The uncle has a suspended sentence for theft, he nicked some power tools from a DIY superstore, but the brothers have no history. They all cooperated readily enough, though the uncle seemed annoyed Toni, as he's known, got involved.' Swift gave an exaggerated bow of his head in acknowledgement of her work.

'We know Madeline knew Lynsey, we need to check any links at school and work and exactly how Jody fits into the picture,' Merry stated but got no further.

'Talking of pictures,' the SOCO, who had taken Madeline's laptop, had slipped into the room as Hayden had been speaking, and now interrupted the inspector, 'you might want to know what was on Madeline Turner's laptop, iPad and phone.' He moved to the front of the room as Merry motioned for him to continue, using an iPad to show the others samples of what he had discovered. 'I'm still going through, checking dates, etc. as some of the files and photos have been moved around, probably transferred from older tech. There is also a lot of stuff stored in the cloud and on different app sites. Most of what I've found so far are selfies of her in different poses, both partially clothed and nude, though often in underwear, and in a variety of places. These include a few photos of her posing with men, though only showing their private parts and no faces.'

'Maybe we should have a national database of men's dicks,' Hayden muttered to Rosen who pulled a face, as the SOCO continued.

'A lot of the outdoor selfies were taken around the canal path, Wapping Woods and the central library.'

'Book worm was she?' Rosen quipped.

'More about all the quiet corners and no CCTV,' the SOCO explained, unsmilingly. 'She seems to be using the photos to attract men to her website, on which she is selling advertising space. Everything is all very soft core, much of it from this year. She claims to be eighteen…'

'Any regular fans?' Lukula interrupted.

'We have a list of subscribers, under 3000 which is microscopic for a website of this type, few originate in the UK and hardly any resubscribe beyond an initial one month free trial. The five top spenders all originate in the far east and account for about eighty per cent of the revenue paid to the site.'

'How much has she made doing this?' Hayden wanted to know, causing Rosen to mutter something about her needing to stick with the day job, which in turn caused the two DCs from CID to chuckle.

'To be certain we need more time but roughly three or four grand, which in internet terms is nothing,' the SOCO explained, 'the site is amateurish, which might give it some appeal but you would have to spend a lot of browser time to find it.'

'The UK subscribers?' Lukula asked, wanting to bring things back on track.

'We will be following up but I need to hand this over to a specialist, they would be able to get a lot more out of this than I can. However, there is other stuff on here you should see first,' the image on the iPad shifted from a slide show of stills to a video shot, as Merry and Lukula recognised, in Madeline's bedroom. 'I reckon these were taken on her laptop camera and I doubt if the step-father was aware. The first two videos show her giving him a hand and partial blow job, the last one depicts them groping each other, then he masturbates over her.'

'Do you have date stamps for these?' Merry asked, he had moved to see the screen better and was watching closely to see if the acts being performed were anything less than consensual or constituted a rape.

'All of them were taken when the girl would have been between fourteen and fifteen,' for the first time the SOCO smiled, knowing he had produced a good result.

'That's good work,' Swift stated, getting to his feet, 'I'll go with Julie to arrest him and bring him in for questioning, we will need a team to go over the flat again. Under the circumstances we should bring the mother in as well, so we will need to notify social services. Hayden can you deal with that?'

'The mother alibis the step-father for the time Madeline was killed,' Merry cut across the sudden activity. 'His brother provided one for Lynsey's murder, and he is vague on where he was when Jody died.' Swift and the others had stopped and were again listening to the inspector, intrigued by his line of thinking. 'The trace evidence found at both of the first two killings shows a potential link, although the threads found are from fairly generic clothing material. We don't have anything yet from Madeline Turner's crime scene. However, it suggests that the killer was wearing a black, cotton and polyester jacket or top; the colour would have hidden any blood splatter. There were shoe prints from Jody's scene, though they couldn't be solely, forgive the pun,' – not that anyone listening smiled – 'attributed to the killer, there was a clear print at the edge of the bushes where she was dumped. A size five which is small for a man, but Alan Turner is on the short side, about five three or four.'

'It's a bit of a jump from porking his underage daughter, to killing her and two other girls,' Rosen pointed out. 'He doesn't have any priors either.'

'But, he used to take Madeline to and from work, so he could have seen the other two girls in the area,' Lukula sided with Merry, though not addressing Rosen's point.

'What is his motive, the videos were taken two years ago, so why now?' Swift wanted to know, his gut telling him Matthew was onto something but he wanted it laid out.

'Her rather expensive MacBook was a sixteenth birthday present from her step-dad. It's still on her Facebook page,' the SOCO revealed, thinking he had more than earned his wage for the week.

'And, Madeline was saving for a salon of her own after she finished her course,' Merry pointed out. 'Her mum said Maddy had a practical head on her shoulders, although perhaps not in the way she thought, so it's possible she expected more than a laptop from the step-dad.'

'It's certainly a line of questioning we should take with Turner,' Swift agreed warming further to the idea, beginning to wonder if things, at last, were coming together on the case.

'They didn't seem to have a lot of money,' Lukula pointed out, she had moved next to the SOCO and was looking through the iPad with him as she spoke, 'finding money for the Mac would have been a struggle. If Madeline was pushing Alan Turner for more then it's possible he was starting to look for another way out.'

'Everyone knows that with an unexplained death we always look at the family first,' Hayden joined the bandwagon. 'So it's possible he hoped to divert attention by attacking someone else first.'

'He's seen Jody and Lynsey at the Berner Centre and starts to follow them,' Merry continued, expanding on his theory. 'He picks Jody first because she's been sacked and there is no obvious connection with his daughter, she also started to hang round St George's so it's easier for him to plan an attack.'

'Only Nowak is arrested for killing Jody and his plan falls apart,' Swift could now see a clear picture and the lines of questioning they needed to take with Turner, 'after a couple of weeks he realised he is going to have to start again and this time goes after Lynsey Hensley.'

'Here is something else,' Lukula suddenly piped up, turning the iPad to show the team. 'Recognise the hair colouring?'

Everyone peered closely, but it was Rosen who had worked on Jody Grahame's case who got it first, 'Jody had those rainbow streaks in her hair.'

'They are not cheap, and difficult to do properly yourself,' Lukula explained, smiling as another puzzle piece fell into place, 'but Madeline has examples of her work on her Facebook page, nails and hair colouring, Jody probably got it done cheap for being Madeline's model.'

'Right we need to get moving on this,' Swift was convinced and wanted action. 'Hayden, take Constable Porter and bring Maureen Turner in, we'll see if she changes her story once she realises what her husband has been up to. Matthew, I want you to see if you can take the brother's statement apart. You said Turner's alibi for Jody's killing was already flaky but pull it apart in any case. If we can shake Turner's alibis we may get him on the back foot. David, I want you to coordinate with forensics, to go over Turner's flat and van, check if he has a lock-up and get that searched as well.'

'He's a builder so don't forget to check his recent places of work,' Merry put in, 'perhaps Barry could look into that and sort it?'

'Good thinking,' Swift acknowledged, nodding his approval of Youlden's role, 'Julie, you are with me, we will arrest Turner for sex with an underage girl and then work up to the killings. Any questions? No? Excellent.'

The incident room quickly emptied out leaving Rosen and his administrative team to get to work. No one needed to tell Rosen and his team what they had to do. It was their job to ensure all the information from forensics, witness statements and what the various teams of officers were discovering ended up in the right parts of the system and were all cross-referenced. Rosen might not be the most senior member of the team, other than in years, but he was the spider at its centre creating a coherent net of evidence to catch and help convict the killer. And, although he understood the inquiry team's animation and excitement at having someone in their crosshairs after the false leads and dead ends they had previously faced, he recognised that there remained too many holes in the net for them to be certain of their man. It was also his job to identify those holes and ensure they were cleared up, he knew he had more to do than anyone else.

The family liaison officer sat in Mrs Hensley's kitchen drinking tea, she seemed to drink endless cups of tea in her role, so much so that she couldn't face the beverage being served at home.

'There must be something?' Joanne Hensley insisted, in the course of a few days she had come to trust the FLO, the woman's businesslike approach, advice and straight talking had quickly won the grieving mother over; the officer was the prop she had so desperately needed. 'It's all over the news about this other girl being killed in Wapping Wood. The phone hasn't stopped ringing, although I haven't answered it,' she had followed the FLO's advice to get a temporary pay-as-you-go mobile and only gave the number to her immediate family and the officer, everything else was ignored or tuned off.

'I spoke with DI Merry before coming here,' the FLO confirmed. 'He has a number of new leads that the team are following up. Not least of these is that he has discovered that the young woman who has been killed worked in a nail bar near to where Lynsey worked and we believe she did Lynsey's nails. They went to the same school up until last year, so there are links that might point to a suspect.'

'Lynsey did have her nails done a couple of times,' the mother remembered, 'it wasn't like her but I told her they suited her.'

'It is very early days, so you shouldn't get your hopes up but they have a strong lead and they intend to question a man who might be able to provide more information.'

'A man, you mean the killer?' Joanne was shocked, somehow she didn't feel ready for this. She was still coming to terms with her daughter's death and didn't have any emotional room left to deal with the killer. Revenge and justice could wait.

'It's far too early to say, it may or may not lead to charges being brought. You shouldn't get your hopes up.'

Joanne had no hopes, hope suggested a future and she could only think about the past. She focused on the memory of Lynsey showing off her sparkly nails, sharing a moment of 'girls' talk' with her mother.

'OK, it might have been later than I thought,' Dave, Alan Turner's brother, conceded as Merry upbraided him with logic, 'it must have been just after four when he arrived.'

'In your statement you said you both knocked off early,' Merry was reiterating the events again, each time finding a small detail that didn't tally, slowly breaking down Turner's alibi, 'and he went to the bank to get some cash. He didn't use an ATM for some reason, but the bank can't confirm seeing him, nor were there any deposits or withdrawals from his account that day.' Dave shrugged his agreement. 'You had drunk a pint and text him to find out where he was and then deleted the text,' again Dave shrugged. 'So if I get our techs to go through your phone,' Merry waved the phone, taken under warrant, which he had melodramatically placed in an evidence bag before the scowling Dave, 'and retrieve the time stamp of the text, what do you think it will show the time as...?'

'After four thirty,' Dave deflated, he wanted to help his brother out but if they retrieved the text then it would show he was lying, 'he came in and we had a couple of pints. But I swear on my life, we didn't leave the place before six.'

Merry nodded, he didn't care when they left the pub, the fact was Turner couldn't now account for his whereabouts at the time Lynsey Hensley was killed. What's more Dave had already told the police that his brother wasn't at work on the afternoon Jody Grahame had died. Turner claimed he had gone for a pint but couldn't remember where and the CCTV at the bookies he thought he might have visited showed he wasn't there.

'You'll need to come with me to the station,' Merry informed the increasingly pissed-off Dave, 'to give a revised statement. I'm not cautioning you, but you'd do well to keep in mind that if I discover you make any more false statements I will be charging you with obstruction.'

'I'm going to let Turner stew in the cells over night,' Swift explained as he, Merry, Lukula and Hayden compared notes on the day's events at a local pub. Rosen had, unsurprisingly as a recovering alcoholic, stayed at his desk working on HOLMES2. 'With the video and photographic evidence Turner could hardly contest having sex with Madeline, I expect that his solicitor advised one hundred per cent cooperation so he could mitigate on remorse when it goes to trial.'

'Arresting him in front of his wife was a good move,' Lukula applauded the govenor's tactics, 'Shook her to the core, so I don't think she will lie for him.'

'Gillian did a nice job on turning the knife as we took her in,' Hayden stated with a grim smile. 'She pointed out that child services would *probably* let her have her son back in her care providing she wasn't charged, of course.'

'Although she hasn't withdrawn her statement that her husband was with her,' Merry confirmed.

'Not yet, she spent the first half of the interview denying any of it was a possible, then spat acid and bile when we went over the evidence with her,' Hayden told them. 'I suspect by morning all her husband's gear will be in the tower block rubbish bins and she'll be singing a different song when we re-interview her.'

'Perhaps I can add some weight to that,' Merry suggested, not wanting to tread on Hayden's toes but thinking he could add to the pressure they were putting on Mrs Turner to reconsider her statement. 'Now that Turner doesn't have an alibi for when Jody and Lynsey were killed bringing your boss into the interview will show her how much you doubt her story.'

'Turner still says he was home when Madeline was killed,' Swift told them, finishing his pint and looking to Merry for another round. 'Though he has said he forked out for the laptop to keep her quiet. He hadn't known about the videos until she emailed one to his phone a month before her sixteenth. He also agreed she was pressing him for help to pay for driving lessons and a car. It was when I asked if he remembered seeing Lynsey and Jody around, when he was taking Madeline to and from work, that his lawyer twigged we were moving towards something more and he started to shut things down. I left them in no doubt where I was going on this, so he can have a night in the cells to stew on it.'

'Not for me,' Lukula said, at the offer of a second drink from Merry, 'I'm driving.'

'Nor me,' Hayden said, 'I need to get home, hopefully I will be in time to read the kids a bedtime story.'

'Bugger it,' Swift added, 'that reminds me I have to phone the chief, she's keen to keep a lid on any media hysteria and wants twice daily updates. At least she was pleased we were able to announce a significant lead on the murders and Turner's arrest at the press conference. So I'd better make a move myself.'

'Cheap round for me then,' Merry smiled. 'I'll have one on my own.'

'Oh. As we're talking about the chief superintendent being pleased, Trotsky the loan shark was arrested and charged this morning, CPS didn't want to wait any longer,' Swift said, looking more than a tad smug, as he stood to leave with Hayden and Lukula. 'It was also noted that the tip you passed onto Gangs about those two girls worked out, the third girl rolled over and there will be further charges being made regardless of how the current case pans out.'

'Something for me to celebrate on the team's behalf,' Merry waved the others off. He'd spoken with his wife earlier in the day to say he didn't know when he'd be home and that he might simply kip-down in the incident room if things got really busy. She'd been understanding, more so than her parents would be at him missing another family meal but that was the life of a detective inspector.

So he was in no rush and when he struck up a conversation with Jackie, a tall, curvy blond, as he waited for his third pint and a burger, he felt even less inclined to leave the cosy comfort of the old fashioned pub.

# 10

It was an unseasonably cold, wet Sunday in May as Matthew hurried from the tube exit to Leman Street police station. The brutalist sixties' architecture of the Leman Street nick was at odds with the renovated and newly built buildings surrounding it, from some angles it was possible to believe you stood on the set of a film based a century before, from others it seemed futuristic. He particularly liked the silvery statues of horses galloping along a stream that had been created to run down Canter Way, flowing round the glass fronted exclusive high-rise. The effect however was ruined by Leman Street being lined with cars, dirty street furniture and waste bins overflowing with plastic rubbish. And, although the smoky grime of London's old pollution had been replaced with invisible fumes so that buildings might now gleam, lungs still suffered from noxious gases.

The team had quickly dispersed from the incident room, still enthusiastic in the belief they had the killer and it was simply a case of ploughing on until they turned up sufficient weight of evidence. Swift and Lukula had gone to another, nearby, police station where Turner was being held in the cells to interview him a second time, hoping to push him to reveal some incriminating detail. Whilst Hayden and Porter went to collect Maureen Turner, who was staying with family, to continue her interview. Rosen and his team continued their work and the others completed the searches, which now had spread to include David Turner's, the brother's, house.

Merry spent his time moping around, annoyed with himself. In a fit of remorse on the way home he had deleted Jackie's phone number, despite their promising start, feeling guilty at their kissing and groping in an alleyway after leaving the pub. He felt no need for an affair. His wife, Katherine, was loving and more than passionate and enthusiastic in their love making but there was an excitement in the unknown that had drawn him in.

Jackie had been uncaring of his married status and only too happy to kiss and fondle him, working up to a hand job. At a critical point he had sobered up and realised he was remembering the photos and videos found on Madeline Turner's laptop. Thinking of the sixteen year old and her step-father's actions while being jerked off by a woman he'd just met in a pub was hardly in keeping with the person he thought he was. His self-recrimination made Jackie's passionate efforts end less than satisfactorily and their abrupt parting that followed made him feel even more stupid and puerile.

Guilt, frustration and dissatisfaction with himself had kept him awake, long into the early hours of the morning. His mood had not improved over the family breakfast especially as his eldest, Becky, had sulked when he explained he would not be able to finish, as promised, the tree house that day.

Maureen Turner had berated and threatened all sorts of retribution on her husband but had not changed the alibi she gave him. 'I won't lie for him, the fucker,' she had stated with a cold fury, 'but I won't lie about him. I'll not stoop to that.' She had then burst into tears, at the thought of her daughter's end and the part her husband had played in pushing the innocent love of her life into doing such vile things. Eventually the mother had confessed all her own sins: loving such a perverted man, bringing him into their lives, not seeing the signs of what had happened.

Merry stopped the interview and sent the mother back to her family, saying it would be up to child services when her son would be returned to her care from the temporary placement that had been made for him. He then went to check on the progress being made on the various searches, leaving Hayden and Porter to complete the paperwork.

'We need more leverage,' Swift rather unnecessarily informed Lukula, they had taken a break from Turner's interrogation though were debating whether it was worth continuing.

'With the other charges we have on him, he isn't going anywhere,' Lukula philosophically stated. 'We don't have to rush things, something will turn up,' though truth was Turner's categoric denials and the details he offered in answer to their questions were giving her second thoughts.

Turner had started the session with angry and aggrieved denials, 'I loved her like my own,' he told them, then became confused by his own words as he remembered he had confessed to having underage sex with her on more than one occasion. Eventually, he had broken down, crying, repenting his actions, his 'transgressions' as he called them, his lawyer having used the word previously much to the two officers' scornful looks, but wailing his innocence of harming her.

'I'd never lay a hand on her,' he bemoaned, snot and tears mingling round his full lips.

'Except to pull her knickers down,' Lukula could not stop herself, though at least Swift and the lawyer had the decency to make no comment or intervene, as Turner jerked back almost as if the sergeant had slapped him, 'and put your hands all over her. Don't you think that killed something inside her?' Turner made no response, huddling down, sensing the animosity and revulsion the others felt towards him. 'Well?' she demanded, 'How will your

96

wife and your brother react when you tell them you did her no harm?'

'I didn't hit her, didn't kill her,' he finally rasped, understanding for the first time the consequences his actions were going to bring down on his head. He began to cry uncontrollably, in pity for his own plight rather than in remorse for the hurt and pain he had caused.

Swift had responded to the message Merry had left on his phone to call him back, hoping for good news, only to be told there wasn't any. Mrs Turner wasn't recanting the alibi she gave her husband. Although the searches had turned up a number of hammers, and two that were the right dimensions had been sent for detailed analysis, none of them looked as if they had any blood trace on them. They had also found a number of shoes and boots but none fitted the print made at the scene of Jody's killing, all of Turner's had been size seven and his wife's size four.

After a quick coffee Swift and Lukula went back into the interview room to confront Turner and his lawyer.

'I've had a message from Inspector Merry,' Swift told the pair placing a file on the table as he did so, his tone officious and his smile indicating a degree of triumph, 'we have recovered your shoes and hammers. Is there anything you want to say? Any changes in your statement about not harming Madeline?' Turner looked completely dumbfounded at the implication they had found evidence against him in the killing of his step-daughter, even his lawyer looked shocked for a second. 'Your last chance,' Swift stated, tapping the file he had put down on the table.

'My client has nothing more to say on the matter at the present time,' the solicitor stated, tumbling the ruse, as his client sat with mouth open and a terrified look in his eyes.

'In that case we are done for today,' Swift stated emphatically, standing, nodding meaningfully at the file, 'but there will be further questions. I'll resume again tomorrow.'

'Fuck,' Swift swore, annoyed they'd hit a brick wall. 'Worth a try but we will need more than bluster and suspicion to pin him down on this.' Lukula said nothing, she knew the govenor well enough to know he was having his doubts and was pondering where this left the investigation.

At least the blanks they were drawing and the lack of a direction at this juncture gave them an opportunity to make an early finish, giving them all a Sunday afternoon free, hopefully to return Monday, refreshed and full of new ideas. Julie, however, had had her own sleepless night, a text followed by a long phone call with her mother the previous evening had left her worried. Their conversations in front of anyone else were in English but private chats were in French, it was a habit both mother and daughter had maintained since Julie had first learned to talk, making her bilingual.

'It's nothing,' her mother insisted, her accent that of her birth, while Julie's response brought out her Mancunian accent far more than English did.

'Nothing? But you said they need to do an exploratory operation?' Julie was as much annoyed at her mother's determination to minimise the issue for her daughter's benefit as she was concerned for her mother's wellbeing.

'Yes, yes, a biopsy the doctor said. Keyhole surgery that won't leave a scar,' her mother gave a light, derisive laugh. 'Not that I would worry about such a thing at my age. I have no intention of parading myself nude in front of anyone.'

'When, did they say when it will happen?' Julie wasn't to be deflected from the point in hand by her mother's levity, 'I will get some time off and come down to stay.'

'No, I will be fine. We come from sturdy stock,' her mother was equally determined not to make a big thing of the issue. 'Look at my mother, your grandma, she lived to ninety four, and look at the life she had led.' However Julie persisted, for her own peace of mind, and they agreed that once an appointment was confirmed she would stay with her mother for a day or two.

So, as tired as she was Julie spent much of her Sunday afternoon first talking with her step-brother to insist he visit their mother, as he still lived in Manchester, and find out first hand what was going on. And, secondly, to scour Google, for all she could find on the limited information she had prised out of her mother. The results of this had terrified her far more than anything a doctor could have told her and left her troubled by what her mother was really going through. It took half a bottle of wine and a return call from her step-brother, shortly followed by one from her mother, before she felt reassured that they were still a long, long way off of fearing the worst.

Early Monday morning Merry received a text from Swift telling him to meet him at the Royal London Hospital A&E, it was shortly followed by one from Lukula to say she was there and giving him details of where to go. Merry had barely left home himself, expecting to arrive early, and it made him wonder if either of the other two officers ever really slept or took any downtime. Lukula's directions proved accurate and very useful in the sprawling hospital complex, as he got out of the lift he saw Lukula and Swift talking to a attractive woman with a light, coffee coloured complexion, long, black hair and dark eyes in an oval face, her thin lips smiling.

'Matty!' the woman spotted him first as the others had their backs to him, 'What are you doing here? I'm sorry,' she said to Swift, darting forward to greet Merry with a kiss on his cheek, 'but this is a very old and dear acquaintance of mine.'

'He is also the detective inspector I told you we were waiting on,' Swift explained, amused at the warmth of the woman's greeting and Matthew's obvious confusion.

'Doctor,' Merry acknowledged Alima Hassan, who held his right arm, like some long lost relative she feared might run off again, 'it has been a good few years. Not that you look a day older,' he gallantly conceded, his initial confusion put to one side as he beamed down at her.

'Twelve years nearly,' then remembering herself, she stepped away. 'Although you are a few pounds heavier, weren't you intending to sit your sergeant exams once your Masters was complete?'

Julie smiled at the pair, as Swift interrupted them suggesting they could catch-up over a coffee after his business was concluded, trying to remember how long Merry had said he had been married for; twelve years sounded familiar.

'Doctor Hassan is here with a patient, a woman in her mid-thirties who tried to commit suicide last night. A confusion over the woman's real identity, and her attempting to assault the ambulance crew, resulted in the uniformed officers who attended having her fingerprints taken and it turns out they match the prints on the blood covered Tesco bag recovered at the scene of Lynsey Hensley's murder.'

'I have been trying to explain things to Malcom and Julie,' Alima never stood on ceremony by using people's titles and it didn't surprise Merry that she already knew their first names. 'It isn't straightforward, but now you have arrived, I'm sure it will soon be cleared up.'

'Perhaps we should find somewhere quiet to talk? Constable Porter is watching the patient, though given her state I can't see her going anywhere,' Swift explained, taking charge and leading the group back down in the lift and to a table in a busy cafeteria.

'I've worked with Jenny, Leanne as I know her, as her therapist for a number of years, since she was twenty, following an attack that nearly killed her,' Doctor Hassan began, smiling her thanks to Julie as the sergeant delivered four large to go cups of coffee to the table. Alima had taken the seat next to Merry and, from the way the pair continually glanced at each other, Julie would not have been surprised to discover they were holding hands under the table like lovelorn teenagers. 'We diagnosed DID, Dissociative

Identity Disorder or Multiple Personality Disorder in layman's terms. Without digressing it is important you don't start to think in terms of schizophrenia or bi-polar disorder, you should also dismiss pretty well everything you have seen in films about this. Suffice to say it remains a relatively rare diagnosis, more so in Europe than America, and is not without its controversy.'

'Isn't it brought on by trauma?' Lukula stated, determined not to be lectured by the attractive doctor. 'A bit like PTSD?'

'Yes, although the trauma usually occurs at a very young age and is normally the result of physical abuse, in Jenny's case this probably occurred when she was about four years old,' Alima continued, acknowledging somewhat condescendingly the well meant, if not entirely relevant, comment. 'A few years later Jenny Cowan and her older brother were put in foster care with a couple in Fort William. Jenny had her problems but, on the whole, was less difficult than her brother and her symptoms were not recognised until after the attack. I was part of a team, as part of my doctorate, working out of Edinburgh studying this particular mental disorder. Given the rarity of the disease we worked with patients from all over the UK and I was lucky in that Jenny was relatively local. Things went well for a while, then she decided to quit the study and therapy.'

'How did that come about?' Swift asked, still puzzling what this had to do with his case.

'Her participation was purely voluntary,' Alima explained, noticing Matthew's rapt attention, while realising she still had to win over the other two. 'Some sufferers of DID can live relatively normal lives unfortunately many cannot, Jenny was borderline and her symptoms were also somewhat atypical, which is why I don't usually refer to her as Jenny.'

'This is the point where you lost me before,' Swift admitted, 'you say Jenny has ceased to exist?'

'Jenny Cowan, was known for her erratic behaviour, well into her teens, sometimes loving and dutiful at other times rebellious, she could have violent temper tantrums and could be devious and untrustworthy.'

'Sounds like me as a teenager,' Lukula pointed out, making the others laugh, even Doctor Hassan.

'I'd happily look over your case notes,' Alima conceded. 'However, Jenny often insisted that she wasn't Jenny Cowan but someone else entirely, behaviour dismissed by her foster parents and school as play-acting done for attention. Since the attack on her, Jenny Cowan, who would be thirty-six, has never acknowledged that name, and the most dominant personality has been Leanne, who claims to be aged thirty-two. Leanne has an entirely different history to Jenny, though on paper some key aspects of it can't be evidenced. However, to her it is completely real and she is totally sincere when she relates this to anyone. This is also true of John, a Glaswegian in his fifties, also of Jacqueline, thirty and born in Ireland. As well as a scary and violent woman who emerges at times of extreme stress, such as in the ambulance. Then there are the two children, one six and the other eight: Lilly and Meg.'

'These are all made up?' Lukula asked, not at all certain what Doctor Hassan meant by all this.

'No, not in the sense of her knowingly making up stories. Early studies showed these to be distinct personalities, totally different people with different ways of thinking and outlooks on life. Leanne is the most stable in that she is able to cope better with everyday life, though not as you might expect.'

'How is that?' Matthew asked, breaking his silence, his curiosity finally exceeding the surprise, confusion and embarrassment at Alima's sudden reappearance in his life.

'She has little self-confidence, is shy and doesn't interact much with people,' Doctor Hassan explained, 'she has a very limited job and, by keeping all stressors at bay, she tends to maintain a happy medium. However, the status quo she strives for is finely balanced and inevitably one of the other personalities will emerge for a time.'

'So when stressed a different personality takes over and then Leanne comes back,' Swift concluded.

'That is how Leanne would see things,' Alima agreed, then confused them by saying, 'but so would John, Jacqueline and the others.

'How can she be a man?' Lukula asked. 'Surely she must realise that isn't physically possible, so by definition it must be a pretence.'

'When you look in a mirror what or who do you see?'

'I see an attractive woman, a lesbian of mixed heritage, who is dynamic and good at her job.' Lukula stated confidently if tongue in cheek.

'Really, because I just see me,' Alima pointed out. 'I don't see a gender, not even a person. It's just *me* staring back at *me*.'

'If we can avoid the philosophical debate,' Swift stated politely though with the complete self-awareness that he was incharge and thought the conversation well off track.

'I apologise,' Alima acknowledged, her tone somewhat pompous, 'I'll have to treat Julie to dinner sometime, as these are questions about the human condition close to my heart and I love to debate them.'

'In a nutshell,' Merry decided to summarise, 'you are telling us we are dealing with someone who has a number of distinct personalities, each unlikely to know what the other has done or said.'

'Yes,' Alima acknowledged, refraining from patting him on the head as much as she would have liked to have done so.

'So when we are interviewing her we may not know exactly who we are speaking to or whether it is the one who can actually give us the answer we seek,' Merry went on, grasping the situation and the problems it would cause them. 'Worse still we have no way of predicting when the right person we need to interview will emerge.'

'Yes, exactly,' Alima agreed, pleased that Matthew had worked things out so quickly.

'Shit,' Swift muttered, exasperated and leaning back in his chair.

'However, I might be able to help,' Doctor Hassan offered. 'Act as a sort of guide through the maze, help unlock her mind for you.'

# 11

It had started to rain again, a light but persistent rain that, with the overcast sky and cold wind, made the May day feel as if winter had returned. They had parked at the rear of a row of shops, above which was a number of small flats, including Leanne's, and dashed up the concrete steps and along the open landing. Lukula, trudged along in her thin jacket watching as Merry ushered and fussed over Doctor Hassan, concerned she might slip or get wet despite her expensive, figure hugging rain mac and hood. Anderson, his round, black face still wet and glistening from the rain, waited with a two person forensic team for Doctor Hassan to let them in.

'I have her door keys,' Alima had told them as Swift had outlined the various courses of action he wanted to happen, as they sat in the hospital cafeteria.

'The nurse tells me that Leanne or Jenny…' Swift paused realising the confusion that would occur over names. 'I think we will refer to her as Jenny Cowan, until we have a clearer picture. Jenny is under sedation and not likely to be able to answer questions until much later today or early tomorrow. Given Jenny's mental health issues I intend for Doctor Hassan to be present when we interview her.'

'Please, I really would prefer to be called Alima,' the doctor informed them with a modest and becoming smile. 'And, if I may suggest, I think the person to lead on the questioning should be female, it will be less of a threat, but I can brief you all on what to look out for and how to approach her. There will be no telling which personality you will be confronted with first and the trauma of the attempted suicide, that they might interpret as an attack, will be distressing to them. So don't expect any coherent responses at first.'

'If it's empathy you want you might do better with Matthew,' Swift informed her, smiling as he remembered Julie's words at the end of Turner's interrogation.

Lukula shrugged, taking the govenor's comment in good stead, but Alima confirmed she thought Julie would be better. 'Matthew has many talents and skills, as I remember well,' Alima said, thinking back to the two nights they had spent together at a conference so many years ago, 'but empathy wasn't one of them.' Matthew looked as if he was going to say something but didn't, waiting for Swift to continue.

'In the meantime, you,' Swift nodded to Merry, 'and Julie should search her flat, you can take Doctor… Alima with you as she is helping us with inquiries.'

'What does that mean?' Alima asked, her brow furrowing.

'Just what it says,' Lukula told her, 'you are a witness rather than a suspect.'

'I have a meeting with the chief about this and another case,' Swift explained, 'I'll bring her up to date on Turner and how things stand. He's still my favourite for the killings but we need to figure out how Jenny Cowan fits into the picture, how her prints ended up on the bag and the motive behind her attempted suicide but for now she has to be a person of interest. Alima, I know you have already gone over your part in this but I'm sure Inspector Merry will have additional questions,' Swift told Alima, who was wondering how the cosy chat over coffee had become so formal and business like. 'We'll see what the search turns up, before deciding how to proceed.' Swift stood up not expecting to get any questions, adding,

'I'll have Ray dig up Jenny Cowan's old case file, she was a minor when attacked in Fort William but I shouldn't think anyone would object to our seeing it, given the circumstances. Our priority is to work out how her prints were on that bag.'

'Leanne's surname isn't Cowan, is it?' Julie asked, the realisation hitting her, as she answered her own question, 'You said she had a completely different history and that includes her surname, doesn't it.'

'Yes, it's Leanne Solbury,' Doctor Hassan responded, surprised at Julie's sudden animation.

'I've already spoken to her as she is one of Lynsey's and Jody's co-workers.' None of the three officers said anything more, each knowing this was the key they had been searching for.

'Is it always like this?' Alima had asked as they sat in the car, Lukula was driving and Merry had opened the passenger side door for her, his rather old fashioned manners held an appeal.

'Like what?' Julie asked, she wasn't entirely comfortable with the doctor being present, despite Swift's thinking, Alima's role didn't seem clear to her.

'It all seems so restrained, orderly and matter of fact. I expected more rushing about and flashing lights.'

'I leave the high speed car chases and jumping over fences until after lunch,' Julie informed her straight-faced.

'What about Matthew, does he simply crash through the fences?' Alima beamed her most winning smile back at Julie and was rewarded with a beguiling smirk.

'No, he does all the shouting,' the two women shared a joke, as Merry sat in the back of the car deep in thought, his mind still on on Jackie, but also adding Alima into the mix and how his meeting her had nearly scuppered his putative marriage.

The flat was tiny, virtually a bedsit. The entrance door led straight into a small kitchen-diner which also contained a battered armchair and TV, to the rear was a small bedroom, which overlooked the front of the shops, and a shower room and toilet combined. The six people crowded into the restricted space and Merry sent Anderson to canvas the neighbours to see what they knew of the woman who lived here.

'How did you get to find her, when she attempted suicide?' Merry asked, the three stood cramped together in the open doorway as the two SOCOs got to work. 'It was late wasn't it?'

'Yes, I almost didn't come,' Alima explained, watching as the SOCOs donned protective overalls before starting their search. Seeing Merry and Lukula pull on overshoes and gloves, she wondered if she would be asked to do the same but wasn't, being told instead not to move from the spot where she stood just inside the doorway. 'I had given her a pay-as-you-go phone, she didn't own one before, so she could contact me. It had rung a couple of times but went off before I could answer and no message was left. It wasn't characteristic so I decided to come round.'

'There are only four numbers in it,' Lukula told them, wearing latex gloves she had picked up the phone off the kitchen table to examine it.

'That would be mine, her place of work and her case worker,' Alima knowledgeably informed them, 'the fourth could be anything, a local take-away perhaps.'

'She worked at the supermarket with Lynsey Hensley and Jody Grahame,' Lukula informed the doctor as she dialled one of the numbers on her work phone. 'Did she mention either of them or Madeline Turner?'

'She spoke of Lynsey and Jody and of their deaths,' Alima explained as her *Pulp Fiction* ringtone burst into life, Lukula rang off and tried another number, 'but only over the last couple of days. It was the police questioning that disturbed her most, it would have made her feel she had a link to the girls, which she would not have fully understood. As for the Turner girl she never mentioned her.'

Lukula had tried a second number and rang off just as quickly as she had with the doctor, getting the supermarket answering machine, but for the third call, the case worker, she struck up a conversation and went out in the light rain to talk more privately.

'She kept a detailed journal, a diary of sorts, detailing all that she did and felt,' Alima explained, as one of the SOCOs pulled a large notebook out of a kitchen draw, 'it was part of her therapy.'

'When you arrived, you got in using your key?' Merry asked, starting on the list of questions he had mentally prepared in the car.

'No, the door was open, her keys were on the hook over the table,' I took them and her purse when we left in the ambulance. Perhaps I should have turned them over,' but Merry shook his head, indicating she should carry on with her story. 'She was in the middle of the room, where the blood stain is, a kitchen knife on the floor beside her. Her left wrist was cut and bleeding out. I bound the wound and called an ambulance and did my best to comfort her until they arrived.'

'Did she say why she had done it?'

'No, it was the elder of the two children, Meg, who was with me. She complained of the pain and the cloth I'd used to bind her wrist, she wanted aspirin and a plaster. I doubt if she understood what was going on, it must have been terrifying, like waking up to find your wrist slashed,' Alima spoke matter of factly, but she scowled at the recollection. 'In the ambulance Mia came to the fore, she is the one I described as the scary woman. At best she rants at worst she is violent and abusive, I never got her to tell me her name or anything about her. I dubbed her Mia because she reminds me of a self-destructive character from a Tarantino film. The ambulance crew ended up sedating her.'

Merry had a million questions he wanted to ask about Jenny Cowan's mental condition but settled for the one foremost in his mind, 'Are any of the people that make up Jenny Cowan capable of murder?'

'Sir,' as if on cue one of the SOCOs called him into the bedroom. 'You should see this.' Merry told Alima to remain where she was and went into the bedroom, there was barely room to move.

'This,' the SOCO held up a hammer, 'was in the bottom of the wardrobe wrapped in a Tesco bag.' Merry could barely take in what he was being shown, his entire attention taken up with a photo on the bedside cabinet, a photo of Jackie, or at least a younger and more dowdy looking version of her.

'It's a picture of her, Jenny Cowan,' Alima explained as she watched the SOCOs place the photo in an evidence bag on the table amongst the growing pile of items they were accumulating there, 'or, more precisely it is Leanne. I took it years ago, in Edinburgh, just before she left the study. I hoped it might help her focus on herself, who she was and reassure her that it was safe to stay in therapy. She was still getting to grips with the fact that she was only one of a number of personalities that inhabited the same body, understandably, it was extremely stressful for her.'

'You mentioned another one, a Jacqueline or Jackie?' Merry was trying not to panic, though inwardly he felt as if he stood on the edge of a very high ledge looking down into oblivion.

'Yes, very outgoing, a party girl,' Alima smiled at the recollection, despite herself she rather liked Jackie. 'Always a laugh, always joking, easy-going. Everything about her is about appeasement, becoming your friend and trying to manipulate you to do what she wants. The complete opposite of the coping strategy Leanne portrays.'

'We will be taking these for comparison purposes,' the SOCO dumped a number of shoes in evidence bags on the growing pile, 'they are the right size but I'm not convinced of a match. Same really with the clothing, there isn't much that fits the mix of blends and colour we have found on the victims. The other bit of bad news is that the place seems to have been cleaned from ceiling to floor in the not too distant past, the kitchen surfaces and shower have been bleached. And, from the smell, the hammer has also been in bleach. There's also a large shoulder bag, that looks as if it's been bleached inside, that we are taking.'

'That was very much Leanne's way of coping,' Alima explained. 'If she thought one of the others had been to the fore, she would clean everything and wash all her clothes and bed linen.' Noticing the face the SOCO pulled at this, she added, 'Much the same reaction many people would have if they thought a stranger had been living in their home, using and touching all their things.'

'We will need to take your prints for elimination purposes,' Merry informed Alima, desperately trying to maintain focus on the case, whilst all the time wondering what to do about his recent *association* with Jackie, who was now a possible suspect in the murder inquiry.

The three of them, Merry, Lukula and Hassan, had decamped to a nearby cafe, for sandwiches, leaving Anderson and the SOCOs to finish up at the flat. Merry phoned Swift to update him on the results of the search and had also taken a call from Porter, who told him that Jenny Cowan had become violent when she had started to come round and they had sedated her again. There was talk about moving her to a psychiatric ward where, given her recent attempted suicide, she could be more closely watched. Meanwhile Alima and Julie had started to chat, carefully probing each other's history, likes and dislikes, neither yet certain if they would befriend the other.

'I should get back to the hospital,' Alima told them both, obviously concerned by what she had heard, 'at this rate they will keep her permanently drugged. As her therapist I need to be there to help her with the transition, whichever personality is present when she wakes they will need the right support, otherwise the spiral of stress will continue.'

'You never got to answer my question,' Matthew pointed out, 'whether any of the different personalities could kill?'

'That is really two questions,' Doctor Hassan replied, 'and hinges on the subtle differences between capability and ability.'

'Try keeping it simple,' Lukula stated, on the whole she tended to find the jargon that experts used unnecessary and pretentious, 'without the psychobabble and jargon, try to use terms that a typical jury member could understand.'

'Such assertiveness and command in such a pretty package,' Alima almost purred, deciding she needed Julie as a friend and seeing a way to get her to be so. 'I rather appreciate a strict hand. However, it is a very interesting point you make, I must remember that Leanne is a suspect and my work with her could result in serious consequences if misunderstood or put into the wrong context.'

'If *we* could stick to the point,' Merry stated moodily, his temper not improved by the dishwater tea and cardboard sandwiches, he remained undecided and worried about what to do about the predicament he was in and had little patience for Alima's and Julie's sparring.

'I would need to know more about the case and the victims but I can't see how, given the nature of DID that it is likely. Some of the personalities, such as Leanne and Jackie, have the ability to kill, that is the wherewithal to plan a series of murders. However, I don't see them as having the capability, or willingness, to kill as neither resort to violence to overcome the problems they face. Mia is the only one I have met that has been really violent and she only appears at moments of extreme stress and then only for short periods, so she doesn't seem to have the ability to plan. She might be capable of a frenzied, murderous attack if provoked but nothing that required thinking through.'

'Could they work together in some way?' Lukula asked, still trying to fully comprehend the nature of Cowan's gestalt personality.

'No,' Alima kept herself from smiling, knowing Julie would not like to think that Alima thought her question rather dumb, 'it doesn't work that way. Each personality is a separate whole, they don't interact and their knowledge of each other is very limited at best. Leanne has come to terms with the fact that other personalities exist, the notes and observations she keeps give her some insight into this. John seems to have the most knowledge of the others, it is as if he sees them whilst dreaming but he can't interact with them. All of their lives are totally separate, if a personality emerges it does so with no knowledge of what has occurred since their last emergence, they simply wake up with a gap in their lives. John seems to quickly grasp this, he seems to intuitively understand what has just been occurring, and move on. Whilst the others have no recollection or understanding at all. The children, for example simply emerge and continue as if there was no break since they were last active.'

'Is it possible there might be personalities you have never met?' Merry asked, noticing Julie's perplexed look, knowing that her only concern was that this sounded like it would all end up in an 'insanity plea'.

'It's theoretically possible,' Alima admitted, 'although I do not think it likely. Jenny was in psychiatric care immediately after the attack on her, for just over two years. Basically on a drug treatment regime for schizophrenia, before being re-diagnosed as suffering from DID. She was released from care and immediately joined the research study and I worked with her as part of my doctorate programme. I virtually lived with her, in Edinburgh, helping her record everything, looking for the stressors that caused a change. It is why I always think of Jenny as Leanne, as she was the most enduring of them and also the most cooperative.'

'So why did she stop the therapy?' Lukula wondered.

'It was all going well, she was beginning to accept the role the others played in her life, that is how she perceives things as it being *her* life. As such she saw the benefits of the therapy, and how it might give control over her condition. I should explain that by stressor I mean anything that causes a change to a different personality. What we normally consider stress can play a significant part, but a smell, taste or action can be the trigger. With Lilly, the younger child, a significant stressor is the act of taking a bath, it would always cause her to emerge and she could play for hours in the water. Which is why Leanne won't go near a bath and lives in a flat with only a shower.'

Alima paused, ostensibly to finish her foul tasting tea but also to check if the other pair were following her, Matthew seemed to be doing so but Julie looked increasingly distracted.

'The problems started when we moved to phase two of the study. I had been awarded my doctorate by then but Leanne and the work I was doing on the study were still very important to me. The second phase required Leanne to move into a specialist facility, so we could measure changes in her brain chemistry, undertake MRI's and various other regular tests. The aim was to identify any physiological changes associated with the stressors and trigger mechanisms. The long term goal was to produce a treatment, to create a mix of therapy and medication that would help the patient control their condition.'

'Which patient?' Merry asked, causing Alima to give him a knowing smile, Matthew never disappointed her expectations.

'That was exactly the problem, and it was an issue of much debate within the team undertaking the study. We never expected a complete solution, never a total cure. The psyche of those suffering from DID is irrevocably broken, split asunder. What we were trying to do was help the more severely affected take back some control, smooth out the emergences and changes, so that patients could lead more normal lives and hold down relationships and jobs. Leanne saw the outcomes in a different light, she became worried that one of the others might dominate. She was particularly concerned that Jenny might re-emerge and reassert overall control. I explained it wouldn't be like that, that it never could be, but Leanne still left,' Alima shrugged, a gesture oddly attractive on her small frame, causing her breasts to jiggle becomingly, something both Matthew and Julie noticed. 'Though on the plus side, it prompted me to take a new direction. I attended the conference where I met a very charming young police officer and I started on my book.'

'The one called *Sexual Violence: Good or Bad?*,' Matthew had read the book when it was first published, long before it had become a bestseller.

'Yes, I got the idea at the conference,' Alima refrained from winking, noticing that Julie had picked up on her inference about Matthew and that Matthew had obviously continued to follow her career. Doctor Hassan felt she could breathe easier now she had the measure of both officers.

# 12

Having dropped Doctor Hassan back at the hospital, Lukula did not immediately pull away, the heavy rain on the car roof drowning out the muted sound of its engine.

'I checked the numbers on Leanne's phone,' she informed Merry, 'the third was her caseworker and she told me something interesting about Leanne. She had lived in Newcastle prior to moving to London and had a relationship of sorts with a man. It seems to have been an abusive one and she wound up in A&E a few times.'

'Interesting but how is it relevant?' Merry interrupted, causing Lukula to scowl at his ill-tempered impatience.

'It ended in a big domestic bust up, during which she clouted him with a hammer,' Julie smiled at Merry's surprise. 'He was knocked unconscious and, despite the state Jenny was in, he claimed self-defence. The police didn't agree and no charges were brought, which explains why there is no record of her in the system. Jenny was sheltered in a unit who helped with her move to London, her local caseworker has helped her ever since. She told me that Leanne had told her she was meeting with Doctor Hassan but that Hassan has not contacted her or her office, the caseworker sounded a bit put out.'

'It's relevant but circumstantial,' Merry was thinking through the mounting body of evidence and the relative weight of each piece, 'it should be chased up so we can record it as more than hearsay.'

'There was a fourth number in the phone,' Lukula reminded him as she pulled away, tensing herself over what she was about to say. 'I didn't need to ring it as I recognised it. Rightly or not I've deleted it,' Merry's mouth went dry, unable to think of anything to say, of course he had given Jackie his number when he took hers, 'I'm trusting my judgement, that it isn't relevant to the case.'

'No it isn't,' Merry muttered, unable to look at Lukula, almost involuntarily adding, 'thanks.'

They continued in silence. Julie wanted to say something scathing, to tell him this is what you get when you think with your dick, but Merry's face told her it would be pointless as he was already of that view. She knew she was risking her own job and she hoped she was right that it was a small risk and worth taking.

'So,' Swift summarised their findings at the end of a long day, 'on the plus side, Jenny Cowan worked with Lynsey and Jody. Although Leanne might not have socialised with them one of her other personalities, like the one called Jackie, might have. It is possible she also knew Madeline who worked nearby though there is no evidence that Jenny had her hair or nails done recently. Establishing exactly who knew who is a priority,' Swift nodded to Lukula who would be leading on questioning Jenny, supported by Doctor Hassan. 'As is how her fingerprints ended up on the Tesco bag found at the scene and covered with Lynsey Hensley's blood. A hammer of the right size and shape was found at Leanne's, but there was no blood on it as it had been throughly washed in bleach. She also needs to be asked about that. Then there is the shoulder bag found at the flat, it's been cleaned inside with bleach but there is blood splatter on the handle. The blood is the same type as Lynsey's and has been sent for DNA analysis, a match with Lynsey's would certainly clinch things. We also now know that, some years ago in Newcastle, Cowan was involved in an altercation in which she used a hammer. Hayden, can you follow up on that, no charges were brought but get statements and whatever records you can from her support workers and the Northumbrian force.'

Hayden nodded wearily, she had been thinking about what to prepare for dinner, listening with only half an ear to the summary and hoping she could leave starting the task until the following day.

'Her shoe size matches the print found next to Madeline's body, one pair of her shoes is a good but not perfect match for the print. There is no trace of any of the victim's blood on clothing found in her flat, at least nothing on the black coloured items tested so far. Nor is there a match for the fibres taken, though tests are still being run. Matthew has read through Leanne's journal, it is inconclusive in suggesting where she was at the time of the attacks. We know she wasn't at work at those times and not only is the journal blank for Jody's time of death the entries made for the time around Hensley's killing are confused. As for Madeline's death, given the hour, it isn't surprising to find she says she was abed,' Swift paused briefly, partly to check his own notes and partly in case there were any questions.

'Getting an alibi, or lack of one, will also be on my list of questions,' Lukula reassured Swift.

'David has been looking at the CCTV around her flat and the shops she lives over, but hasn't had any luck yet,' Swift continued.

'No, sir, unfortunately the system that covers her entrance way and its approaches is on a 24 hour loop,' Anderson explained, he'd hoped for a more positive contribution, 'but I am looking at cameras in neighbouring streets.'

'If you, Barry and Gillian can continue to work on that and recheck what we have on the CCTV around the crime scenes looking for Jenny Cowan,' Swift smiled encouragingly knowing how laborious and unrewarding, though essential, such tasks could be.

'Were any headscarves, recovered from the flat? I've drawn a complete blank on the woman wearing one who was seen near Lynsey's crime scene but it doesn't have to be a Muslim woman, that was just what the male witness assumed,' Porter pointed out.

'Excellent thinking Gillian, you'll make a DCI yet,' Swift smiled and getting a ripple of laughter as Porter blushed, 'Julie, another item for your list. Anything else we should consider?'

'Just a reminder,' Merry, who had been very subdued since returning to the incident room, stated, 'about how difficult the interrogation will be given Jenny's mental illness.'

'I have spoken with the chief and CPS about developments,' Swift explained, 'and it turns out that Doctor Hassan is something of a friend of the chief. I'm told that her discretion can be relied on and she will act as a consultant in support of the investigation. As there is nothing to suggest that Cowan is mentally vulnerable, it's been suggested we undertake a preliminary interview, while she's in hospital and under medical supervision, to confirm that she is definitely our main suspect. However, all things remaining as they are, we will then arrest her and all further interviews will be undertaken with a solicitor present. We are not to assume anything about her mental state or capacity, an independent assessment of that will occur if CPS require it. Doctor Hassan's notes on the case will be taken into account but will not be the sole basis for any assessment of Cowan's mental health.'

'Just to be clear, sir,' Lukula asked, 'does that mean we can share details of the crimes with Doctor Hassan?'

'Yes, we have the go ahead on that, though obviously it doesn't include any key evidence we are holding back on. Officially Cowan isn't under Doctor Hassan's medical care, though her knowledge of Cowan's condition and the work she has done with her has an obvious value to us in guiding how we deal with the suspect,' Swift confirmed, remembering the chief superintendent's praises for the doctor, whom she had known for some time. 'Doctor Hassan has contacted me to say that Jenny has been transferred to a psych ward where she can receive specialist treatment in more secure surroundings than currently. She is no longer sedated but is extremely tired and confused. She has suggested you and Matthew meet her here at nine tomorrow morning and then go together.'

Lukula nodded, though she was none too happy at Alima's involvement, seemingly based on her being known to the chief, and glanced at Merry who still seemed preoccupied and unconcerned at the development.

'Don't worry, Julie,' Swift continued, noting the expression Lukula had pulled and understanding her concerns, 'Doctor Hassan will still rank as a civilian, she is there to advise and assist you not to direct you. I've sought advice over her role, as she has been Jenny's therapist, however it's clear that the ward doctor, under whose care she is currently, has the role of protecting her medical interests. If that person tells you to stop the interview on medical grounds, then do so, if Hassan suggests you stop then listen to her advice but it will be your call. You can bring her into the incident room but she shouldn't be allowed to wander around freely. Does that clarify?'

'Yes, thank you, sir,' Julie smiled her appreciation, glad she worked for such a perceptive govenor.

'That leaves us with Turner to deal with, CPS are pursuing the prosecution of Alan Turner for sexual assault. Ray and Matthew can you ensure everything is in order for that? As for the killing of his step-daughter evidence is at best circumstantial and his wife still confirms his alibi. However, I don't want the pressure taken off even while we are looking at Cowan, admittedly she is a better fit currently, but it remains an open race and Turner is in the number two spot.'

'An ideal position for the little shit,' Rosen pointed out, causing groans of approval.

'You mirror my own thoughts,' Swift informed Rosen, in complete seriousness. 'So, although I want you to pull up everything you can find on Cowan and pass it to Matthew, I want you to keep digging into Turner, his wife and brother as my gut tells me there is still more to be found on him.' Again Swift paused, glancing around the incident room, knowing what he was about to say wasn't going to motivate anyone.

'As you know, in addition to the spate of local gang related stabbings the rest of the team are involved in, there has been a terrorist incident and now a race-hate attack, sparking fears of reprisals, all involving knives though the motivations are very different. The impact on resources across the Met is dire and manpower is stretched as thin as a gnat's whisker. So I am asking Matthew to continually review his manpower needs to see if anyone can, even if only for a short and temporary period, be released for other duties. I'm sorry, I realise the effort everyone is putting in and that you will all want to see the case through but we no longer have that luxury.' At least Swift had the decency to hang round for a few minutes, in case anyone had concerns they wanted to raise, though none did as they all knew what drove the job these days.

Matthew had been in no mood to speak with Swift, he knew Jenny Cowan was a strong suspect but would be difficult to pin down, it would take time though a smaller team could still crack it. Too add to his concerns he'd had a message from family liaison informing him that Joanne Hensley was being trolled, with some very nasty and unfounded statements about her and her daughter now circulating on social media sites. Merry looked at the examples the officer had sent him, suggesting that Lynsey had been killed because of her and her mother jointly prostituting themselves. Merry contacted the Online Hate

Crime Hub to see what could be done to track and stop the attacks, then contacted the family liaison officer to suggest they jointly visit Mrs Hensley.

Given his recent indiscretions Merry hardly felt himself best placed to offer support to the dead girl's mother but, as he still led the inquiry team, he wasn't going to shirk this. He'd do his best to reassure Joanne Hensley that the team were still moving forward and that they wouldn't tolerate the abuse she was receiving. For what little real good it would do. At least she still had the police on her side unlike Maureen Turner who probably felt the world was against her. One way or another, Merry thought, interviewing Jenny Cowan tomorrow would determine the course of the investigation and whether or not he owned up about his knowing Jackie or kept quiet. Whatever he did he'd keep Julie out of it, she'd done him a favour which he wouldn't forget.

Neither Merry nor Lukula felt at ease listening to Doctor Hassan's briefing, adding to their woes was the fact that they had both dressed for a cold day and the hospital interior was sweltering hot. The doctor responsible for Jenny's medical care had made himself known, told them he would check on his patient regularly and that she had a buzzer to signal any distress she felt, then disappeared again. Doctor Hassan's list of dos and don'ts added to the officers' growing frustrations.

'This isn't going to be much of an interrogation,' Lukula muttered to Merry as they waited outside the room as Alima checked to see if Cowan was ready.

Merry was taken aback as they were ushered in. Though propped up in the hospital bed, looking wan with her left arm bandaged, a drip attached to her right, looking thinner and with her hair pushed back, it was still unmistakably Jackie.

'John, this is Detective Inspector Merry and Detective Sergeant Lukula,' Alima spoke clearly, carefully pronouncing each word as if talking to a confused and slightly deaf elderly patient, despite the alert eyes that scanned the newcomers.

'Good morning,' Lukula began, ignoring what they had agreed as she was determined to take the initiative.

'I'm not so certain of that, lass,' John's voice stunned them both, it was light but throaty with a pronounced Scottish accent, exuding a confidence totally at odds with the frail looking female in the bed. 'First I wake to find myself in this place all cut about, then the police are here to *speak* with me. I assume your visit isn't just a social call?'

'No, John,' Doctor Hassan retook the initiative as both Merry and Lukula seemed lost for words, 'they are here to ask you some questions. Do you feel up to answering them?'

'Fire away, I'm dying of curiosity to know what they want,' John's tone was not sarcastic though his eyes told a different story.

'We are here to ask you some questions about three young women who have been killed,' Lukula asked now feeling on familiar territory, quizzing a suspect. 'We believe you know two of the women, Lynsey Hensley and Jody Grahame.'

'Their names aren't familiar,' John was quick to answer.

'They worked in a supermarket near the Berner Centre, you will have seen them there.' Lukula was savvy enough to realise that it was Leanne and not John who worked with the girls.

'I'm not one much for shopping, girlie,' came the laughing response, whether it was a deliberately evasive response neither Lukula nor Merry could tell.

'Do these help?' Lukula asked, letting the 'girlie' go, passing him pictures of the three girls, 'That is Lynsey, then Jody and finally Madeline Turner.'

John studied each picture carefully, finally saying, 'They are sweet young things, aren't they. All dead you say, such a terrible thing, they have a look about them but no, I don't know them.'

'What do you mean by "a look about them"?' Merry asked, causing Alima to scowl at his insistent tone.

'Ah, the undertaker speaks,' John stated, his eyes dancing with laughter though his visage was solemn enough. 'I thought you were here to measure me for my coffin, Big Man. Tell me how did my arm get hurt?'

'You cut yourself,' Doctor Hassan smiled, pleased at John's lucid responses. 'Do you remember how?'

For a moment John looked perplexed, then said, 'I remember a hand holding mine and a knife, then nothing until I saw the girl in the water.'

'A girl in the water?' Lukula asked.

'Yes, floating,' John struggled with his memory, trying to pick out the details, 'I'd clocked off work from the brewery, I was the nightwatchman, and I'd walked back to town past the ruined castle, past the train station and down by the loch. There was a policeman in the water, trying to lift the young girl, he was up to his knackers in the icy water and it must have been a painful job.'

'Where was this?' Merry asked, interrupting and causing Alima's eyes to signal he had broken the rules once more and should take more care.

'As I told yeah,' John pointed out a touch impatiently, 'on my way home from work. The women were there: three hens cackling, clucking about the girl. "The poor thing," they chattered, "it is no surprise, she was always trouble," they crowed, "the slut deserved it," they chirped. All three women were ever loving but never kind.'

Merry and Lukula exchanged glances wondering what this meant, whilst Doctor Hassan suggested, 'Is it a dream, John? Are you telling us about a dream?'

'A dream, aye possibly, who knows,' John mused. 'A dream can seem like real life and real life a dream.'

'The three women, John, are they the young women we showed you pictures of?' Lukula asked, thinking she had worked out the puzzle. 'Is that why you said they had "a look about them"?'

'I don't think so, the girls remind me of a girl I once knew,' John explained, then smiled and added, 'Or perhaps I just dreamt of her.'

'Was there anyone else with the women, watching the policeman deal with the girl in the water?' Merry asked, keeping his tone calm though his instinct was to be more aggressive and try to rattle the suspect.

'A man,' John paused and screwed up his eyes as if trying to focus on what he saw, 'no, it was two men, one behind the other. An older man at the rear and a young tough at the front, both wearing black, in the shadows.'

'Who is the girl in the water?' but John shook his head, so Merry continued, 'How did she get in the water, had someone hit her, with a hammer perhaps?' John smiled and shrugged, he suddenly looked tired.

'Do you own a hammer? We found one in your flat, wrapped in a Tesco bag,' Lukula asked, sensing they didn't have much time left with John,

'It must be mine if it was in my flat,' John yawned, struggling to stay awake.

'Can you remember where you were on the...' Lukula started to ask but got no further as John slumped to one side, then sat up looking dazed.

'Where am I?' the accent was gone, replaced by one more reminiscent of London, the voice wavering and hesitant and undoubtedly female, 'My arm hurts. Who are you?'

'Hello, do you remember me? I am Doctor Hassan,' Alima said quietly, indicating to the officers to remain quiet.

'Yes, of course, Doctor,' Leanne said, only Leanne referred to Alima as 'Doctor'. 'What is happening?'

Alima began to explain who Merry and Lukula were and why they were there and the two officers started to think they might get further on than they had expected. However, when Alima asked Leanne if she remembered how she had hurt her arm

125

Leanne became agitated and started to cry. As if from nowhere the ward doctor appeared, and seeing how agitated his patient was told Merry and Lukula to leave, allowing Alima to stay as they both worked to calm Leanne.

# 13

Merry had phoned ahead and Swift met up with the trio at the Leman Street incident room. Alima was looking decidedly underwhelmed by the stale interior of the desolate sixties building but had impressed the others by telling them she owned an apartment in the modern glass encased tower block opposite, in Canter Way.

'That must have set you back a bit?' Rosen commented, he and Hayden were the only other members of the team present. The others, taking a break from the gruelling task of wading through the CCTV footage of the various locations they were reviewing, had gone with the admin team for a collective coffee break.

'Proceeds from my book and lucrative consultancy fees cover it,' Alima stated breezily, 'but the views across the Tower of London and the Thames are worth every penny.'

'I'd be happy to afford something under an hour's drive from here,' Rosen commented, without rancour, after all it was hardly the doctor's fault that public sector pay was so poor.

'How did things go?' Swift called the meeting to order, thinking of his own apartment south of the river, although not in sight of the Thames and rather bijou it was convenient for work.

However, his current partner was pushing for them to combine finances and find something more up-market.

'Not good, though I'm not certain what we are judging it against,' Merry explained, he'd made a few cryptic notes in the car on the way back and was looking them over as he spoke, his brow furrowed in thought. 'We spoke with John, that was somewhat uncanny, close your eyes and you'd think of a middle-aged Scotsman, the affable sort you'd find propping up a bar somewhere. Open your eyes and you'd see a fay looking female staring back.'

'It was disconcerting at first,' Lukula agreed.

'You'll find you quickly get used to it,' Alima reassured them, 'just imagine yourself holding a conference call, where you are speaking with a group of people but only one person can answer at a time and you have to carefully keep track of who you are speaking with.'

'How many changes of personality are we likely to have to deal with in each interview?' Swift asked.

'It's hard to say,' Alima admitted. 'It will depend on who you start with and how hard you push. They will all have gaps in their memory so pushing them to remember things will always be a stressor. My therapy sessions tend to meander with one direct question then two or three general ones to ease back. It might pay us to rehearse a set of questions so the flow can be maintained without the pressure.'

'Excellent idea,' Swift agreed. 'I can't see things going forward much until we have a clear picture of what Jenny knows.'

'I don't understand why John seemed to remember another person's hand on his during the suicide attempt,' Merry commented, still pondering his notes.

'I suspect he briefly started to emerge during the attempt and then quickly faded, so his recollections might be muddled,' Alima reiterated, she had told him so in the car and was annoyed he'd raised it again here, 'or it could have been when I was there and trying to bandage her arm. I'm still not certain who made the attempt, I'm most suspicious of Leanne but I didn't get to question her that much, the ward doctor was concerned how agitated she was becoming. The fact is if I'd been able to work with her longer I believe she would have stabilised and we'd have made more headway.' When a breakthrough came Doctor Hassan wanted no doubt in anyone's mind that it was down to her intervention.

'I still think that what John was trying to tell us in someway links the past with present,' Merry stated, knowing Alima had taken a very different view in the car, dismissing John's ramblings as 'just a dream'.

'How is that?' Swift asked, noticing Lukula's nod in agreement and Doctor Hassan shaking her head.

'Jenny Cowan,' Merry summarised the case notes that Rosen had pulled up, 'was a vulnerable, blonde-haired, seventeen year old when she was attacked. Hit over the head and left for dead in an icy pool, within the grounds of the ruined Inverlochy castle. She was found and saved by a local policeman, in the *wee small hours*, on his way home from a night shift. There was no evidence of robbery nor sexual assault but, given her background and her strange ways, various possible motives for the attack were considered: was it a man she had been leading on, was she buying or selling drugs? The suspects they turned up all had alibis, including her brother who seems to be a nasty thug, and in the end the investigation petered out. Unlike our victims, but against all expectations, Jenny recovered. She was already thought a strange and wayward individual but her behaviour became even more erratic until her doctor had her sectioned. If this doesn't ring any bells with our current case, then I don't know what does?'

Alima sat tight-lipped, annoyed but not saying anything as Merry spoke, she didn't want Jenny's past being dragged up, at least not like this, but then she decided to take a risk, 'The connection is obvious, though I feel conflicted as Leanne's therapist in pointing it out.'

'Which is what?' Merry demanded, surprised Alima had conceded his point given how strongly she had so recently argued against it.

'Although each of the personalities exist as separate individuals they will share a collective id,' Doctor Hassan explained, feeling herself reassert control with each word she spoke. 'It gives them all a common framework of references and understanding. So it is possible they all, or at least some of them, share some memories especially of traumatic events but they will see them from very different perspectives, possibly even as dreams.' She paused realising she had lost her audience. 'I believe John's dream is how he perceived the attacks. The various elements of the dream are symbolic of what he *witnessed,* that one of the personalities is responsible for the killings.'

'That is going to be difficult to record as evidence and put before a jury,' Rosen commented before anyone else could speak, echoing the collective thought that this was too vague to constitute a lead.

'This isn't going to be a typical case,' Swift ruefully stated, scowling at the thought of how things were going to bog down in the collective experts' psycho-babble. 'Matthew, can you and Doctor Hassan work on setting up a series of interviews, Cowan's fingerprints on the bag are enough to justify her arrest.'

'Can I suggest,' for once Merry felt strongly enough about a line of inquiry to challenge his superior head on, 'Julie and Hayden do that with Alima. It will take time for all parties to become settled with Jenny and her many personalities for anything productive to come out of the interviews and, frankly, I think female interviewers would be less intrusive. In the meantime I'd like to go to Fort William and get more background on Jenny Cowan's case, along with the incident in Newcastle,' Hayden nodded in agreement as she hadn't had much response from the Newcastle force to her requests for information. 'It would add weight and understanding to any motivation we put forward, otherwise we are relying a great deal just on the Tesco bag evidence and her own muddled testimony.'

Before Alima could think of anything to say that could argue for keeping Merry in London, Swift had agreed, 'Excellent idea, Matthew. This could end up in an diminished responsibility plea and, though we won't have any say in that, the more we can produce to show prior actions, motives and factors that explain the killings the better,' Swift sat back, looking satisfied. 'Things are definitely coming together, I feel it in my water. We still have a way to go yet, although I'm hoping you can release more officers, especially once the review of CCTV footage is complete; things are tight, very tight.' Swift tapped the desk, no doubt echoing the mood of the chief superintendent's briefing to her senior staff.

'It will only be a couple of days,' Merry apologised once again to his wife, Kathy, 'I rather talked to the govenor into letting me go so I can't back out.'

'It's fine,' Kathy told him, again, amused he should think she was upset, 'Mum and Dad love to stay and they will look after the girls when I'm at the school governors' meeting the day after next. I'm just glad to see you have some of your old enthusiasm for the job back.'

'What do you mean?' he still felt guilty at leaving his wife and daughters, as much because of his indiscretion with Jackie as going to Fort William on his own.

'You are not really suited to a nine to five job,' Kathy smiled as a thought struck her, 'That young female sergeant isn't going with you is she? The attractive one with the nice figure and *come-to-bed eyes.*'

'She doesn't have come-to-bed eyes and she isn't into men,' Merry protested, smiling, knowing when he was being teased.

'She'd probably break my arm if I so much as looked at her in the wrong way.'

Hayden had phoned Lukula to apologise as she was running late, something about one of her children being taken ill during the school run. Lukula had told her not to rush as Jenny Cowan's legal council, Ms Robeson, was still getting up to speed and meeting with her client.

'It didn't start well,' Alima sighed taking the seat next to Julie in the ward's waiting area. 'Despite everything I told the solicitor she still addressed Leanne as Leanne *Cowan*. Leanne was none too pleased but seems to be cooperating.'

Lukula nodded, not in the mood to chat, she had received a text from her mother telling her she had a hospital appointment arranged, much sooner than she had expected and Julie was trying to work out if she could get time off.

'Everything alright?' Alima asked, more out of politeness than real concern.

'Just family,' Julie gave a half smile to signal it was just one of those things and not Hassan's business.

'Ohh, family, that's never an easy situation is it?' Alima, raised her eyebrows in sympathy, seeing a way to get closer to Julie. 'I'm forty but being single my parents still talk to me like a teenager: "you should be married" and "you've passed up on children, such a pity", endlessly badgering me.'

'You're forty?' Julie was genuinely surprised as the doctor didn't look older than her.

'Oh, that's cheered me up no end,' Alima was decidedly pleased at the unintended compliment. 'Yes, I'm forty, over the hill and all washed up.'

'Hardly, you look stunning and I'm surprised you aren't married you must have had lots of offers.'

'I have,' Alima's smile broadened at the thought, 'but men can be such arseholes. Matty is a prime example, when we met he was such a gentleman, reserved but earnest. However, he didn't think to mention that he was only a few days off getting married until after we had sex.'

Julie wasn't surprised, given what she had recently found out about her boss, but had no intention of gossiping about him either. 'Women can be just as bad,' was all she said, thinking back to the brunette sergeant from the Gangs Unit.

'I've been lucky then,' Alima confessed, 'I've had two good relationships with women. In both cases it was me that could not make a commitment.'

'Snap,' Julie confided, realising she wasn't particularly surprised at the doctor's revelation about her being bisexual. Then adding without thought, 'We would be a disaster as a couple.'

'My excuse is my parents,' Alima decided to push on the door that was opening between them. 'Papa is from India and is a well known medical researcher, Mama is from Egypt and was an economist working for a large bank. Papa is also a devout muslim and Mama a christian, but when they met it was love at first sight. All obstacles of family, race, religion were overthrown in the face of their all conquering love. Growing up with such a romantic view of love makes finding the *perfect partner* difficult.'

'Wow,' Julie couldn't help being impressed, she thought her own family history was exotic, but Alima had her beat, 'sounds an interesting story.'

'Add two older brothers into the mix, one a successful TV producer in America and the other a barrister, and you begin to see why I have high expectations and a competitive streak that is a mile wide,' Alima laughed.

'Money as well,' Julie assumed, pulling a face of mock disapproval. 'God, some girls have all the luck.'

'I'm also a great cook, my talents are endless,' the pair briefly locked eyes and Alima decided to take another step. 'You should try my ful medames or hawawshi.'

'Sounds exotic,' Julie sighed, her best and most enticing smile on her lips.

'Why not come for dinner? It will give us a chance to get to know each other and compare who has the most difficult family,' Alima smiled back, hoping the date would be sooner than later, with Merry in Fort William the closer she could get to Julie the more she could insinuate herself into the investigation.

Leanne wasn't happy, she just wanted to be left alone, her left arm hurt and she didn't like the drip attached to her right. She was worried about her job and what the manager would say about her not going to work, although the new woman, Robeson, told her not to worry about that. Leanne didn't much like the assertive and confident Robeson. She also disliked the police sergeant, Lookyloo – or something like that – who sat looking stern and asking lots of questions. Questions Leanne didn't like or know the answers to. She wasn't happy either that her therapist, her doctor, had brought these two women into her room. The hospital bed and the room were the only things Leanne did like. It was how she imagined a hotel room would be, with the nurses waiting on her and the ward doctor being so kind.

What is more Leanne was worried as she didn't know how she had cut her arm, though Sergeant Lookyloo seemed to think she should. And, why should she have a hammer in her wardrobe? She remembered another time with a hammer, one that belonged to a man, but the man had hit her when she told him to go away. That hammer had gotten her into trouble so she would never want one in her flat. Nor did she shop at Tesco's, she got a small discount where she worked and bought what little she needed from there. Yes, she knew Jody, a little, but Lynsey hardly at all and Madeline Turner not in the least, although she did walk past the hair and nail bar to and from work. She didn't normally go to any of the parks Lookyloo mentioned, though she did like to sit in Rope Walk Gardens when the weather was nice. The questions went on and on until she pulled the bedclothes over her head and buzzed the buzzer for the nurse, falling asleep before he came.

Merry arrived at Fort William station on time, having dozed on the train he felt refreshed and strode through the barrier and into the small concourse of shops, the entire station was hardly bigger than his local tube.

'I'm Sergeant Allaway,' the plainclothes officer greeted him, her accent softer than John's had been, she was tall, broad at the shoulder, dark haired and looked bored. 'You were easy to spot amongst the tourists and locals,' she informed him before suggesting that he drop his overnight bag at the hotel before starting.

Merry had expected a car waiting as they emerged from the subway leading from the station into the town centre but came out into a large, open square with a green in front of him, a row of shops to his right and an outdoor gear shop on his immediate left, before emerging into the square. Almost opposite from where he stood, across the green, was an imposing grey stone building which turned out to be his hotel. He had assumed Scotland would be colder and wetter than London and could not have been more wrong. The sky had only just sufficient clouds to emphasise its otherwise endless blue, the sun was a bright, crayon yellow and the air warm and mellow.

'I was told you'd want to see the foster parents first,' Allaway stated, still looking bored. 'They live nearby so we can walk.' Merry didn't complain, he was happy to stretch his legs after the train journey and they crossed the Parade, which was what the green was called, and then followed a street lined with gift shops, cafes and restaurants to suit every tourist's taste.

'Unless you want something fancy I'd suggest you eat at the hotel, they do a good meal there,' Allaway, informed him as they turned up a small side street, little more than an alley, that climbed up the hillside, emerging onto a row of grey stone houses. 'The bar is well stocked as well and a lot of the locals drink there.' Merry paused to look back over the roofs of the shops down at the expanse of the narrow loch that the town sat beside.

The foster parents were little help. Despite their fostering experience they freely admitted they had not been able to cope with the Cowans, brother and sister, who had been placed with them thirty years previous. Things had gone well at first, better than expected, they had two elder foster children in their care at the time who had helped with the younger newcomers. But, when the older ones left home, then Jenny and her brother, Albert or Alby as everyone knew him, became too much for the couple.

'We did all we could,' the foster mother explained, her rheumy eyes, moist with tears, 'but Alby had a wicked soul and was a big lad, he'd threaten Father,' she nodded to the lanky, old man who sat sullenly silent in the corner, 'whenever he told him off. The police became regular visitors and Jenny would act up.'

'Act up? In what way?' Merry asked, sipping the hot, strong tea he'd been given without being asked.

'She was in a world of her own,' the old man suddenly broke his silence, 'always pretending to be someone else, messing around and laughing one minute, being angry and throwing stuff the next. The school complained more about her than Alby, though he got expelled often enough.'

'Jenny was out late when she was attacked, do you remember where she had been?'

'With boys, I expect,' the old man stated, anger in his voice even after all the years that had passed, 'doing her drugs, I expect, causing trouble.'

'Now, Father,' the foster mother remonstrated, 'she did little more than what most teenagers get up to.'

'She ruined our life is what she did,' it was too much for the old man and he got up and left the room, they could hear him banging around in the kitchen beyond.

'After Jenny was attacked, all sorts of things were said,' the old woman explained, dabbing at tears, 'things about us, about Father mainly, and how he had treated the children. After all we had done for them, it was too much, even our friends stopped talking to us and he stopped going out to the pub. Life became bitter for him.'

'I'm sorry to hear that,' Merry sympathised, noticing Allaway still looked bored.

# 14

'You shouldn't pay too much attention to the old couple,' Allaway told him as she drove him from the hotel, where she had parked, to the police station in the centre of what was still known locally as the new part of town. 'Jenny used to tell that she was given regular smacks with a belt and put in the cupboard under the stairs as punishment.'

'Did that come out in the investigation?' Merry asked.

'No, I knew Jenny, we were in the same class at junior and secondary school, me being A for Allaway and she a C for Cowan,' Allaway explained, smiling for the first time since they had met. 'I wasn't a close friend, no one was, and her brother was a couple of years older, he was a real shite and was more out of school than in. However, this is a small town, at least this end of it is and everyone knew about the Cowans.'

'Was she into using drugs?' Merry asked as they pulled off the main road.

'Oh yes, and a lot more besides. Sold drugs as well and never said no to any boy,' Allaway informed him, pulling up and getting out of the car, 'I thought you'd want to see where she was attacked.' They followed a well worn path through open woodland running alongside a green field and shortly came out at the ruined castle on the banks of the Lochy river. Only the walls remained, though the worn pathways criss-crossing the site showed it to be a popular tourist attraction.

'She had been dumped in a dip, over by that wall,' Allaway explained, like a tourist guide pointing out the sights and giving a brief history of the place. 'It's been filled in since, but was half-full of rain water and even in the late spring it gets cold here, so she was lucky not to die.'

'She was found by one of the local police?' Merry asked, wondering how this landscape tallied with John's dreamscape

'Yes, before my time and when there was an office up beyond the Parade, he was on his way home on his bike around dawn. He apparently liked to watch the sun come up over Ben Nevis.'

'Which is where?' Merry puzzled, assuming it a long way off.

'It's the big rocky thing behind you,' Allaway pointed out, assuming Londoners spent all their time dodging traffic and pedestrians and never looked up. Merry turned, having had his back to the mountain since getting out of the car, and took stock of the huge mountain and its snowy top. 'The big pipes running down the side have to do with powering the smelting plant over the way and the small factory, over to the left, is the Ben Nevis distillery.'

'The file said Cowan was hit over the back of the head and left for dead. And, although there were other injuries, rape was quickly ruled out as a motive?' Merry asked, eventually turning back, he could see why someone would be happy to stand there looking at the view as Ben Nevis had a singular majesty of its own.

'Hmm, poor cow. From what I know, her clothes were all in place and the medical examination showed no signs of rape nor was there any evidence of a robbery either. No weapon was recovered, in fact virtually no other evidence was found as she'd lain in the water all night. She remembered nothing of the attack and was in hospital a long while recovering, eventually she was transferred to Edinburgh,' Allaway sighed, thinking back to the time and her own so different youth: a time of dances, boys and the wonder of a promising future, 'I never saw her again.' Allaway paused, taking in a deep lungful of the bright, clean air before saying, 'There was no arrest, no real suspects either come to that. It was a DCI from Glasgow who came up to lead the investigation, he looked at the connection with drugs and her brother, but threw in the towel after a couple of weeks and went back. A local man, DC Proctor, kept up with the case for sometime afterwards, he told me all about it when I joined up, it was a bit of a cause célèbre with him.'

'Do you know what happened to the brother?' Merry asked as they walked back, passing a small group of hikers.

'Left, just after the DCI from Glasgow went back, I think he went to Newcastle but he's in prison now. Some of your mob from the Met caught up with him when he moved to London: selling class A drugs, GBH, possession of an unlicensed firearm, resisting arrest and pretty well anything else they could think off. I think he's in Belmarsh currently and won't be out for another decade or more at least,' Allaway told him as she started the car then, catching sight of Merry's expression, explained, 'I keep Procter informed, he's moved to Mallaig, since retiring, but still pesters me for information.

'Talking of which, Jenny often travelled to Mallaig and had just returned from there before she was attacked. It was assumed she had either been to see her supplier or was selling drugs there herself. She must have come back on the late train, the castle isn't too far to walk from the station so it was possible she was meeting someone but whether it had to do with drugs or something else we don't know. Toxicology showed she had traces of drugs in her system but there was no evidence of her carrying anything. Nothing really added up but, then, nothing ever did with Jenny.'

'Jesus, you look stunning,' Julie's jaw literally dropped as Alima opened the door to her apartment, dressed in a silky, dark brown, off-the-shoulder dress which was intricately patterned with pin-points of white. The dress's colour complimented her golden skin, as did the lightest of coral pink lipsticks and matching varnish on her manicured nails. Her high heels emphasised the curve of her shapely calves and thighs and she had put her hair up in a simple knot that suited her oval face. 'You might have said you were dressing in your finest.' Julie tugged at her faded denim jacket covering a plain white tee shirt. At least her jeans were fashionably distressed and horizontally slashed a number of times across her thighs, although her comfortable, beige sandals looked well used.

'Actually, you look quite sexy as you are,' Alima assured her, then threw caution to the wind and taking Julie by her waist, kissed her. Not a welcoming peck on the cheek but a full kiss on the mouth, the tip of her tongue invitingly parting the other woman's lips. Julie, without thought reacted as her body and nature wanted, her own tongue pushing into Alima's mouth, pulling her close, momentarily their bodies pressing into each other.

'The great thing about Egyptian food is that it can remain heated for a long while before it spoils,' Alima told her, pulling her into the luxury open plan apartment. 'Let me give you the tour first. That's the view,' she pointed across the open plan, glass fronted living room as she tugged Julie along by the hand, 'living area, kitchen, bathroom through that door, guest bedroom there and in here is the master bedroom with kingsize bed,' she breathlessly explained, starting to undo Julie's jeans.

'Hold on,' Julie brought proceedings to a sudden halt, her stern voice making Alima believe she had over-stepped the mark, but with one smooth movement Julie turned Alima around and pulled down the zip on her dress. Alima shrugged and stepped out of the dress, wearing only the skimpiest of knickers, her high heels and lipstick she turned back. Her smiling, inviting, eyes fixed wantonly on Lukula's. 'Fuck me!' Julie stated in a hushed whisper, intending to add 'you are gorgeous' but Alima acted before she could speak, taking Julie's exclamation as a command and, covering her mouth with a kiss, pulled her onto the bed.

Dianne Allaway had arranged for Jenny Cowan's old doctor, who had treated the girl during her childhood and teenage years to meet with them. The elderly retiree was spritely and only too willing to help, talking at length about Jenny's troubled upbringing, the suspicions and reports to the foster care service about the often unexplained bruising and occasional broken bones that he saw Jenny and Albert for; reports that came to nothing. How he had seen her after the attack, how changed she was, being almost mute and unresponsive, with occasional unexpected outbursts of violent rage. He also remembered filling in the forms to start proceedings to have her sectioned and later providing background information for the study she was eventually placed on and the name of the professor in Edinburgh who led it, Professor Macalby. However, he had no recollection of Alima Hassan.

It was late when they finished so it seemed only polite, given how smoothly Allaway had organised his itinerary, to offer her dinner. She made a quick call to check that her sister was OK to look after her children, two boys, her husband having been given the boot some years previous. And, being in no hurry they had a drink in the bar afterwards, swapping stories of old cases and what it was like to live in the scenically idyllic Fort William as opposed to the cosmopolitan grandeur of London.

'The world's greatest city,' Matthew informed her, offering another double Ben Nevis ten year old signature single malt whisky. Which she accepted, then another and another, until they wound up in his room for an hour of sweaty, if satisfying passion. Then she had to dash off, swaying slightly as she went, taking a taxi home wondering how she might explain herself to her younger sister, who was normally the one being lectured for coming home late with the smell of whisky and a man on her lips.

The next morning, after a full Scottish breakfast, Merry left early for Edinburgh, feeling slightly worse for wear and a complete dick for once again being the unfaithful arsehole he was. At least he had text Allaway as he waited for the train, thanking her for acting as his guide, introducing him to Ben Nevis and sharing her passion for scotch whisky; he'd have liked to have said more but what was the point? He had to change trains to get to Edinburgh, but he had phoned ahead and had plenty of time before his meeting with Professor Macalby, over coffee and cake at The Elephant House.

'I do not remember ever actually meeting Jenny Cowan, Inspector,' Professor Macalby informed Merry, his mid-Atlantic accent telling both of his American birth place and adopted home in the UK, 'though I'm well aware of her condition and background history from the many reports I received as part of my research project. I published our findings six years ago but it raised more questions than answers about DID, so we have embarked on a much bigger study in collaboration with an American university.'

'These notes you have been so kind to collate for me,' Merry, was flicking through a slim A4 folder with papers and data about Jenny Cowan that Macalby had given him, 'seem to indicate that the project was already underway when she joined.'

'Yes, new subjects were still being referred, though Doctor Hassan was very lucky to identify Cowan,'

'Why was that?' Merry was pleased at the comprehensive file and he wondered if the professor had given any thought to confidentiality but then it was his experience that the general public rarely did when dealing with the police, perhaps that was just a concern of corporations and the guilty.

'DID cases are relatively rare and often hidden by misdiagnoses, as in Cowan's case, so Doctor Hassan was lucky in finding her subject,' Macalby, a small man with thin features and piercing eyes, sniffed before adding, 'Although, no doubt it was the result of considerable hard work and researching of patient records. As I recall she had a tendency to rush, which made me question some of her results with Cowan, though my concerns were never proven as Cowan left the study before phase two, which would have thrown a spotlight on any inconsistencies.'

'Inconsistencies?' Merry puzzled, noticing an attractive Japanese woman taking a snap of the elephant pictures on the wall behind the professor. 'Didn't Alima Hassan receive her doctorate based on the work she did with Jenny Cowan.

'Yes,' the professor stopped smiling, having posed as he thought for the tourist snap, 'her work tended to the superficial. I had my concerns about some of the evidence she used in her doctoral thesis, nothing I could pin down at the time. Had Cowan remained in the programme and Hassan's work put under greater scrutiny in phase two...' Macalby paused for dramatic effect, 'Well, to say the least it would have been extremely embarrassing for her if I had been right. That book she went on to publish only proves my point and undoubtedly it dented what little academic status she had. It was more about popular culture, puerile and sensationalist, rather than rigorous academic research. Of course, it would have made her a pretty penny.'

'You haven't kept in touch with either Doctor Hassan or Jenny Cowan, professionally or otherwise, I take it?' Merry, asked wondering if the professor was jealous of Alima's publishing success. He'd read her book and had found it oddly bland given its subject matter, although he'd put that down to a matter of taste as it had sold very well.

'No,' the professor seemed surprised at the question. 'Doctor Hassan remained in Scotland for a while, I believe, using her brother's holiday home as a base for writing; rather less bustle in

Mallaig than this place I suspect. As for what happened to Cowan I have no idea.'

Matthew's stopover in Newcastle was more rushed than in Edinburgh, but the detective sergeant who had dealt with Cowan's case was happy to meet him in a cafe on the station concourse. Matthew again received a slim file of papers, which the DS seemed reluctant to part with, placing it on the table between them but keeping a hand on it.

'She was in hospital for a couple of days,' the large rather dour looking man said, his local accent was very marked and Merry had to concentrate to make certain he followed what was said, particularly over the noisy chatter in the cafe, 'if she'd not used the hammer he would have gone down for ABH. However, the truth got blurred.' The DS petered off, realising he was repeating himself and Merry checked his watch thinking he needed to start for his train.

'Given the bad shape she was in no one really doubted her side of events, but it was proving it that was the problem,' the sergeant continued, paused again and then finally started to say what had been troubling him from the start. 'Thing was she'd bought the hammer a couple of days beforehand. She denied it, of course, said she'd never seen it before and it must have been his, but we found the receipt in her handbag.' The DS finally lifted his hand off the file allowing Merry to take it. 'Don't read too much into that,' he warned as Merry got up mumbling his thanks, 'it weren't the first time he'd done her over, so we all thought he had it coming and she was never charged don't forget.' Merry was going out the door, but waved to show he'd heard.

Merry's phone had cut out once already as the train sped towards London, the signal strength fluctuated from mediocre to poor, but he finally got through to Proctor in Mallaig, using the number Allaway had given him.

'I've nothing to add,' Proctor told him sounding annoyed, not appreciating how much of their conversation Merry had missed. 'The chief inspector they sent up from Glasgow was a shite investigator and turned up nothing of worth. I had a theory of my own but the man I had in mind died so nothing was proven and it'd be no use raking up the past, of no help to anyone.'

'I understand, 'Merry said, speaking loudly to compensate for the poor reception, which did nothing to endear him to his fellow passengers, 'but if you can give me a broad outline of what you found, who you looked at it might be of help. Allaway said you had done a lot more digging than the original investigation.'

'That's true enough, not that it took much effort to do more…' then the line cut out again and Proctor, no doubt annoyed by the further waste of his time by another incompetent inspector didn't answer when Merry tried again. The unsuccessful phone call did not improve Merry's mood as he transferred to the overcrowded tube in the middle of rush hour, it was an incomplete question that was failing to form within his mind that was nagging at him, like a word he thought he should know but could not remember.

Julie was having a mixed day, she had not been able to continue questioning Jenny Cowan as her solicitor had raised issues about her client's mental state and ability to answer questions while recovering in a psychiatric ward. Rather than argue the point Swift had recommended waiting until the patient was released before formally arresting and detaining her. He was in no doubt of Cowan's guilt but their suspect wasn't going anywhere and it would give the team more time to collect evidence. Having done some paperwork, Lukula had a late lunch with Alima and the doctor had pointed out how stressed Julie was looking, suggesting they spend the rest of the day at a spa.

Julie was not the sort to shirk her duties but she had racked up some long days and in practice felt there was little she could do until Merry returned, so was easily persuaded. At the all female spa, Julie was pleased at the number of compliments she received from staff about her well toned, lithe body. Though was increasingly jealous as Alima flirted with the young attendants, she wasn't used to feeling so needy of an exclusive relationship and was surprised at the depth and strength of feelings she had for Alima after such a short time. Although the good doctor made it up to Julie, relaxing her beyond measure and reducing her to a tingling jelly-like state when they were alone in the showers. Alima's enjoyment of the situation was gilded by the knowledge that it was in the spa that she had first met Chief Superintendent Jackson.

They had stopped on the way back to Alima's apartment at Julie's flatlet so she could get fresh clothes, Alima noticeably not making any comment on Lukula's untidy rooms. Back at the doctor's much more spacious apartment in Canter Way, Julie was happy to leave the cooking to Alima. However, Julie soon grew bored and decided to check her emails on her phone, only to discover the battery had died. It was as she looked for a charger in Alima's modern, functional desk that she came across a sheaf of printed papers, notes about the case and Jenny Cowan.

# 15

The desk was in a home office space within the luxury apartment, around a corner and out of sight of the open plan kitchen, with the dining and living space in between. However, as if sensing something was wrong in the quiet that had descended on the apartment, Alima put down her cooking utensils and crossed to the cubby hole she called her office.

'What are you doing?' the doctor demanded, turning the corner and seeing Julie intently reading her notes. 'Those are private.'

'Jenny Cowan confessed to you?' It was more statement than question and if Alima sounded outraged at the invasion of her privacy Lukula's tone was strident and accusatory, 'You told us Jenny Cowan never presented herself to you, not in the original research study nor since. Yet you say it was her who attempted suicide and she confessed to the killings.'

'Please, Julie, it isn't how it sounds,' Alima struggled to remain calm, inwardly panicking and realising how things would look to the sergeant, she needed to explain so as to keep Julie on her side. 'I didn't lie, I just didn't tell you and Matthew everything,' then seeing Julie's face grow hard and disbelieving. 'Please, my darling, just let me explain.'

Julie was thrown by Alima calling her 'my darling' – it reminded her of how close they had become and she hesitated long enough for Alima to pour them both wine and sit down in the living area. It also gave Alima time to think and decide on an approach she thought Julie would accept.

'You are right, I should have told you and I'm sorry I didn't,' Alima began, looking unhappy and contrite. 'When I went to Leanne's flat and found her bleeding out, I realised that Jenny was the most likely personality to have attempted suicide. It was a guess based on her medical history, as a young teenager she had self-harmed and her years of remaining *hidden* also suggested a very disturbed and *hunted* personality. As I bandaged her arm I realised it wasn't Leanne nor any of the others I knew, so I risked calling her Jenny. It was an educated guess but she responded, she was almost passing out and I was concerned another personality was emerging, but it was Jenny that said "I've done it now, I've killed four of me".'

'Just that? Those exact words?' Julie was now more puzzled than angry.

'Yes, then a very frightened Meg emerged and I focused on keeping her alive until the ambulance arrived,' Alima explained, her head hanging in shame for what she had done. 'When we spoke at the hospital and I was told of your suspicions I decided I could help the investigation more by not saying anything about it.'

'How?' Lukula was thunderstruck at the idea.

'It wasn't conclusive and I knew given Jenny's mental state how difficult it would be to establish her involvement. Afterwards I even spoke with your chief superintendent, who is a friend of sorts, and explained how I could help and in return I would use my experiences to write another book.'

'You told her what Jenny had said?' Julie could hardly believe this.

'No, only that I know the patient well enough to help discover exactly what she knows. Look, I've told you that I thought

Matthew was partly right about what John told us at the hospital. To me it suggests Jenny has resurfaced and her memories and thoughts are bleeding into his dreams. As you know, I've already said that I believe Jenny could commit a murder on impulse but to kill three girls in succession is more than impulse. I have a theory as to how to bring Jenny out into the open and have her tell us what she has done and why, what is driving her to kill. However, it won't be easy,' Alima tried to keep a balance between pleading for understanding and being apologetic for what she had done.

'Surely you can appreciate how quickly things could become confused if the interviews are not handled correctly,' Alima persisted. 'Just think how things would have turned out if you had simply sprung this on Leanne or one of the others, it would have been utter confusion.' Alima knew she had won the point as Julie finally nodded in agreement, her frown of annoyance turning to one of exasperation as the doctor's words sunk home. 'Once we can interview her in a consistent way, taking our time and managing the situation to bring out and maintain Jenny's presence, then I am sure I can get her to give a meaningful confession. To give you more than just vague words or second-hand dreams.'

Lukula had to admit interviewing Jenny Cowan wasn't easy and, the more she reasoned it, the more she began to realise that Jenny's confession was far from being that. Alima had hardly lied, just not given her complete opinion of the facts. She looked at the crestfallen and unhappy Alima and it pulled at her heartstrings, she didn't want to hurt her new found love, 'You said something about a book?'

'Yes, I want to write this all up, use a real case to show how psychology can help the police in their interrogation techniques when dealing with the mentally ill,' Alima couldn't help sounding enthusiastic, seeing Julie teetering in her favour. 'I know I may sound like a bit of a commercial whore, no better than a journalist hunting for a story to sell. However, I really need another book deal and I promise that you, Matthew and the others will all be shown as the great police officers you all are.'

'You should have told us, though I have to admit we would have jumped in feet first had we known,' Julie conceded. 'Police size sevens,' she waggled her bare feet, pulling a wry smile of conciliation.

'I should have trusted you, I'm sorry,' Alima slid across to kiss Julie. 'I should be punished, I know.'

'Good thing I have my handcuffs with me,' Julie smiled, responding to the kiss in kind.


At the morning briefing the following day Lukula had a glow and shine about her that caught everyone's, except Merry's, eye. To the inspector everything was a uniform and indistinguishable grey, a murky picture puzzle in his mind he could not complete for lack of all the pieces. Had he slept it might have come to him on waking but he had tossed and turned, partly from the guilt that pricked him from having slept with Dianne Allaway, partly from recognising how little time he had spent with his family recently and, partly because he could not define what it was he believed was missing from the case. How could he start to look for something if he didn't have any idea what that thing was? It was the need to achieve a greater clarity of the whole picture and identify the missing pieces that made him insist they should investigate further before considering their next steps with Jenny Cowan.

'I realise the evidence is somewhat *limited*, CPS wouldn't disagree with you on that,' Swift stated, determined to remain calm, he had never seen Merry as frustrated and annoyed as currently, though he understood that being told the investigation should be wound up was cause enough for any good detective to question if they had found out all they could about a suspect. 'Unfortunately, the recent terror incidents have pushed the entire Met to its limit and, reluctantly, I've had to agree to release more officers. Hayden is needed elsewhere while Ray and his team could support other investigations part-time, though they would still be based here and you will have first call on them.'

'Jenny is due to be released tomorrow morning, we can arrest and detain her then, even on what we have now,' Lukula stated, determined to bridge the rift between Merry and Swift. 'We've arranged to visit Albert Cowan in Belmarsh this afternoon, to see what he can give us, but from what you have told us about her time in Fort William and Newcastle, it tends to confirm that she should be our focus at the moment.'

'I don't think we are ready to arrest her just yet,' Merry stated, it didn't help that he couldn't formulate his concerns clearly enough to convince the others, but then conceded, 'but I agree we should interview her again before deciding on how to proceed, assuming her solicitor agrees.'

'That's the point, Matthew,' Swift patiently explained, 'unless we arrest her I suspect her lawyer will cry foul again and advise her client that she has nothing to answer. Cowan's prints on the plastic bag justified searching her flat, hopefully the DNA from the blood on her shoulder bag will clinch things. In the meantime we should push on, get her interviewed on tape, and not let up on the pressure.'

'Very well,' Merry shrugged, 'but we should have Doctor Hassan present, to help make sense of who is saying what and how the parts all relate.'

'Fine,' although Swift didn't sound too pleased with the idea, 'have it set up so she can listen in and suggest questions directly to you from outside the room. However, remember it's not for us to determine the impact of Cowan's mental state on her guilt. That, thank God, will be for the court to decide,' Swift, somewhat high-handedly, pointed out.

Belmarsh is situated south of the Thames on the site of the old Royal Arsenal, in Woolwich, and it reminded Merry of childhood rides on the Woolwich ferries, in the days when it was still possible to go below decks and watch the engines in operation. From the outside the prison was a mix of supermarket redbrick and razor wire, while the inside was modern nondescript with more than a dash of high-security. Albert Cowan was of medium height but a muscular and heavy set build, his dark hair and unshaven face matched the darkness of his eyes and sour, world weary expression. Neither Merry nor Lukula could detect any family resemblance with Jenny Cowan beyond the slightly hunted look in his eyes, a product of their common upbringing.

'I'm DI Merry, this is DS Lukula, we have a few questions to ask you,' Merry paused, but Albert simply maintained his silent stare, uncertain whether he should look menacing or simply bored. 'You don't look anything like your sister,' Merry continued, unexpectedly switching from the impersonal brevity of his introduction to a more personal tone.

'No,' Albert's monosyllabic response said much less than the puzzled expression that passed over his face about why his sister had been mentioned, as it helped Merry if Albert didn't know about his sister's suspected involvement with the killings.

'I'm sorry to inform you that she is in hospital, physically she is fine and due to be released but there are concerns about her mental health,' Merry informed Cowan as matter of factly as he could, he wanted this to sound routine and mundane.

'Hardly news, she's been a nut job for as long as I can remember,' Cowan informed them his bored expression returning.

'She was about six or seven when you were both put into foster care, you are four years older than her, is that correct?' Merry asked, unnecessarily consulting his notebook.

'There abouts,' Albert agreed, adding, 'our dad was a drunk and ma was a prozzie. Life's a bitch ain't it.'

'How was life as a foster child?' Lukula asked, Albert had been eyeing her since he had been brought in, it was about four years since he had been this close to a woman, at least one that didn't have a cock and false tits.

'Shit, is that why you are here? Bit late on checking up on that old pair of bastards, aren't you?' Albert scowled with disdain, he had no feelings about his life, it was what it was, but there still remained a deep well of anger in his gut at the memory of his foster parents, especially the old guy.

'No, as deserving as that might be, although we are aware you and your sister had a hard time of it, particularly your sister,' Lukula sympathised. 'She ended up in a lot of trouble because of her upbringing, didn't she.'

'Did she?' Albert mused, smiling as he glanced around at the walls, to suggest he had troubles of his own.

'She got involved with drugs and boys quite early on,' Merry stated. 'Did you have anything to do with that?'

'She didn't need much persuading,' Albert shrugged, he had little feelings for a sister who at one moment was loving, another in a rage and at other times pretended not to know him.

'Although you were involved in persuading her?' Merry didn't expect and didn't get an answer, 'There are quite a few who thought you were the one who attacked her at the ruined castle.'

'I was in Glasgow at the time.'

'Unfortunately, no one could be found to confirm that,' Lukula pointed out the flaw in his alibi.

'So what? I was questioned and never arrested or charged,' Albert sat back, crossing his arms, feeling no need to be defensive.

'Did you see her after the attack?' Merry asked.

'I went to the hospital when I came back from Glasgow but the police were there. After the police had questioned me I went back to Glasgow and I haven't seen her since,' Albert was bored again, glancing up at the clock on the wall.

'You were in Newcastle about the same time she was, you didn't meet up?' Lukula asked, the plan she and Merry had agreed on during the car journey to the prison was coming to a head.

'No.'

'But you went back to Mallaig before you went to Glasgow?'

Merry asked, his tone still neutral and unconcerned, his eyes still on his notebook.

'Yes,' Albert stated, growing impatient. 'It'll soon be dinner.'

'Not much longer. You went to Mallaig to meet with your supplier, is that why Jenny went there the day she was attacked?'

'I don't know why she went,' Albert, suddenly alert, skated over the reference to his supplier, thinking himself on safer ground talking about Jenny. 'She hadn't been happy for a while, kept on and on that she weren't Jenny but someone else, saying she'd had enough paying off a debt that weren't hers.'

'Oh yes, her debt,' Merry looked up from his notebook, 'was that to her supplier or someone else exactly, my notes aren't clear.'

'Your notes are way off,' Albert informed him, happy he had sidestepped the issue about his involvement. 'It was her job to pay off people, only she'd spent the money she'd been given so had to pay it back in kind. Why do you want to know for now?'

'The supplier left the area after the attack on Jenny, did you ever see him again?' Lukula asked.

'No, it was Jenny into drugs and that, not me,' Albert responded, once more wary and defensive.

'Was there anyone else up in Mallaig she might have seen that day?' Merry asked, sensing that Albert was going to clam up soon. 'Or anyone she was expecting to meet back in Fort William when she returned?'

'I was asked that before, at the time, and I said then I didn't know nothing about the attack or who might have done it. I still don't,' Albert was wondering where all this was leading to, his mind trying to catch-up as they seemed to jump from one line of questioning to another.

'Did Jenny have any close friends, either in Fort William or Mallaig?' Merry suddenly jumped at a long shot like a gambler putting his last pound on an outsider.

'No, not Jenny,' Albert seemed surprised at the thought, 'she ain't the kind to make friends. There was some Asian tart in

Mallaig, she was pretty as I remember but stuck up. She hung about, bought a few pills, she'd chat with Jenny a bit but I don't know if they were friends exactly,' Albert paused, willing himself to shut up until he could grasp the angle the two filth were trying to play. 'Why are you here?' The interview wound up quickly after that, as Albert's cooperation fizzled out.

'Where did that get us?' Julie asked as they pulled away from the prison carpark.

'Nowhere,' Merry admitted. 'Just trying to confirm what was in the report Dianne Allaway gave me. I still think we need to unravel more about Jenny's past to understand how she fits into the deaths of the three girls, I still think that is what John was trying to tell us. The reality is we don't have that much on Jenny, apart from the Tesco bag and a bleached hammer. Oh, and she has the same shoe size as the killer, at least we think it is the killer's shoe size.'

'There are things we know about her background: she is mentally disturbed, has had violent episodes and you said the Newcastle police thought she planned the hammer attack on her abusive boyfriend. Even if she only purchased it to defend herself with, it shows intent,' Lukula pointed out. 'And, if it turns out to be Lynsey's blood on the shoulder bag that was found at her flat, we have her.

'It's just that Jenny Cowan sounds more like a victim than a suspect: abused as a child, attacked as a teenager, a brief and abusive relationship as a young woman, now this?'

'We can question her on our own terms tomorrow when we bring her in, maybe that will throw more light on all this,' Lukula tried to remain optimistic in the face of Merry's black mood. 'You know Alima thinks somewhere deep inside Jenny's shattered psyche these killings are Jenny's way of hitting back.'

'Shit, shit, shit, shit,' Lukula muttered under the wailing of the siren, infuriated at herself for the morning's disastrous events.

'I'm sorry, sir,' Merry was trying not to shout into his phone, but it was hard making himself heard above the siren and Lukula's swearing, 'but the hospital seems not to have recorded our interest in Cowan, nor our instructions about not releasing her before we arrived.' Swift interrupted Merry's explanation once again to angrily explain this was policing 101 and he expected more from his two senior and supposedly experienced officers. Merry calmly listened, feeling noble at taking the heat for Lukula who had failed to ensure the hospital clearly understood the situation, before continuing, 'They have their own staffing shortages, sir, and apparently it isn't uncommon to release patients late on a Friday, instead of when planned on a Saturday, so the relief staff working at weekends aren't overly taxed. If I'd known I'd have detailed an officer to keep a watch on her, but given how securely they oversee their patients I thought it an unnecessary drain on manpower.'

Merry didn't doubt that his words and tone were as a red rag to a bull and, for one reason or another, he probably deserved the dressing down Swift proceeded to give him.

'Yes, sir, I will sir, though that is another reason I phoned you, sir,' Merry found himself smiling at the number of sirs he could insert into a sentence, 'we are on our way to her flat now, sir. Unfortunately, it being Saturday and what with our own manpower shortage, there isn't anyone at the office to get the necessary alerts out. Hopefully Jenny will be at her flat but we should put out an alert across London, stations and bus terminals, etc. We know she doesn't have a passport, but she has links to Newcastle and Fort William, so I hoped, sir, you could get someone to initiate things.'

There was a deep intake of breath at the other end of the line before, 'You are a fucking idiot!' Then the line went dead, though Merry suspected it wouldn't be the last he heard from Swift that day.

There was no sign of Jenny Cowan at her flat, the neighbours hadn't seen her for days. Lukula phoned Doctor Hassan, as Merry drove them to Leanne's place of work, but Alima couldn't help with any suggestions as to where their suspect might have gone. Leanne's work manager hadn't seen her either and was surprised that the officers thought she still had a job after her absence. Merry tried to console Julie, who still blamed herself, by saying that it was probably the fun loving Jacky who was out partying and would no doubt soon reappear back at Leanne's flat.

Back at the Leman Street incident room they helped the still smouldering Swift, pulled in from his weekend break, set things in motion, including getting a PC stationed outside Leanne's flat. Then Lukula was off out scouring the neighbourhood in her car while Merry stayed to listen to another lecture from Swift.

'Tough day?' Kathy asked her husband as he wearily slumped into the armchair.

'Yes and then some,' Merry said giving a half-hearted smile, he'd resolved that if he was going to be in Swift's bad books he might as well go the whole hog and had booked tickets to Fort William and Mallaig, 'The bad news is I'm back up to Scotland first thing in the morning. So I'm afraid the treehouse won't get finished as planned.'

'They'll be teenagers and have other interests by the time you finish, at this rate,' Kathy pushed herself into the chair next to him for a kiss and a hug. 'Though at least I won't have the worry of them falling out of it and breaking their necks,' she quietly laughed, glad they'd have the night and breakfast together.

# 16

Mallaig was bright, clean and bustling with happy tourists, while Proctor was gloomy, unwelcoming and his house stuffy and smelling of dog.

'I told you when you phoned you are wasting your time,' Proctor informed Merry before he was barely over the man's threshold.

'I only have a couple of questions,' Merry reassured him, 'I simply need to know more about Jenny Cowan's background, what led up to her attack.'

Proctor, as an ex-copper, was resigned to helping a colleague and made them both a cup of tea, talking through the serving hatch between the kitchen and combined living and dining room.

'Nice place to retire,' Merry commented, making himself comfortable, while keeping a wary eye on the Labrador that lay watching him from its blanket in the corner by the TV. 'Are you married?'

'Was, kids grew up and moved on, as did the wife,' Proctor gruffly called back, 'she never took to my hours and the job but stuck it out until the kids flew the nest.' The resignation at the inevitability of a lonely retirement made Merry think of his own marriage and how he took it for granted by assuming his passing affairs somehow didn't matter. 'You wanted to know about Jenny Cowan?'

'Yes, I've spoken to her brother and he seems to suggest she was more involved in drugs than was in the original report.'

'She was caught up in it more because her brother pushed her into it than anything else,' Proctor emerged with the tea and sat in an armchair, tapping his knee to beckon the dog over to lie at his feet, a position they were both obviously used to adopting.

'Did she have a history of violence, recorded or not?' Merry asked, the tea was hot and strong but the milk too creamy for his taste.

'Not as such, not to get her arrested. She'd occasionally cause a scene, fly off the handle, it might end in a slap or two. It was usually all over nothing and ended as quick as it started but it wasn't always her fault and it wasn't always her giving the slaps; she wasn't well liked. We got called out a few of times, but she had a habit of running off after any flare up, so we were usually more concerned about finding her and taking her home than the disturbance.'

'You believe the final attack on her was related to drugs?'

'Aye, not that the DCI who investigated thought so. Although, whether he was here to cover it up or was simply an arse, I can't say,' Proctor huffed, his disdain for what had happened only too evident.

'Why should he do that?' Merry pressed on, waiting for Proctor to decide just how much of what he knew to reveal to the officer from the Met.

'Mallaig was just a part of a much bigger puzzle,' Proctor poured some of his tea into a saucer and set it down for his dog to lap. 'Drugs came up through Latvia, then into Denmark and by boat to Ireland. There were innumerable stops on the way to feed Sweden, Germany, France, Scotland and Northern England A fishing boat, out of Mallaig's small harbour, would meet another boat out in the North Sea, drugs were swapped for money and then returned to port. Twice a month Alby Cowan drove the truck with its cargo of fish and cocaine down into Glasgow and brought back money for the next shipment and to pay all the locals involved, including various officials, to look the other way.'

'Alby organised this end?' Merry could see him as muscle but not as a key figure in an operation of the scale Proctor was describing.

'No, he was far from the brains,' Proctor snorted laughter at the question. 'It was a Glasgow based gang that was behind the Scottish end of things, but they had a man based here who was the owner of the two fishing boats that did the pick ups out at sea. Not long after Jenny was attacked a joint European task force shut the whole thing down. The boat owner disappeared, probably dropped into the ocean, and shortly after Alby ran off to Newcastle. As I remember Jenny was put into an asylum for a while and then moved to Edinburgh.'

'She was attacked because of her involvement with this gang?'

'Yes and no,' Proctor stated unhelpfully, then seeing the inspector's annoyed expression, explained, 'Jenny could be a lovely girl and she was bright, occasionally she'd have these temper tantrums, like car rage but without the car. But, she could also be muddle headed and not know one end of a spoon from the other, so making her the go-between who took drugs and money up and down the rail line between here and Fort William to pay off the locals and Alby was a risk. Rumour had it she'd lost or spent some of the money that weren't hers and the man she should have paid off whacked her a bit too hard.'

'That would be the man who found her?' Merry had already put two and two together. 'That's why you won't say, fellow officer and all.'

'Not like you think,' Proctor growled, surprised, annoyed and yet relieved the inspector from London had worked it out, 'he died in a car accident when on duty about a year later. I had the proof by then but saw no reason in depriving his wife and kiddie of his pension so I shelved the file.'

'He could have killed her,' Merry remonstrated, though realised that in Proctor's place he would probably have done the same.

'I think he lost his temper and hit her harder than he meant, then went back later to muddy any evidence found that could incriminate him, the rest you can work out.'

'Do you still have the file?'

Proctor sat for a minute, stroking his dog whose head was on his knee, then he got up and went upstairs. Merry listened to the man's footsteps on the boards above his head, then went to meet him at the bottom of the stairs.

'It's in your hands now,' Proctor told him, handing over a box file full of papers in a Tesco bag-for-life, 'literally, it's all there, copies of everything from the original investigation plus my own findings, not the physical evidence of course but it's all cross-referenced. It's up to you what happens next.'

'My interest is in how Jenny Cowan is involved in the death of three young women, not a corrupt copper whose been dead for years,' Merry said as they shook hands and he thanked the retired constable. Proctor could at least say he had finally done his job having now passed on the file but Merry just felt he had wasted his time as he hadn't really learned anything more about Jenny Cowan than he already knew.

Merry was tired by the time he got back to Fort William, he'd had to wait for the train and had taken a slow walk round the small, scenic harbour in Mallaig along with all the tourists, but the day had turned grey and wet, matching his mood. Dianne Allaway, whom he'd text as he'd set off from London, was waiting for him, dressed up for the dinner he had promised her. He was hardly scintillating company and the sex that followed the meal lacked passion. Allaway left him, no doubt, thinking the scotch they had consumed on their first encounter had made it seem more special and exciting than it really was. Merry's inability to fully meet Allaway's expectations only made his mood darker and, despite his exhaustion, kept him awake. In the end he relented, ordered a bottle of Ben Nevis whisky to be sent up and started to go through the papers.

Halfway into the box file he found a pack of witness statements, three from Mallaig, from when Jenny had boarded the train, two from a passenger and the conductor on the train and two from workers on the Fort William concourse who saw her disembark. All but one of the witnesses to her journey from Mallaig to Fort William, mentioned that she travelled with a young, Asian looking woman who wore a headscarf, something more noticeable in those climes twenty years ago. It was assumed the woman was a tourist, she never came forward and was never found, a photofit was compiled and Merry spent a long while contemplating it before falling asleep.

Merry left on the first train, checking his connections he had decided to eat breakfast in Glasgow, texting his wife to say he missed her and when he expected to get home, which wouldn't be until late. He also text Dianne Allaway, thanking her for the evening and apologising if his company was less than she deserved as he had been so tired. He got a 'smiley face' from his wife and nothing from Allaway, which was probably better than the 'pile of poo' he deserved. Lukula wasn't answering her phone, so he decided to face up to Swift and phoned him to explain how he had spent Sunday and why he wouldn't be in the office today. The call didn't go well.

On the Glasgow to London leg of his journey Merry had a number of calls with Rosen, occasionally disrupted when the signal died.

'He's not a happy bunny,' Rosen informed him of Swift's

mood, 'you must have caught him as he left the incident room, looking for you and Julie, we could hear him down the corridor'.

'Into every life a little rain must fall,' Merry stated philosophically, though it wasn't clear if he referred to his own, Swift's or both. 'I gather from what the govenor said, amongst other things concerning his general disappointment in how I am conducting the investigation, is that Cowan is still missing.'

'Yes, CCTV picked her up entering her flat late on Friday night and then leaving with a bag at five in the morning but nothing has been reported since, not even a suspected sighting,' Rosen informed him. 'The govenor is thinking about having a press release put out, appealing for help in locating a suspect in a murder inquiry, but can't decide if it will be worth the cost in manpower to sift through all the calls it will generate. Given his mood I wouldn't be surprised if you end up doing it all on your own, at least Julie's using her time wisely.'

'Doing what?' Merry asked, ignoring Ray's backhanded jibe at his trip to Scotland.

'Re-interviewing family, friends and work colleagues of the victims to see if there is any link between the girls and Jenny Cowan. I've been onto the tech boys to get them to review all the social media stuff and the victims' phones to see if anything has been missed that might be a link. I've explained about Cowan's different names, at least the ones Doctor Hassan has given us.'

'Anything else, what about CCTV?' Merry asked, thinking again of the photofit picture he'd found in the box file Proctor had given him.

'Another sore point with the governor. I had to inform him that although all the CCTV footage seems to have been gone through, a number of follow-ups that were flagged haven't been done or completed. Only a couple from the crime scenes but a number from the Berner Centre and around Cowan's flat.'

'What did he expect, cutting back on the manpower before we had finished,' Merry was aggrieved, although Swift might have a point about his jaunt to Scotland, the cuts were not his fault and he'd spoken against them.

'He said he should have been given specifics about what was outstanding and the potential cost in man-hours,' Rosen stated, his tone neutral, not wanting to take sides in a disagreement in which both parties were wrong. 'However, I said Hayden could probably cover it in a couple of days at most, so we are getting her back.'

'Anything else we have missed?' Merry was growing increasingly despondent, although in practice he knew everything that could be done was being done and, perversely, Cowan going missing was giving them the time he'd asked Swift for in the first place, to do it.

'Bad news on the blood on Cowan's shoulder bag handle,' Rosen started with the worst, 'the fumes from the bleach used to clean the inside of the bag, when sealed in the evidence bag, seems to have corrupted the blood. They can't get DNA as a result and as Jenny has the same type of blood as the Hensley girl, so we are screwed on that one. Otherwise, nothing new from forensics, given the speed and simplicity of the attacks that is hardly surprising. We also have the definitive toxicology reports now, again nothing surprising: opioids and cannabis, small amounts in the Turner girl, more in Jody Grahame, nothing of note in Lynsey Hensley. We still have unidentified fingerprints from the bench in St George's Gardens, nor do we have an exact match for the footprint at Jody's crime scene. No viable witnesses have been found, the identity of the woman in a headscarf seen at Swedenborg Gardens is still unknown. There are boards up at the scenes appealing for witnesses, but the canvassing of the areas and the press appeals have produced a lot of work but nothing of any use.'

Merry broke off to get a cup of coffee, resigned at how thin their case remained, then phoned back, 'So, apart from her working with two of the victims, the plastic bag and bleached hammer we found in her flat and her shoe size, the only concrete thing we have to connect Jenny Cowan to the killings is her prints on the bloody Tesco bag bound in Swendenborg Gardens.'

'Although forensics say Cowan's fingerprints form a pattern which suggests she had done more than just touch the bag but actually gripped the hammer inside the bag. However, the plastic bag found in her flat had been wiped clean, like everything else,' Rosen commiserated. The lack of leads was more common than most officers liked to admit, most only remembered the leads that broke the case, but then Rosen didn't feel that his career rode on solving the killings so could be more relaxed about such things. 'Normally that'd be suspicious but Doctor Hassan has said excessive cleaning is part of Leanne's normal behaviour. Not that Cowan's behaviour is consistent: compulsively cleaning one minute and carelessly leaving her fingerprints on the Tesco bag that held the murder weapon the next.'

'What would we do without the good doctor,' Merry, somewhat ungenerously muttered, realising the inconsistencies, as with most of the ambiguities of the case, resulted from Cowan's multiple personalities. Any half-decent defence lawyer would have a field day.

'Not much if the govenor is anything to go by,' Rosen informed him of Swift's change of mind. 'He's gone off to speak with her, as our expert consultant, to help us unravel and understand the working of Cowan's mindset and motivations.'

'All well and good, but without more links established between Cowan and the victims, we don't have anything. Even if she confesses it won't help the case that much if her brief argues diminished responsibility, especially given her multiple personalities,' Merry bemoaned, knowing Rosen already knew this.

'We also need to link her to the other crime scenes. Some blood, trace or DNA would crack it but there's been more than enough time for clothing and shoes to be disposed of,' Rosen pointed out, realising it didn't help but at least gave him the opportunity to sound sympathetic to his boss's problem.

'You know, that's a point,' Merry puzzled at the inconsistency he'd spotted, 'if Jenny had disposed of the clothing and shoes she wore to get rid of any evidence then why hang on to the hammer? Even having washed it in bleach you'd think she'd dump it?'

Much later, tired and hungry from his travelling but now on the Dockland Light Railway heading for Woolwich Arsenal for another prearranged meeting with Alby Cowan in Belmarsh, Merry had a final call from Rosen.

'Thought you'd want to know,' Rosen told him without any preamble, 'they have picked up Turner and he is in custody now.'

'What?' Merry wondered, the train was packed and he was having trouble maintaining his balance as the carriage swayed and rattled along the track with his bag and file in one hand and phone in the other.

'You hadn't heard?' Rosen realised his error, 'Saturday night a group of men pushed their way into the Turners' flat. Fortunately the mother and son were staying at her sister's but Alan Turner and the flat got smashed up. Seems he went into hiding but failed to report this morning, which is a violation of his bail, so he's been picked up having been spotted by uniformed as he was getting a takeaway.'

'Let me know if anything else turns up,' Merry said unenthusiastically, 'but I'll be in first thing in the morning.'

'Come wearing a stab vest, the govenor is still on the war path,' Rosen cheerily told him.


'Do you recognise this woman?' Merry demanded, his ill-temper sounding in his voice as a warning to Alby that he wasn't in the mood to play games, putting the photofit of the woman in a headscarf, from the file Proctor had given him, before the prisoner.

'No,' Alby stated, wondering at the inspector's second visit in so short a space of time. Not that he minded as he didn't get any other visitors and it broke up the routine of the days, that flowed into weeks, months and years of endless repetition.

'What about her?' Merry held his phone up, showing a still of the hijab wearing woman from the CCTV taken at Swedenborg Gardens.

'Could be the woman in the photofit or just about anyone else,' Alby stated, finding the question amusing.

'What about her?' this was a picture of Alima he had taken from her blog.

Alby studied the picture, despite himself the sudden remembrance made him speak, 'Yes, I remember her, I think. I can't be completely certain as she looks older, still a nice bit of skirt though. It looks a lot like Jenny's mate from Mallaig.'

'Was she involved in selling drugs? Same as Jenny was?' Merry was tired and he thought his voice lacked conviction, he struggled to believe that Alima would do such a thing, and it was almost as if he wanted Alby to say no.

'Not that I know,' Alby stated. 'What is this about?'

'You said she bought drugs from Jenny?' Merry persisted, he was relived by Alby's answer but wanted absolute certainty that his faith in Alima was justified.

'Just for pleasure, don't think she was supplying anyone,' Alby stated, deciding he'd clam up again as it might help prolong the interview and keep him out of his cell for a bit longer.

'Did you see any more of Jenny after she left Edinburgh? You were both in Newcastle at roughly the same time?' Alby only shrugged in response, 'Your sister is implicated in the killing of three young women. Her friend from Mallaig is her therapist, currently helping us build a case against her.'

'Really?' Alby was completely stunned, his sister might be strange and full of rage at times but he couldn't believe she'd kill anyone, then he thought again, 'I'm not surprised.'

'At what? Your sister killing three young woman or at Doctor

Hassan being involved with her still? Merry realised he wasn't handling this well, was losing the initiative.

'So, she's a doctor is she?' Alby sat back, stifling a yawn, or at least making a show of doing so. 'I remember she was a student, done well for herself then.'

'You think your sister capable of killing?'

'She was always getting angry,' Alby confided, 'and would fly into a temper over nothing. So she was capable, yes she was, she could work herself up enough to kill,' adding as an afterthought, 'Although she might not intend to. She could also be loving and liked the boys when she was in the mood and at other times she'd be quiet as a mouse. But she didn't always know who she was or remember what she'd done.'

'What about when she was in a rage? Did she remember what she did, who she got angry with?' Merry asked, trying not to sound overly interested, just tying up a small detail before moving to his next question.

'Jenny had an angry soul,' Alby stated, smiling at the recollection of all the blow-ups and temper tantrums, 'she might pretend to be someone else after and not to remember but Jenny could be a scary bitch when she got the wind in her sails.'

By the time he got home Matthew could hardly keep his eyes open, if he hadn't been so hungry, he'd probably have gone straight to bed.

'Something wrong?' he asked Kathy as he wolfed down the fish and chips he'd stopped to buy on the walk home from the tube.

'No, nothing that can't wait,' Kathy smiled, knowing Matthew was too tired and had too much on his mind for her to say anything now. She'd wait until morning to tell him about the conversation she'd had with her headteacher at the end of the day, where she had been told that the school needed to save a large amount of money to balance its budget, given the recent cuts. The head had warned her that she was about to be made redundant.

'OK,' Merry smiled assuming it was just another errant pupil his wife was worried about, she took her responsibilities very seriously he thought. 'Want a chip?'

# 17

Matthew slept well and rose early, wanting to get to work and catch Lukula, promising his wife they'd talk that evening. Despite their lack of progress on the case and not having any clear plan how to proceed he felt refreshed and ready to tackle the situation head on.

'We have fuck all,' Merry summed up Julie's listing of the evidence they had accumulated, it was no different from Rosen's list of the day before and only emphasised how little they really had.

'But she has lied,' Lukula persisted, she still felt raw at having bungled Cowan's arrest and read more into Merry's tone than was meant. 'Leanne did work with Lynsey when she first started and was seen talking to her and Jody Grahame occasionally. She had even had her hair done once at the hair and nail bar.'

'Only no one at the place can remember if Madeline Turner was there at the time,' Merry reminded Lukula of what she had only just told him, 'she was doing work experience then and there was no record of her being there. You also said the manager remembered the bubbly blonde when you showed her the photo of Leanne, which hardly sounds like her, more like Jackie.'

Lukula bit her tongue to stop herself saying something sarcastic – about him knowing more about Jackie than her – but she didn't want to antagonise her boss and it would be a low blow in any case.

'Nor is there mention of her doing more than asking Jody and Lynsey about work, no suggestion she socialised with them in any way. Nothing on social media I take it?' Merry was trying to be constructive but was only too aware it sounded like he was criticising what Julie had done while he had been in Scotland.

'Neither Cowan nor Jody Grahame had any social media presence and Lynsey Hensley was pretty limited,' Julie began. 'Madeline, as we know, was all over the internet for all the wrong reasons and mainly as her alter ego, MaddyTease, no mention of anything linked to Cowan or Leanne, John and co. Although a couple of small things of interest have come up.'

'Ohh?' Merry asked, realising the extra effort Lukula had put in since the mess up at the hospital. 'What's that?'

'Madeline had a large number of contacts listed on her phone,' Julie explained, trying to sound enthusiastic about the tit-bit, 'and we've traced all but one of them. It so happens the same number is on Lynsey's phone, a pay-as-you-go number. We can't trace it but it shows they had one contact in common.'

'OK, but hardly useful if the number is untraceable and the phone has been dumped,' Merry was less than impressed by the news.

'Also, Madeline had a scheduling app, to keep up with her college work, nail bar appointments, plus her social and website life,' Julie raised her eyebrows, still wondering how a sixteen year old could be developing an online soft core porn business to finance her future; enterprising just didn't come into it. Although Maddy was hardly in the same league as the millionaire internet teens that were often quoted in the papers. 'It shows she had met a CW a few times recently, including the day she died, and seems to have earned a bit of cash as a result, a figure of two hundred and fifty being shown against each visit.'

'Do we have any idea who CW is?' Merry was wondering what Julie was leading up to, hopefully not another dead-end.

'No, the initials CW don't link with anyone we have come across so far. Although they're worth keeping in mind,' Julie pointed out, trying not to sound as if she was clutching at straws. 'However it started me thinking and I've checked out her financial situation. It turns out she has quite a bit stashed in a savings account, even taking account of what she earned on the internet and from part-time work. Also, Jody had managed to fund her drug purchases despite not having a job, so she was getting money from somewhere. Even Lynsey seems to have had a healthy bank balance for a student, though her mother did describe her as thrifty. My point is that if they were all getting extra cash from somewhere that's an avenue we should look into?'

'Possibly,' Merry agreed without enthusiasm. 'Jody had been on the street when she was younger and God knows how far Madeline was prepared to go for money. But how does that link with Lynsey? She was anti-drugs, clean lifestyle, shy even and too bright to get messed up in anything illegal.' His own words, however, sparked a thought, 'Not that being bright doesn't stop you from doing something stupid. One of the things I found out in Scotland was that Alima knew Jenny Cowan long before she was admitted to the research project.'

'Really?' Julie was surprised, she couldn't think that anyone had asked Alima exactly when she had first met Jenny but was surprised she hadn't mentioned this.

'Her brother had a holiday home up near Mallaig and it seems she knew Jenny and was buying drugs off her,' Merry explained noticing Julie suddenly looked upset: both annoyed and hurt at the same time. 'Of course she might not want to advertise a youthful indiscretion. She was still a student at the time and it was only a relatively short while after that she *discovered* Jenny as a DID sufferer, which got her onto the research project. Apparently it earned her a few brownie points so she might not have wanted to admit she already knew Jenny and it was just luck and not dedicated research and analysis that had located her.'

'But you have to admit her knowledge of Jenny has helped us,' Julie went on the defensive, determined to see the best in Alima's actions and that they represented something more altruistic than just serving the doctor's own ends.

'To an extent,' Merry admitted. 'Certainly she brought Cowan to our attention. The confusion she created over Jenny's identity caused the uniforms responding to check Cowan out carefully, leading us to match her prints with those on the Tesco bag, that's the one solid piece of evidence we have. She also helped us sort out each of Cowan's different personalities. Although, from what everyone, particularly her brother, has said Jenny sounds like the violent personality Alima calls Mia, the one who is always angry.'

'Then you have Jackie, the party girl who can't say no to boys, who is a bit like Madeline,' Julie continued the line of thought. Then glanced at Merry and felt embarrassed at her boss's embarrassment at her words so she quickly continued, 'While Lynsey, the vulnerable and shy one, is like Leanne, trying to get on with her life despite everything.'

'And, Jody is the drug addict, with no family and no one to care about her, almost invisible, there's also elements of Jenny in that description, minus the violent outbursts,' Merry said, thoughtfully. 'Each victim was vulnerable in some way, each a facet of Jenny's shattered personality. Was that what marked them out?' he wondered out loud, 'Is that Jenny's motive? Is that enough to justify killing?'

'That tallies with Alima's thinking,' Julie agreed enthusiastically. 'She has said she thinks you are right about John's dream, the women represent aspects of Cowan's different personalities and the men are her abusers. She believes that she can use Jenny's attempted suicide to help elicit a confession.' Julie explained without thought, pleased to be boosting the part Alima had played.

'When did she say that?' Merry asked, thinking he remembered Alima suggesting it was most likely to have been Leanne who had attempted suicide.

'Sorry,' Julie said, rapidly covering for herself and Alima, 'I haven't had time to tell you, but I've talked with Alima and she says she now suspects it might have been Jenny who attempted suicide and that she saw the other three victims as reflections of herself, killing herself off in four steps.'

When Merry spoke with Swift he thought he'd be updating him on some new and unforeseen progress, hopefully justifying and covering up for his going AWOL to Scotland. Much to his annoyance Matthew found that Swift was already aware of everything he had to relate. The DCI had met Doctor Hassan for coffee, who had expounded at length on her theories about Cowan's motivations. Hassan had even suggested that Jenny had hinted at a confession of sorts, something Merry hadn't known and made him wonder if Julie knew but had kept it back from him.

Alima had managed to convince the previously doubting Swift that she was indispensable to extracting a full confession, using Jenny's desire to self-destruct against her. Swift had enthusiastically agreed and made it clear to Merry that although he would be putting the questions to Cowan, when she was apprehended, they would be the questions that Hassan devised. Merry felt himself in no position to complain, his standing with his govenor being at a very low ebb, as a result of the time he had wasted and the various errors made on the case so far, not least of which was Jenny Cowan's walking out of the hospital.

With Hayden still following up on the Berner Centre CCTV leads that had been left incomplete, Lukula still interviewing people about possible links between Cowan and the victims, Rosen chasing up the technical staff and trying to track down possible sources of the victims' financial well being, Merry had left himself two tasks. One, to speak with the various mental health workers to see if they could shed light on any connections between Cowan and the victims and, secondly, to visit the victims' families to update them. Although family liasion officers would be working with the families he felt it was also timely to speak with them directly.

Jenny's case worker was little help, being alternately defensive of the work she'd done with Leanne and impatient of the time Merry was taking up in her busy work schedule. She had seen many sides of Jenny Cowan: including Leanne, Jackie and Meg, but nothing of John, Lilly nor the rage filled Jenny. She referred to her client only as Leanne Solbury and knew very little of Jenny Cowan or her background other than as a name on Leanne's file that she had paid little attention to. She certainly knew little of Doctor Hassan's work with her client and didn't consider her to be officially involved with Leanne. Fortunately, It was a different story with the manager of the CAMHS centre.

'I am so sorry, Inspector,' Liz, the manager, apologised after having reiterated that Lynsey's and Jody's times at the centre didn't overlap. 'I'm more than happy to check again, but after your last visit I spoke with both Lynsey's and Jody's doctors and checked our files on both, and I can't find any connection between them.'

'You've been very helpful,' Merry smiled. 'I wouldn't be taking up more of your time but if there is any link with the names I've given you it would be a tremendous help.'

Merry was left with tea and biscuits whilst the manager went to ask about Jenny, Leanne, Jackie and John, to see if Lynsey or Jody had ever mentioned them. Twenty minutes later and the manager reported back that the names meant nothing to either doctor and they had checked their notes, which being kept online these days meant they could be quickly searched for names or key phrases.

'I really am sorry,' the manager reiterated, 'Lynsey's death has struck everyone here quite hard, we were very proud of her recovery and how well she was doing.'

'She wasn't paid for any of her voluntary work she did here?' Merry asked, a long shot he thought if ever there was one, given the definition of voluntary work being that it was unpaid.

'No, she gave willingly of her time, happy to help others,' the manager's tone hushed and in awe of the paragon of virtue, as she now considered Lynsey to be for her occasional help at the centre. 'Though she may have been paid expenses for taking part in the research study I told you about.'

'I thought that was data collection only and didn't directly involve the girls?' Merry was suddenly alert, his inquisitorial tone making the manager uneasy, causing her to feel she had let the inspector down more than she had thought.

'With some one-to-ones with certain individuals to help put the data into context. It was done with the girls' permission and, as I said, they were paid expenses to compensate for their time. I can look up the researcher's name, they'd know who exactly was seen and the amounts paid.'

'Did their parents know?' Merry asked.

'Jody had turned eighteen by then but Lynsey would have needed her mother's agreement,' the manager explained as she searched her computer for information about the research project. 'We weren't directly involved other than to put the families in touch with the researcher, it only involved five or six girls as I remember, all of a certain age,' then growing frustrated at not finding the contact information she was looking for, the manager stopped typing and took a different approach. 'Actually, it'd be quicker if I phoned Doctor Hassan, she'd be able to give me all the details…'

'Doctor Hassan? Alima Hassan?' Merry asked dumbfounded.

'Yes, she sponsored the project,' the manager could see she had hit on something, from the inspector's expression. 'I explained when you were last here. She is a prestigious author and expert in her field and has done some consultancy work with our therapists. Though her methods weren't always appreciated by some of the older staff, she was always full of praise for what the centre has achieved.'

'Was she involved with the girls directly, did she work with them at all?' Merry tried to keep his rising concern in check. It may be nothing, simply an innocent omission, however it was another connection to the case that Alima should have mentioned and that threw increasing doubt on the validity of her advisory role.

'Never, that wouldn't have been appropriate,' the manager reassured him, 'Doctor Hassan is not the sort of person to ignore best practice and protocols.'

On reaching home Merry thought he would be able to put an increasingly bad day behind him, he hoped to gather his thoughts and recharge his batteries, but it wasn't to be.

'Redundant? That's what she told you?' Having spent the final part of the afternoon with the mothers of two recently deceased daughters', both murdered, he could think of worse news but he had come to rely on a stable home environment to see him through the stresses of his job, so the news unsettled him more than perhaps it should.

'She was very clear that there was nothing official as yet and technically she shouldn't be telling me,' Kathy quietly explained, herself still hardly believing what she'd been told and hoping it would blow over, a simple misunderstanding. 'The decision and restructuring package has yet to be agreed by the governors but the head wanted to warn me, given all I have done for the school.'

'All you have done and they are sacking you?' Merry was indignant, it seemed to him it was his wife that carried the school.

'They can optimise savings without impacting on teaching staff by cutting down on the pastoral care side, obviously they can't do that so easily on the curriculum side,' Kathy tried to sound reasonable, not taking it personally, even so she burst into tears.

There had been a lot of tears that afternoon, born of pain and anger. Merry had arranged to meet both mothers', Lynsey's and Madeline's, along with their family liaison officers, for a personal update. They had listened patiently to his briefing: there was a suspect but they were still gathering evidence, that it was a case of methodically sifting and checking through each line of inquiry until eventually they would have a solid case on which to charge someone. There followed all the usual questions, but growing anger at the trolling and press coverage.

'They've wrecked my flat,' Maureen Turner, angrily turned on him, after he offered some inane platitude about seeking grief counselling, 'how will counselling help with that? There's graffiti all over the place, it's disgusting, we can never go back so where will me and my son live? My husband might deserve to be treated like this but I don't? You should be doing more.'

'We are investigating the attack and property damage,' Merry tried to reassure her, 'and will work with the local council so they understand your plight,' he nodded to the FLO so he would know to follow up on both issues.

'What about the things that people are saying and writing about us?' Joanne Hensley, who had been the quieter and more reserved of the pair, suddenly joined the fray. 'It isn't right, we're victims not suspects.'

'I understand, I really do. Our press office is sensitive to what is released but we can't control what the papers print,' that sounded like meaningless bullshit even to Merry's own ears but what else could he say. 'As for the really disgusting and nasty online comments, though they have died down, we have a specialist unit trying to trace them back and won't give up on that. I know it's hard to accept but, for the moment, the best route is to have these sites taken down and not respond to them.'

'I just want peace to grieve,' Joanne said, desperate, angry and pleading. 'I don't want understanding or condolences. I don't want lies or people asking me how I am. I want these people, who seem to enjoy feeding off others' pain, to leave me alone. Just peace, that's all. An end to it all and to be able to bury my daughter.' Maureen had burst into tears halfway through this and had moved to hold Joanne's hands in mute support. Both FLOs looked as if they were holding back tears, both had spent many hours in the company of the two despairing, grieving mothers.

'I can't promise you that,' Merry spoke in a quiet, even voice into the tear filled silence that followed the intense outburst, 'I can't promise to change the world or the people in it, but I will move heaven and earth, all that I can possibly do and more, to find who killed your daughters.' They muttered their thanks, though their eyes still accused, and no one in the room thought what he said was enough, it never could be. Words on their own were futile even if they were expected and well meant. What was done could not be undone, could never be mended, could never fully heal.

At two in the morning, weary from having spent the evening going over lists of evidence, formulating priorities for the investigation, as well as reviewing their household budget to see if they could make ends meet without Kathy's income, Merry got up to do the one thing he felt might give him some peace of mind and enable him to sleep. He copied a couple of pictures from Doctor Hassan's blog and then used Photoshop to dress her portrait in a headscarf, like the one in the photofit and CCTV picture and printed off the results. Making up a file of the different photos, composites and photofits, all of which bore striking similarities to each other while at the same time were nothing like each other.

He was none the wiser and couldn't even rationalise what he was trying to do. Alima had obviously made some bad decisions which undermined her role as an expert assisting the police. If this was the case it made himself and Swift culpable for not doing sufficient background checks, though in their defence none of this could have been discovered had not Merry delved so deeply into Cowan's past. And, they did have the chief superintendent's recommendation of Hassan.

However, none of this rid Merry of a nagging doubt, a doubt he could not define, that plagued him. The puzzle unresolved he finally fell asleep in an armchair.

# 18

Jackie was embarrassed at wolfing down the breakfast roll but she was hungry and had not refused Matthew's offer. She had been surprised when the two uniformed officers had approached her outside King's Cross station, she had been sat outside a cafe nursing an empty cup of coffee wondering what to do next as she had no money left. They had spoken to her for a little while, unsuccessfully questioning her about Jenny Cowan and Leanne Solbury, before asking her to go with them to the police station. She had been polite and honest and made no objection to their requests, why should she be otherwise?

At the police station a detective sergeant, whose name Jackie didn't quite catch, asked her the same questions as the uniformed officers had, with as little success, and then left her alone with an odd tasting cup of tea which she barely touched. Eventually he came back, explained she was under arrest on suspicion of murder and told her she had the right to remain silent, unless it harmed her defence and something about questioning and court. She agreed she understood her rights mainly as she was tired, increasingly bored and too fed up to have him repeat them. Then she was driven off, by yet two more uniformed officers, and she assumed she was being taken to prison to await trial. However, she was pleasantly surprised when she arrived at Leman Street, partly as she recognised the place but more because Matthew was waiting for her.

Swift had phoned Merry, not long after the inspector had arrived at the incident room, telling him that Cowan had been picked up, arrested and was on her way to Leman Street. Swift was absolutely clear that Merry was not to interview Cowan, she was simply to be kept safe until her solicitor arrived. Swift and Hayden, with Doctor Hassan's close support, were going to conduct the interview and over the course of the day Swift expected to get a confession, Hassan had assured him the attempted suicide was a cry for help and the work she had done with Leanne when she was in hospital had paved the way. However, Swift didn't say Matthew couldn't take the suspect for breakfast.

Jackie had a nice smile, both inviting and shy at the same time, her eyes warily glancing around as she ate. She held herself more upright than Leanne, having a confident posture which showed off her shapely curves as she was not afraid of attracting admiring glances. Her voice was equally attractive, being soft with the slightest hint of an Irish lilt.

'You can have another,' Matthew told her, the glass fronted cafe in Canter Way had pretensions above the typical greasy spoon but the breakfast roll did look inviting and he fancied one himself now.

'You must think me a pig eating it so quickly,' her embarrassment, at discovering he was a police officer, fading as they smiled at each other, 'but I can't remember when I last ate.'

'Do you remember being at the hospital?' Merry asked, waving at the waitress to bring two more rolls and tea.

'Vaguely,' she admitted glancing down at the grubby bandage on her left arm. 'They said I could go and gave me some pills as I left.'

'Where did you go?' Merry wanted to know, surprised at how

pleased he felt speaking to Jackie, it was more a comfortable chat between old friends rather than an interrogation.

'I do remember you,' she stated with a shy smile, pouring them both more tea from the pot the waitress had brought. 'In case you thought I'd forgotten.'

'I'm glad,' he told her truthfully enough. 'I'd have liked to take you for another drink but under the circumstances I can't. As you are under arrest... being a policeman you understand, I can't be your friend...'

'I understand,' she tried to reassure him, very few of the men she had known bothered to be as nice to her as he was being and she wasn't the sort of person to get someone else in trouble if she could avoid it. 'It's kind of you to buy me breakfast.'

'Where did you go when you left the hospital?' he asked.

'To the pub, same one we met in,' she explained, wondering if he'd understand that she had hoped to find him there, but he gave no indication of doing so. 'Then I must have gone back to the flat, as I woke up there. I thought I'd get away for a few days, so I changed and packed some stuff.'

'Oh, why was that?' The rolls arrived and he passed one to her, indicating with a smile and a nod that she shouldn't stand on ceremony and tuck in.

'Don't know, just felt I needed too. I can't leave them behind, I know that, but at times I like to feel I'm going off, getting away by myself, you understand,' she explained, unabashed at talking with her mouth full, they had already shared enough intimacy not to be put off by a few poor manners she thought. 'I couldn't think where to go exactly, but decided on Newcastle, as I've lived there before.'

'Do you mind talking about the others?'

'I prefer not to,' she pulled a face. 'Doctor Hassan explained to me about them and my condition when I lived in Edinburgh. I try not to think about them and just get on with my life.'

'You've known Doctor Hassan a long while, from when she

184

was a student. Do you remember her from Mallaig?' Merry asked wiping his mouth on a napkin, he felt sorry for Jackie, she seemed nice, so ordinary and chatty, not at all like the mousey, shy Leanne, nor the aggressive Jenny he'd learned so much about.

'No, not really, I may have met her then,' Jackie pondered, 'but I get confused. Leanne mentions the doctor in her diaries, they are sort of like my own but written by someone else,' she smiled at the guilty thought. 'I always read them, when I can, so I know what she has been up to. I never really liked Hassan, she went on all the time about how important the research project was and how I needed to listen to her. But, from what she wrote in the diary, Leanne seemed to like her.'

'This was during your time in Edinburgh, not from before?'

'Yes, Leanne's diaries from that time were all taken by Doctor Hassan as she said they were part of the project. All her ones from Newcastle got dumped, I don't know how but Leanne wrote about how upset she was about it. I never kept any of my own, I didn't want her or the others reading them.'

'What exactly have you been up to over the last few days?' Merry was keeping an eye on the wall clock behind Jackie, knowing he didn't have much time before Swift would find out she was missing.

'I booked into a Premier Inn, I think I slept there but don't remember going back, all my stuff must still be there,' Jackie, didn't seem particularly put out by either the gaps in her memory nor the loss of her things, it had happened often enough and was just the way her life worked.

'Did you find a boyfriend to stay with?' Merry guessed, Jackie wasn't the type to stay alone for long.

'We stayed in the hotel together, though it may have been his room,' Jackie admitted, she wasn't embarrassed by the fact that she'd picked up a man but hoped Matthew wasn't jealous or angry; she didn't like it when people got angry with her. 'He was going to drive me back to London but something must of happened as I woke up back on the train. Good thing I'd kept hold of my purse and ticket in my handbag. Then the police found me at King's Cross and brought me back to you.' She smiled at him in what she hoped was a becoming way that would make it clear he could have her again if he wished.

'Do you remember the night we met?' he asked, reading the desire in her eyes.

'Of course, it was fun,' she put her hand on his, giving it a gentle squeeze as she winked and smiled broadly.

'What about the night before that? Do you remember where you were and if you were with anyone?'

'I'm not very good with days and dates,' she explained, wondering why he wanted to know, 'I remember a lot and the order of things but not always exactly when.'

'We met on a Saturday night, I was wondering if you were out or with someone the night before on a Friday,' he explained, but seeing her smile fade he added, 'I'm not upset if you did but it may help you if you can remember.'

'There was a man,' again there was the shy, becoming smile, she was a passionate woman and she knew it, didn't apologise for it, 'someone I'd met, that I knew from some weeks before. I had spent an evening with him and then a night when I bumped into him again in a pub, that could have been the Friday or it may have been a Thursday.'

'Do you remember his name?' Merry asked, knowing they should be heading back. 'Or the pub where you met?'

'It was the Hungerford, on Commercial Road, I often go there, and I think he was called Billy,' she explained, glad to see Matthew wasn't the jealous type, not all her boyfriends were as understanding of her needs. 'He worked there, behind the bar, or his mate did and he was helping him as it was busy.'

'OK, one last question and then we need to go back, do you know any of these girls?'

Merry spread the pictures of the dead girls out on the table and Jackie studied them, shaking her head at each, then going back to Madeline Turner, 'I think I've seen her, somewhere but I haven't a clue where or when.' Matthew's phone rang as she spoke and he could see it was Swift, but he didn't bother answering it.

'Come on, we need to get back,' he told her getting up. Outside, before they turned the corner where they would be seen from the police station, he suddenly pulled her to him and they kissed. 'It's best if we pretend we don't know each other, you understand,' he told her and she nodded, even if she didn't fully understand why. 'I'm on your side but it's better no one else knows.'

Swift did not believe Merry, he didn't even bother giving the impression that he believed him. Merry had told him that Cowan had complained of being hungry, couldn't remember when she'd last eaten and was agitated by the arrest. Given that he thought it best to keep her calm, he'd decided to take her to a cafe, the Leman nick being anything but calming.

'She is hardly a flight risk,' Merry explained, knowing he had flouted PACE regulations, which determined how detainees should be treated, and that he could be suspended.

'Although you had lost her once already,' Swift pointed out, his tone hard and disapproving. Everyone else in the incident room was keeping their head down apart from Alima, who was quick to side with Merry, saying that keeping Cowan calm and stable was the best thing to have done. Alima had glanced over at Julie, expecting her to speak up for Matthew as well, but she seemed inordinately busy on her computer. Lukula was desperately trying to think of something to say that would help rather than make things a lot worse for Merry whose breach of police protocols was breathtaking.

'I see,' Swift, his face a study of barely controlled anger. 'Under the circumstances I will conduct the interview, I was in two minds about letting you run with it but this has made my mind up.'

'Yes, sir, I have plenty of paperwork to be getting on with,' Merry stated truthfully, though the message was plain enough, he'd fucked up once too often and Swift no longer trusted him.

'Your workload isn't my primary concern about your current performance,' Swift informed him, leaving the incident room with Doctor Hassan and Hayden, carrying a file of evidence prepared for the interview, in tow. 'Performance being the operative word for a clown show like yours.'

Merry waited long enough to be certain Swift had gone to the interview room where Cowan and her solicitor were waiting, before turning to Julie and motioning her to follow.

'Where is it we are going?' Lukula asked, feeling as if she'd been volunteered for a suicide mission, she had nothing against an officer showing a bit of initiative and going rogue occasionally but Merry seemed to have taken to it like an alcoholic falling off the wagon.

'The Hungerford Arms on the Commercial Road, just down from Watney Market,' Merry explained. 'Jackie told me she had seen a man, by the name of Billy, who works there on the night Madeline Turner was killed. At least she thought it was the Friday but could have been the Thursday, either way I thought it worth checking out.'

'And you didn't think to mention this to the govenor?' Lukula stated despairingly, 'If he finds out about you and Jackie, he will suspend you.'

'My actions might have been morally suspect but she wasn't even known to us at the time I met her so I can't be suspended for that.'

'But taking her out of custody for breakfast, given your history it will look decidedly suspicious,' Julie felt annoyed, not only because he'd acted so idiotically but also his taking the blame for her mistake in letting Cowan get away from the hospital was now gong to make the whole thing seem ten times worse. 'If he'd given you a dressing down it might have been better but as it is he's obviously seething and…'

'Forget him and focus on the job in hand,' Merry stated, surprised just how calm he was feeling, somehow being on Swift's bad side wasn't bothering him. 'It's Alima's involvement that's concerning me.'

'What do you mean?' Julie demanded, suddenly on the defensive.

'She's known Cowan for a long time, youthful indiscretion or not she seems to have bought drugs from her in Mallaig as a student,' Matthew ticked off his concerns. 'Then she uses Cowan to get on the DID project which led to her getting her doctorate. Then Cowan runs scared and leaves the project before the professor in charge has a chance to conclusively review Alima's data. Now she has picked up with her again in London and suddenly Cowan's in the frame for three murders.'

'What are you on about?' Julie puzzled, she'd pulled into Buross Street and was waiting for a parking space, unconcerned at blocking the short, dead-end turning. 'So she has been Cowan's therapist since Edinburgh, so what? OK, she knew her before then and it opened up an opportunity for her but that's hardly suspicious.'

'That's just the half of it. Yesterday I visited the local mental health services office and the manager told me that Doctor Hassan was well known to them and she sponsored a research project that just happened to included Lynsey and Jody,' Matthew was using Julie as a sounding board, knowing what he had discovered was strange but could be no more than coincidence.

'Ahh, I see your point,' Julie's tone dripped sarcasm as obviously as a bucket with a hole drips water. 'A well known clinical psychologist sponsors research at a mental health facility. Wow, Sherlock Holmes would be astounded.'

'Cheeky cow,' Matthew laughed, causing Julie to smile, the tension between them ebbing away as they shared the joke.

'However, good old fashioned policing made me get the manager to pull up everything she had on the project and I checked with the university supposedly involved. Not only didn't they know anything about such a project, the post graduate student named as conducting it had left the university over a year ago and returned home to Hong Kong.'

'There has to be a mistake,' Julie could hardly believe what she was hearing, Alima wasn't like this she knew her too well.

'This all happened a couple of months before Jody was killed,' Merry went on, surprised at how shocked Lukula was, it was beginning to dawn on him that there was more between Julie and Alima than he had realised.

'It's just a coincidence, odd I'll admit,' Julie didn't believe her own words but neither was she going to back down, if you couldn't trust and stand up for the woman you loved then what was the point?

'Look,' Merry pushed on, 'she's a chancer, she used Cowan to get onto the DID project and then to get her doctorate. When I contacted the university they said that she had worked with them on a consultancy basis but they had parted company when her work didn't prove to be up to the standard they required.' Merry paused as a car left the turning and Lukula manoeuvred to take the space, for a moment it looked as if another driver was going to pull in front of them but Lukula hit the siren and sent him packing.

'Right,' Lukula stated, more calmly than she had felt a moment previous, 'so she had a bit of bad luck and did something stupid, so what?'

'This is our expert, the person we are allowing to direct the questions we ask our murder suspect,' Merry pointed out, causing Lukula to swear under her breath as the penny dropped. 'She was obviously fishing for something with the local mental health service and two of the girls she has been looking into have been killed. What worries me is she has seen an opportunity again…'

'Her new book *Unravelling the Mind of a Killer*,' Julie groaned in realisation, then went on to explain, 'She's desperate for a new book deal, that's what she's angling for.'

'Exactly, she's got herself involved in the middle of the case, convinced us all she has a special insight and all the time I think she's plain out of her depth and simply floundering: not waving but drowning.'

'And us with it,' Julie realised the crap storm they were creating for themselves. 'Jesus! Have we fucked up?' It was a decidedly rhetorical question.

Billy, it turned out was a forty year old, out of work builder who helped out at the pub for cash in hand, his wife having a small part-time job and he was worried that he'd lose his benefits if his tiny income was declared. Once they'd assured him they weren't going to say anything about his occasional work at the pub he readily talked about Jackie – a 'lovely and loving woman', as he described her. He was absolutely certain they had met for the second time on a Thursday, as he'd covered for his mate in the bar that afternoon while the landlord was out on business, and he'd spent the first half of the night with Jackie when his wife was doing a late shift on her cleaning job.

'What about when you first met her?' Merry asked.

'That'd be a Friday in April,' Billy explained with a wide smile of remembrance, 'that was a day and a half, it was the wife's birthday so I had to satisfy the lovely Jackie in the afternoon and my wife after bingo in the evening. Not bad for a man of my age.' He grinned and winked, then stopped, realising that Julie was glaring at him as she would at dog shit stuck on her shoe.

'What was the date?' Merry persevered.

'The 14th, Friday 14th April,' Billy confirmed, trying to look contrite under Lukula's disapproving stare.

'Right, we'll need a statement,' Merry informed him, Swift wasn't going to like this, the afternoon of the 14th April was when Jody Grahame had been killed.

# 19

'What is happening?' Doctor Hassan patiently asked, she had been surprised when Swift had suspended the interview with Cowan, just as she thought they were getting somewhere. She had waited, sipping the coffee that Hayden brought for her, while Swift went to speak with a man that Matthew had brought in. But now she was getting annoyed at being left out of the picture.

'Matthew has found a man who claims to have been with Jackie at the time Jody Grahame was killed,' Julie told her, having studiously left Alima alone as she wanted some distance between her professional and private life.

'That isn't possible,' Hassan looked genuinely shocked. 'We were making progress and, with another push, I am certain I can get through to Jenny. It is only too clear that Leanne and John have concerns about what has been happening recently.'

'Whatever their concerns,' Swift stated, entering the incident room and catching the end of Hassan's comments, 'Jackie, that is Cowan, has a strong alibi for the 14th April. Mr William Craig spent the afternoon with her, he knows her address and could describe the interior of her flat. As I've been saying to Matthew, that leaves us with a problem.'

'We still have Cowan's fingerprints on the plastic bag found beside Lynsey Hensley's body, it has Lynsey's blood and DNA on it and forensics can demonstrate that the hammer used on her was wrapped in it, it's as close to a smoking gun as we are likely to get,' Merry informed them. He was back in Swift's good books after a brief dressing down for ignoring PACE regulations in dealing with Jackie but it had brought them a result, even if an unwanted one.

'Her background points to a motive,' Lukula agreed, glancing at Alima, the cogs of whose mind could clearly be seen working as she scowled in disapproval at this sudden turn of events.

'Perhaps the killings are not related,' Rosen pointed out. 'There was a gap of four weeks between Jody and Lynsey's killings, while Madeline's murder followed quickly on from Lynsey's.'

'You had arrested someone for Jody Grahame's death, hadn't you?' Alima asked, trying not to sound like she was clutching at straws, mindful that she didn't want the others to think she was biased.

'Nowak,' Julie remembered.

'He's helping us with another inquiry,' Swift, told them his mind still pondering what to do about Cowan, 'as part of that he has admitted to selling drugs to Jody earlier in the day but was elsewhere when she was killed. We now have him on CCTV going toward the Albion pub just five minutes before she was attacked, we believe he was going there to buy new stock from his supplier.'

'Still Ray has a point,' Lukula said.

'What do you think Matthew?' Swift asked, his deferring to Matthew leaving no doubt in anyone's mind that he now thought of him in a new and better light.

'I think the first question to resolve is why would Billy Craig lie about being with Jackie?' Merry could immediately tell that only Alima thought this likely. 'The second is to review whether the killings are linked or not, as Ray has suggested, and, the third point, have we overlooked a possible suspect?'

'I've been reevaluating everything we have done so far,' Rosen chimed in before anyone else could speak, determined to prove his own hypothesis wrong, 'I've even taken into account the recent follow-ups Hayden has been looking into. I have to say that there is strong evidence linking the killings: the manner and places where the attacks occurred, the girls are all linked with the Berner Centre and are of a general physical type and age. As well as some circumstantial evidence: Jody and Lynsey both used Madeline's hair and nail skills, Madeline and Lynsey had the same untraceable phone number in their contacts, Jody and Lynsey have links with mental health services, Lynsey and Madeline both went to the same school.' Rosen paused, mentally checking he hadn't missed a point before continuing, 'There is no one we have questioned so far, apart from Cowan, that remains a viable suspect, but there are still a few gaps around following up on CCTV from around the Berner Centre so a new lead is still possible. Of course, another public appeal might draw in more witnesses and there's still the witness from Swedenborg Gardens we have never identified.

'Thanks, Ray, a clear and succinct summary. Although I can't see why Billy should lie,' Swift stated.

'So, we're back to square one,' Lukula despaired, 'looking for a new lead at the Berner Centre?'

'You are all underestimating Cowan,' Doctor Hassan stated assertively, having realised how to play this setback to her favour and come out in a stronger position as a result. 'You have all fallen into the trap of assuming that because Jenny Cowan has a mental health problem that she is also unintelligent. Nothing could be further from the truth.'

'What are you getting at?' Merry asked, intrigued at this turn of events.

'I'm sorry to be so blunt,' Alima stated, asserting her professional authority, 'However, none of you understand how Jenny Cowan's mind works and, as a result, you are missing the obvious. If you were investigating a close knit family who all lived in the same house, you would be more suspicious of what each person told you about the others. The difference here is that the personalities concerned don't know what the others have done, but they are not stupid and can make educated guesses. Leanne and John have both shown they are capable of working out, to an extent, what has been going on and if they can then I'm certain Jackie can. Jackie is also the most manipulative of them all, she is the one who fought most against any restrictions put on her as part of the Edinburgh study, but she never approaches a conflict head on…'

'What is it you are trying to say, in layman's terms?' Lukula interrupted, feeling she was losing the plot and not liking the high-handed side of Alima that was emerging before her.

'If Jackie is fearful that Jenny has committed these crimes and as a result, her own future is at stake, then she might have found a way to get this Billy to lie for her. She can be highly persuasive,' Doctor Hassan was pleased to note the concerned looks the others were giving each other.

'Jackie was clear about reading everything Leanne wrote in her diaries,' Merry confirmed. He certainly knew how persuasive Jackie could be, that mix of vulnerability and sexual appeal she exerted was a strong pull to any man, it appealed to a basic programming wired into heterosexual men.

'Certainly John and Leanne have indicated a knowledge of the actions of their other personalities, including Mia, whom Doctor Hassan now believes is Jenny. The interview we were halfway through shows as much,' Swift acknowledged, now in half a mind to press ahead with Cowan's interview.

'Then we should continue,' Alima stated, seeing Swift wavering. 'If we keep pushing, as we have agreed, Jenny will emerge and I am certain I can get her to confess.'

'That still leaves the problem of Billy's alibi,' Lukula pointed out, she didn't want to be the one to rain on Alima's parade but the doctor's pushing to be the one to solve the case, just to boost her future book sales, riled Julie's own professional standing. 'Once Cowan's solicitor is told she will have a field day.'

'Nor is Jenny's confession likely to be that coherent,' Merry put in, 'under the circumstances a useful brick but not the killer blow we might hope for in a normal case.'

'That's true, it might be a tactical mistake to proceed,' Swift stated, as Alima shot darts at Julie and Matthew whom she had hoped would be more supportive of her. 'It will give us a much stronger case if we can break Billy's alibi and *then* get Jenny's confession, otherwise it looks muddled. Plus I have an idea of how to do it.'

It was not the complete win Doctor Hassan had hoped for but she nodded as if giving Swift consent to continue, Lukula noticed the arrogant action and felt part of her affection for Alima break.

'I'll speak with Cowan's solicitor and explain we are releasing Cowan on bail pending additional investigations,' Swift decisively stated, smiling at Hassan's negative body language but putting it down to no more than her own professional self-worth. 'Hayden I want you to lead on round the clock surveillance of Cowan, I'm going to pull in additional support to cover this. Julie, I want you to take over from Hayden to follow up on anything outstanding from the Berner Centre. Matthew, I want you to work with Ray, see if you can break the link between the girls' murders, see if you can come up with alternative scenarios that still match all the evidence. If you can't the case will be more solid for the attempt. If Jackie is as manipulative as Doctor Hassan suggests then I'm sure she will contact Billy Craig and it will throw up something we can use.'

'No, Mum, everything is OK,' Julie reiterated, though it was far from being the truth. 'I know it's late but I just wanted to let you know I'll be down for the weekend. It's all agreed with my boss and the case I'm working on is at a bit of a stalemate so I can get away.'

It was late and her mother sounded tired so she finished the conversation sooner than she wanted, things had gotten difficult with Alima and she had hoped to discuss the situation with her mother who had that knack of giving sound advice by simply listening. Julie had gone for a meal in Soho with Alima, which had gone well until they had bumped into Sergeant Mehta, out with her colleagues for a night of fun.

'You've not heard?' Mehta shouted over the noise in the club, 'I'm leaving, this is my leaving do.' Mehta swept her arm round to indicate half the club's clientele, she beamed a bright smile, exhilarated by the music and her impending freedom. 'I'm sick of the cuts, what they've done to the job, the impossible targets. I can't get out fast enough.'

Julie didn't know what to say. She understood Mehta's motives as the sergeant was far from being the only one to quit but her experience would be missed and Julie told her so, at the same time wishing her a great future. When she turned back Alima was far from happy, not only hadn't Julie supported her at the meeting but now she hadn't thought to introduce her to her colleague.

'It isn't about support,' Julie told her, exasperated, wanting to ask about the misgivings Merry had raised about Alima but the club wasn't the place to do this, 'this isn't an academic exercise, people's lives and futures are at stake.'

'You know how much this means to me, the book and everything,' Alima felt her frustration surging and she felt slighted that Julie hadn't bothered to introduce her, as if she were some inconsequential flirtation, 'given our connection I assumed you'd understand. Of course I want justice to be done but I need to be a central part of the case, otherwise how can I write the book?'

Julie just stared back for a moment, her concerns about Alima and her role as expert consultant were whirling through her mind. Perhaps those concerns were not really that significant and no more than innocent lapses of judgement, easily explainable coincidences. Indecision kept her mouth clamped shut on a dozen things she could have said. Maybe she should have dragged the doctor from the club and insisted they discuss things, cleared the air and put Julie's mind at rest. Perhaps Julie should simply have given Alima the benefit of the doubt and pulled her onto the dance floor, reassuring them both with a grinding dance and kisses. Unfortunately her temper got the better of her and she left the club without a further word, leaving a shocked and angry Alima behind.

Merry had told the FLOs that he would be meeting with the two mothers in the morning, news of Cowan's release would be out by then and he wanted to put it into context for them, explain it wasn't the step back they might assume. He was experienced enough to know such news was never easy for the grieving family but the meeting went far worse than he expected. Maureen Turner became angry and stormed out, fuelled by Merry explaining the chief suspect had been released, while they investigated further leads, proving to be one repetition of events too many for the grieving mother.

'You keep arresting people, saying you have someone then releasing them,' Maureen angrily said, rising and casting around her, partly in appeal to the others present, partly to ensure she wasn't leaving anything behind as she seemed to be increasingly forgetful of late. 'Firstly it was that perverted little shit of my husband, may he rot in hell, now this woman! You know nothing, clutching at straws, giving us false hope, then taking everything away from us.' She paused at the door searching for the right words, wanting something hurtful to say, that wasn't an obscenity, 'You don't care, not about us, not about my poor girl, still laying on a cold slab waiting for a decent burial. It's just your job! So don't come here with your "sorries" and "things are progressing", it's all just bullshit.'

Joanne Hensley had collapsed in on herself as Maureen's voice rose to a screaming shout, she understood every word the woman said but didn't have the emotions left to feel angry. It was all just words: what the FLO said, what was in the media, what the inspector said, her family and now what the other grieving mother said was *just words*. Nothing could describe the void in which she existed, the vacuum of emotion at the centre of her raw pain.

Matthew didn't feel much like going back to the office, Billy was uppermost in his mind but he knew that patience was required at this stage of the investigation and Swift was right, give them time and if something was amiss with the alibi Jackie and Billy would give themselves away. Instead he opted to deal with his second concern and this he thought should be tackled face to face.

'I didn't expect you,' Alima stated, opening the door after a quick tidy of her apartment. She had gauged the time Matthew would take getting to her floor after he had spoken with the concierge in the lobby and she could either tidy the place or make herself respectable. She correctly judged Matthew would prefer her disheveled.

'You look relaxed,' Merry commented entering the apartment noticing the lavish decor and spectacular view but focusing on Alima's short, flowing summer dress which showed off her legs and breasts to their best advantage. 'Are you off out?'

'No, as you speculated, just relaxing,' she held up a glass and a teacup for him to choose his beverage and he indicated the teacup despite a sudden need for wine. 'On days like this I love to just sit and gaze at the view, the sparkle of the sun on the river.'

'Summer has certainly arrived with a vengeance,' he admitted, feeling sticky in his jacket and tie despite the air con.

'So, to what do I owe the pleasure?' she asked as they sat on the long corner sofa which dominated the middle of the living area and gave great views through the ceiling-to-floor windows, she had curled up almost opposite him, her legs showing to their best advantage, and pleased that he continually peaked to check out her lack of underwear.

'Nothing really, just to let you know that things are not as bad as they seem,' he sipped his tea and wished he'd thought to remove his jacket, so he could benefit more from the cool of the air con. 'I understand you want to push on but sometimes a slower pace gets better results.'

'How clichéd,' she laughed, moving her legs to ensure he had the perfect view and wondering if he was thinking about the film *Basic Instinct* and the irony of the situation, 'a phone call would have done.'

'I also wanted to talk about your time in Mallaig with Jenny Cowan,' he decided, for once, to take the direct approach hoping to catch her off guard as she was obviously trying to distract him and, he had to admit to himself, she was succeeding, 'during your student days.'

'Oh, that,' she shifted her position, sitting up but still giving him an eyeful. 'Yes my student days were, well, my student days. I suspect you weren't as straight-laced when you were a student as you are now.'

'You'd be surprised, I was very studious,' Merry smiled, he liked Alima and didn't want to assume the worst just yet, but he did need some points answered. 'Although it isn't just that which concerns me, more that you haven't said you have known Jenny from before the Edinburgh project.'

'I didn't think it relevant and, to be frank, it hardly shows me in a good light does it,' she was laughing at him, amused at his thinking and not afraid to show it, she had no secrets from her old friend. 'Hello, I am Jenny Cowan's therapist and I'd like to help you get to the bottom of her involvement in the murder of three girls. Oh, by the way, she used to sell me recreational drugs when I was student.'

Merry laughed, she was right it was an understandable avoidance of the truth, and she still looked like a student, despite her mature, knowing eyes, she possessed the gaiety of a much younger, carefree time in her life.

'I realise that. Do you mind?' Merry finally removed his jacket and loosened his tie as she acquiesced to his need with a nod, 'it doesn't usually bother me, the heat that is.' He wondered if his explanation sounded lame and whether she assumed it was her revealing, loose fitting dress that was making him feel hot. 'Although there is something else,' he continued, determined to keep the initiative, 'you also knew two of the girls, Jody Grahame and Lynsey Hensley, before they were killed.'

'God! You are good,' she stated with genuine admiration, she had forgotten how much she really liked him. 'You should be chief superintendent by now,' she sat up, straightened her dress and folded her hands in her lap, like an errant schoolgirl up before the head. 'Truth is things haven't gone well for me recently. My last book did well, as you know, at least for a short while. There was even talk of a film but then sales dropped and so did everything else. I had various consultancy jobs, that I procured based on my public image, but they petered out and my last big contract ended in a bit of a row,' she glanced at him looking for a sign of sympathy, but seeing only that policeman's blank look of mild suspicion on his face, she couldn't help but laugh. 'Oh, come on, you could at least try to look like you cared. I know, I got ahead of myself, took on too much and it all fell apart. I'd bought this place on the back of my success but there is still the upkeep, I have to pay the bills. So, I started to look round for an angle.

'I'd come across Jenny again by then, simply bumped into her one night, although it was Jackie not Jenny. Then Leanne emerged and seemed in need of help so I became involved again. It made me think that perhaps I could find other cases, similar types to show how basically comparable childhood issues could spark different mental health problems. I won't bore you with the details but my problem was how to find such cases as organisations don't just hand over patient details, even to a respected clinical psychologist as myself. I made one or two direct approaches but realised it would be very long winded so I made up a white lie about sponsoring an undergraduate researcher, somehow it made everything seem more acceptable.'

Alima stopped, Matthew's expression still unsympathetic, still judgmental, just like her father who criticised every little thing she did and made her feel she achieved below his expectations of her. 'Oh, fuck you!' she told him suddenly angry and unrepentant, she got up to pour herself another wine, not offering him any. 'Just sod off and go tell your little police friends what a real fuck up I am.'

Instead Merry stood up, took her in his arms and kissed her, tugging at her dress so it slipped off her shoulders, picking her up in his arms and carrying her to the bedroom, the direction of which she pointed out with her foot.

Thank God that men think with their dicks, she thought to herself, relaxing again, blanking her mind to put up with the hour or so that lay ahead.

# 20

It was going to be another hot, late spring day. Matthew's daughters were rushing their breakfast and his wife, Kathy, was preparing for the school run while snatching mouthfuls of her own food, insisting he take it easy. Merry watched the domestic scene counting his blessings but also pondering the debit side. He had explained his lateness home yesterday and the various bites, scratches and bruises Alima had inflicted on him during their rough sex as having been the result of his helping two British Transport Police officers arrest a violent drunk.

Kathy had been both aggrieved that he'd gotten involved, at the same time admiring his heroism for doing so. She obviously had no recollection of his having arrived home many years ago, when they were only a few days from their wedding, from a weekend conference with similar injuries due, he'd told her, to slipping on the hotel stairs. Then as now he'd swept Alima off her feet, she had been a speaker at the conference and they had chatted first over lunch then dinner, winding up having cocktails in the bar. She'd explained that her Muslim heritage required her to be modest in public while her Christian half allowed her to drink and flirt. They had discussed the book she was researching, about the good and bad of sexual violence, they laughed and were comfortable in each others' company, like old friends.

Having sex that weekend seemed natural, they recognised a kinship in each other. Matthew had literally never even fantasied about having sex in the way he did with Alima, it was wild and feral yet they came to it without hesitation. For days afterwards he had thought long and hard about phoning her, throwing everything out and running to her, even after his wedding he kept thinking back, asking himself had he done the right thing. However he couldn't hurt Kathy, he knew he loved her.

What Alima offered was something passionate and intense but not love. Now he had two daughters there was no doubt in his mind he'd made the right decision, even assuming Alima would have wanted him. Yet Hassan pulled at his wild side which was so deeply hidden within himself he barely knew it was there. He had no doubt that his casual, short-lived affairs and one night stands were no more than some desire to recapture that intense passion. Rarely did he come close to doing so, they just led to frustration and guilt.

As he watched the girls and his wife finish their whirlwind breakfast ritual, kiss him goodbye and rush out the door, Matthew was completely certain that, after last night, he had banished any residual desires he had for Alima. A philandering arsehole he might be but he realised on which side his bread was buttered and was content with domestic bliss and a passionate, loving wife.

Julie Lukula was also contemplating her love life. She had come to work early, wanting to drive to Manchester that afternoon so she had a full weekend with her mother, and was working through the last of the CCTV clips Gillian Porter had left unchecked, due to her early departure from the team. Julie had avoided Alima as much as she could yesterday and was now *Alima free* for two nights and Julie realised the drug of their lovemaking was wearing off. Had she been so naive to mistake the physical chemistry and passion of their lovemaking as something more meaningful? She didn't think so, love had been there, perhaps only fleetingly but it had sprouted then withered as Julie's doubts had surfaced, like weeds strangling the new growth. Her doubts, however, were proving hard to pin down in concrete terms. There were certain character traits Julie disliked: Alima's self-centred world view, her attempts to manipulate the case, her occasional flashes of arrogance. However there was something else, something that fuelled Julie's suspicious nature that she couldn't put her finger on. Then it was staring her in the face.

Porter had labelled a whole series of CCTV clips from the different locations as 'Headscarf – Hijab' they had all been marked as reviewed and followed up by Hayden, apart from one, nestling in a batch of CCTV clips from the Berner Centre. And there, caught on a street cam, was Doctor Hassan in a hijab, pausing outside the hair and nail bar, possibly leaving it, in the act of putting on a pair of sunglasses.

At first Lukula was incredulous, only after she had printed a series of stills and noted the dates and times, which spanned a period from before the killings occurred up until Lynsey Hensley's murder, did she start to wonder if this was more than mere coincidence. To be certain she spent a couple more hours checking other CCTV images from the same street cam, finding a number of shots of Alima in different headscarves but with the same sunglasses, come rain or shine.

'Where's Julie?' Swift wanted to know, he'd spent the morning firstly with the chief superintendent and then CPS, mainly on other matters but also mentioning their yo-yoing murder case, which may or may not be moving forward.

'She's out, following up on the last of the CCTV footage,' Rosen explained. 'I'm not certain if she will be back today as she mentioned wanting to get off early to visit her mother.'

'Matthew?' Swift asked, remembering Lukula had told him

her mother was ill and he'd agreed to her taking time to visit. Police officers, despite common opinion, still being human and having a life outside the job.

'Out getting sandwiches, he's been going through the CCTV footage from the streets around Cowan's flat on the 14th April, seeing if he can spot Billy or her,' Rosen felt like he was having to cover for his colleagues though in reality they were both doing their jobs, it was just that they both gave off the same clandestine vibe that they were following up leads of their own.

'Did he find anything?' Swift asked, having assured the chief that they were making progress and he was hoping not to be contradicted.

'From the various expletives being liberally thrown about I suspect not, unfortunately the coverage around Cowan's flat isn't that great.'

Swift didn't have to wait long before Matthew appeared with sandwiches and coffee to which, unbidden, he helped himself liberally.

'I want a briefing Monday, at ten,' Swift told Merry between mouthfuls, 'everyone except whichever pair is on surveillance. We need to decide on a way forward as I can't justify surveillance for more than a few more days. If Billy Craig's alibi is still standing by Wednesday I think we should pull Cowan back in and focus on the Hensley killing, as we can link her to that.' Merry nodded in agreement, slightly aggrieved that half his lunch was going down Swift's throat. 'Trouble is, interviewing Cowan is like pulling teeth and, despite what Doctor Hassan believes, I'm not convinced we will get anything,' Swift drank some sips of coffee, to wash the sandwich down before continuing. 'The problem is Hassan doesn't understand the limited time we have with the suspect, nor what a court of law requires from a confession, vague assertions and generalised indications aren't going to cut it. If we are no further forward I doubt if the chief will approve my spending more man hours on the cost of a further public appeal.

I mooted the possibility of a re-enactment and she looked as if I'd suggested hiring Hollywood starlets to play the leading parts.'

The two men munched on, pondering their own thoughts until Merry's mobile dinged at the same moment Swift's did. It was an email from Porter with a video attached. It took them a moment or so to work out what they were watching. Porter was in a pub, the Hungerford Arms' Merry thought, holding her phone and muttering as if making a call but her phone was pointed at a couple sat at a table just down the bar. It was Cowan and Billy Craig. The pair were, heads leaning close, discussing something that couldn't be overheard by Porter or her phone's microphone. Then, just as they were starting to wonder if Porter might have tried to get closer to hear something, Jenny Cowan calmly reached into her pocket and pulled out a roll of bank notes, a thick roll of notes with an elastic band to secure them, and passed them to a surprised but happy looking Billy, who gave her a thumbs up and a wink. It was like watching a pair of comedy crooks pass a bag marked 'swag' between them.

Julie was getting impatient, she'd wanted to get away before the rush hour started and already knew that wasn't going to be achieved. Her time at the hair and nail bar had been a waste. The manager and staff vaguely remembered the headscarf-wearing customer, though they were confused as to which of their customers it was. Nor could they pick Alima's photo out of a selection that Julie had prepared for ID purposes. On a long shot she had tried at the supermarket where the girls worked and the woman on the till was fairly certain, possibly, that it was Hassan she remembered speaking with Lynsey; possibly, maybe, Jody as well. As time ticked on Lukula tried the black youth who had been at Swedenborg Gardens and seen the headscarf-wearing woman.

He wasn't at home but at college, or so his mother told the sergeant and she also provided Julie with his mobile number. Julie text the lad, saying she needed to speak with him urgently and to be waiting at the main reception. When she arrived he wasn't there, so she phoned, he didn't answer, she text again, increasingly frustrated and annoyed. Then asked at reception and was told there was a second reception on the other side of the college. Halfway across the campus, the youth phoned back and, as if in a farce, asked where she was as he'd been waiting and needed to get to his class.

'Do you recognise any of these women?' Lukula asked, having finally tracked the youth down and laid the selection of ID photos before him on a low table, between their chairs, in the lobby.

The youth, pleased at seeing the attractive sergeant once again and only regretting that none of his friends were around to see them talking, carefully studied each photo and then tapped one saying, 'That's her, the woman I saw at the gate of Swedenborg Gardens.'

'You're certain?' Lukula checked as the CCTV still of Alima outside the hair and nail bar, in a headscarf, wasn't in brilliant focus.

'Yes, I even remember the sunglasses,' the young man beamed, pleased to be helping. 'Did I mention them before? She wasn't wearing them but she had them in her hand, just putting them on or taking them off. I remember now because they were designers, not cheap.'

'OK, what about these, do you recognise any of these women?' Lukula spread out another set of photos, this time of women without headscarves.

'That's her,' there was no hesitation this time and he pointed straight to Alima. 'She's good looking, with or without the headscarf, as her bone structure and her eyes are unmistakable.' Then seeing the sergeant's surprised look, the youth added with a shy smile, 'I'm studying Art and Photography.' Lukula gave him the full beam of her smile as a reward for his help and had him sign, date and say where he'd seen the woman in the photos before, and explained he'd be called on to give a formal statement, before she dashed off.

Now she could place Hassan at Swedenborg Gardens at the time of Lynsey's death and, with Merry's evidence of her researching the girls, it was highly suspicious. However, Julie wondered if she was letting her emotions get in the way and was now reading too much into the evidence, wanting to cast Alima in a bad light. There was no doubt that Alima's involvement with the case was at an end but did this new evidence add up to more that just coincidence and conniving on Alima's part? It was already late in the day and Julie needed to reflect on what she had found out, so she decided to brave the frenetic Friday rush hour traffic and head for her mother's. A day or two of normality, away from the incident room and the others, would help her put her thoughts in order and ensure her perspective of events was reasonable before she went about opening up a can of worms.

'Hello Billy,' Merry said amicably as he seated himself opposite the startled Billy who was still in the same seat as when Porter had videoed him and Cowan earlier. 'Can I get you a pint?'

'What? Oh, yes, it's Inspector Merry isn't it. You startled me for a moment,' Billy smiled, trying to regain his composure and doing his best to sound as if he had nothing to hide.

'Sorry, you did look preoccupied,' Merry's face a blank and his tone neutral, 'no doubt you were working out how to spend all your money. I assume you won't be telling your wife about your little windfall?'

'What?' Billy glanced round, wondering how the inspector knew so quickly about the money Jackie had so unexpectedly given him.

'The money Jackie gave you,' Merry went on, knowing a few facts were excellent leverage at getting at the truth, 'to pay you for the alibi you gave her.'

'No, she didn't give me anything,' Billy was quick to deny, not wanting the officer to get the wrong idea, 'I was with her like I said.'

'On your wife's birthday.'

'Yes, like I said.'

'You'll be treating her then?'

'What?'

'Your wife,' Merry clarified, 'a belated present. I'm sure she will expect it after I've spoken to her, to see what she can or can't corroborate about that day.'

'No. What? You can't,' Billy objected, wondering what had brought all this shit so suddenly down on his head.

'I can and will, if I don't get the truth.'

'I've told you the truth, on my word,' Billy stated earnestly, even crossing his heart, a hangover from his school days.

'Your wife is the least of your worries,' Merry reassured him, the slightest of smiles at the pleasure he would feel when arresting the errant Billy, 'it's a long jail stretch for abetting a murder. Do you think your wife will hang around once she knows you've been fucking the delectable Jackie behind her back?'

Billy had gone pale and his mouth worked for a moment or two before he stammered, 'I swear on all that's holy I haven't lied, I've told you the truth.'

'That you were with Jackie on the 15th?'

'Yes.'

'Your wife's birthday?'

'Like I said, the 15th April… no, you've got me confused, turned around. It was the 14th,' Billy felt the pub was revolving.

'So your wife's birthday isn't on the 15th?' the inspector seemed puzzled at Billy's confusion.

'No, the 14th April, my wife's birthday is 14th April,' Billy stated, once again certain of his facts.

'You saw Jackie on the 15th then?'

'No,' Billy almost laughed, he was clear about the dates, 'it was the 14th.'

'Of May?'

'Yes, 14th May… no April,'

'You really don't seem that certain,' Merry concluded.

'You are twisting everything and confusing me,' Billy's voice had risen at each step of the conversation and now most of the pub was quiet and listening to his confused answers.

'It will be good practice for you,' Merry stated in a clear, loud voice, relishing his role before the audience of the pub's clientele. 'When you are stood in the dock, answering charges for aiding and abetting a murder, the prosecution will do all they can to show the jury what a liar you are.' Billy had sat bolt upright, his body quivering like a bow string, unable to think, no answer coming to mind. 'I wonder what your wife will say when she's called as a witness? We've already got Jenny dead to rights, of course you know her as Jackie don't you? Are you sure which girl you fucked and when?'

Billy got up, his back straight, he swivelled round to find the nearest exit and marched out, rather like some puppet soldier his limbs jerking in an oddly coordinated way.

'I'll give you until Monday, to consider your statement then I'll be down on you,' Merry called out after him. He waited for a moment and then got up and calmly sauntered out, half expecting the late afternoon pub goers to give him a round of applause for the stirring entertainment.

'He was rattled,' Merry explained to Swift on the phone, as he walked back to his car, 'although he stuck to his story, but only just. He is definitely the weak link of the pair, so if we leave tackling Cowan about the pay-off I think we are more likely to get a result.'

'I agree, I don't think she will break cover as easily as Billy. If we keep the surveillance going over the weekend, Billy might just pop round to see her,' Swift conjectured, feeling that the alibi was about to break. 'If he does I'll have them pulled in and we can confront them both.'

'I would put money on us not needing to wait for a solicitor for Billy. I can't see him clamming up, he's close to breaking point.

We just need to let him simmer a while, let the thought of a long stretch in prison work on his mind, then I'm sure he will crack,' Merry stated with certainty, he knew Billy's type too well, knew he wouldn't hold up as the pressure built on him.

'It would be best to catch the pair out but if not we'll bring him in on Monday in any case,' Swift almost sounded gleeful, glad to be on the same wavelength as Matthew, he felt the team was firing on all cylinders again after a small bump.

'At the very worst we can still link Cowan to Lynsey's killing, although we'll need more than her prints to be certain of a conviction,' Merry ruminated, 'I'm surprised she didn't try for an alibi on that one.' Then, considering that Swift seemed happy with the news he'd been given, decided to venture, 'You know I can't help feeling that Doctor Hassan's involvement is simply confusing things.'

'I agree,' Swift came to a decision as Merry spoke. 'Despite the chief's recommendation of using her I believe we'd be better without her. Although, to be fair, I think she is right that we have underestimated Cowan, she's a much more subtle actor in this than I've certainly given her credit for. However, on Monday the gloves will be off.'

Before heading home for the weekend Merry called Ray, knowing he would be the last to leave, 'Can you get details of Doctor Hassan's recent bank transactions?'

'As we are paying her expenses, I can get them easily enough,' Rosen had seen it all and wasn't fased by the request, 'though I'd have to be a bit inventive as to her status in the investigation after all she isn't a suspect. Is she?'

'Not exactly, it's just that I've been wondering where Cowan got that roll of money from,' Merry explained. 'Let's just call it an *elimination*, for our peace of mind.'

# 21

Julie's mother was all smiles and good cheer, despite looking tired, she was obviously determined her daughter should not worry about her. In reality it simply made Julie worry more. Her grandmother had been the same, up until her very end she had denied anything was wrong, that there had been nothing for anyone to worry about. It reminded Julie that the women in her family were both fighters and deniers. Denial was something that gripped her now, she thought. It wasn't so much that she wanted to protect the woman she loved, as she realised she no longer loved Alima. It was, however, that she couldn't face the fact that a woman she *had* loved should be so duplicitous. It was coming to terms with this that decided her to phone her boss, at least it got Julie out of helping in the kitchen as her step-brother and his wife prepared Sunday lunch while her mother was entertained by her grandchildren in the garden.

Matthew had also spent most of the hot, summery weekend in the garden, finishing the tree house. To him it was a large wooden box, stood on stilts, with holes cut in it and a dodgy looking rope ladder for access. To his daughters though, it was just the right mix of fairy castle and trolls cave, no doubt it was his wife's artistic flair for the furnishings and painting the exterior that made it magical in his daughters' eyes.

Saturday evening had been spent with his wife, emptying a bottle of wine and discussing what to do about her redundancy. The restructure, apparently designed by the deputy head in charge of curriculum, decimated the school's pastoral care team whilst leaving curriculum intact. Kathy explained she could have cried on seeing it, despite being pre-warned, but had refused herself the self-pity, as she saw it. She would of course apply for the single deputy post remaining, combining curriculum and pastoral, but would also start thinking of other options. The likely redundancy payout was less than Matthew had expected but they agreed that, with care, it should tide them over until something came up.

Merry was in the middle of helping prepare Sunday lunch when Lukula phoned, and he went into the garden, where his daughters played in the tent they had made under the tree house, to talk. It was a short conversation, as Julie told him her findings and the suspicions it raised in her mind about Doctor Hassan.

'It puts her at the scene of Lynsey's killing,' Lukula pointed out, 'which is bad enough, but given what you discovered about her and that she has visited the nail bar at the Berner Centre a number of times, it raises serious concerns about how much she hasn't told us.' Julie hesitated at the final step before taking it but then plunged on, 'It might even suggest she is colluding with Cowan, perhaps trying to protect her patient rather than helping the police solve a murder.'

'We are going to have to tell the govenor first thing tomorrow,' Merry concluded, stating the obvious, 'I've been in touch with Hayden and surveillance hasn't revealed anything new.' Swift had drafted in additional officers to ensure a round the clock watch was kept on Cowan and Billy, the cost of manpower involved was going to test the chief superintendent's textbook calm manner, 'and he will be wanting Cowan and Billy Craig brought in Monday. He's already agreed Alima is a liability and can't be used as a consultant any more but I will need to explain that he should also have her brought in for questioning. It's time she was completely honest with us.'

There was a pause as Lukula gathered her strength and set aside her pride to tell him, 'You know I can't be involved in that, don't you. Since meeting Alima I have gotten close to her, started a relationship with her. I shouldn't now be involved in interviewing or investigating her.' Julie had expected a degree of surprise from Merry but up until this moment she had simply been having a relationship with a civilian consultant, hardly unethical and certainly not contrary to any police procedure, so she wondered at the length of the pause in the conversation as Matthew considered what he'd been told.

'I didn't realise,' he finally stated, having moved to a corner of the garden furthest from any prying ears, 'so I hope you understand… that is I wouldn't have… You know Alima and I had a fling years ago, before I was married.'

'Don't be daft,' Julie laughed, amused that he should be worried about a liaison from so long ago, then registering his embarrassed tone the penny dropped and she went silent,

'Well, seeing her again after all those years,' his embarrassment was tangible, Julie could visualise him looking down at his feet, unable to face the world for the guilt of what he'd done, 'it sort of rekindled my old feelings, that is our old feelings…'

'You fucking bastard!' Lukula said with cold rage. 'You shit, you just couldn't keep it in your pants for once could you?' The line went dead, Julie couldn't slam her mobile down but she could hurl it across her step-brother's garden; much to the astonishment and amusement of her niece and nephew.

Monday morning Swift pondered what Matthew and Julie had told him, 'Hassan's much more deeply implicated in this than we had cause to believe,' he repeated again, as if saying it for the sixth time somehow made the assertion more acceptable, he could see that her involvement in the case so far was not going to play well, neither politically nor legally; it had 'career-ending cock-up' written all over it. 'She is almost certainly a witness, possibly an accomplice, to Lynsey's killing. And, from what Ray has dug up about her finances, she seems to have supplied Cowan with the money to pay off Billy Craig for providing an alibi. Although it's possible she doesn't know the use it was put to given that she obviously didn't warn Cowan she was under surveillance.' Swift tapped the report Rosen had handed him showing that Hassan not only had significant debts, and various unaccountable outgoings but that she had withdrawn money from a number of ATMs, in the early hours of Friday morning, that added up to £1000. 'Added to that she seems to have managed to bed my two senior investigating officers.'

Julie managed to keep her mouth shut but the anger contained within her breathing and facial expression caused Matthew much discomfort, much more so than Swift's disapproval. Julie's relationship with Alima could not be held against her but Matthew was married, a fact which hardly made his actions censurable in this day and age but still put him decidedly on the moral low ground.

'Right,' Swift began decisively, inwardly he was amused at Merry's obvious discomfort. 'I'll take Ray and arrest Doctor Hassan, we'll have forensics go over her flat and car, put everything on a legal footing given she has, at the very least, potentially perverted a police investigation. Matthew, you and Julie,' he wasn't going to let the pair off easily they needed to get over any personal difficulty and get on with the job, 'bring in Cowan. Forget all this DID crap and treat her just as Jenny Cowan, use whatever name she responds to but otherwise do it by the book. At the moment I would be comfortable with a charge for the murder of Lynsey Hensley. I'll have Hayden go pick up Billy Craig, she can arrest him unless he comes clean in the first five minutes. We could be waiting on a number of solicitors, so it's likely to be a long day.

What's more the searches will take time, in addition to Hassan's flat I'll want Cowan's place re-examined and Craig's if he doesn't change his story. So it'll be a while before we have a full picture. Any questions?'

'Not a question,' Rosen chimed up, knowing what he was about to say wasn't going to endear him to either Merry or Lukula, 'but another point to note. When I was looking at Doctor Hassan's details for her bank account something rang a bell about her address. You may remember we had a report back from the tech guys who'd looked at Madeline Turner's phone and she had a note in her scheduling app. We thought CW was the initials of someone she was meeting with and the number 250 was an amount of money. Well, 250 Canter Way is Hassan's address: CW 250.'

Billy took less than five minutes to recant his statement. By the time they reached the station he was telling Hayden he'd been confused, that he had seen Jackie on the 14th April but in the early evening, not the afternoon; his wife swapped her shifts so often he'd been muddled.

'The money you were paid had nothing to do with it?' Hayden asked, sounding anything but convinced by his change of heart.

'I didn't ask her for any money,' Billy went on, desperate now to be believed, 'she just turned up with it. "Thanks for the favour" she said, then told me not to try and see or speak with her again. She hardly seemed to know me at first. She wasn't her normal sweet self at all but was stand-offish, almost angry with me, then went off without a by-your-leave. Obviously I wasn't going to say no to the money, so, when the inspector saw me shortly after I was confused, didn't know what to say or do. But, over the weekend I decided it was my *civic duty* to tell the truth, no matter what, and was just leaving for the police station when you knocked at my door.'

'So what have you done with the money? We'll be needing it as evidence to trace where the notes came from,' Hayden informed the crestfallen Billy, doing her best not to smile as she had no sympathy with his plight.

It was late in the afternoon by the time Doctor Hassan's solicitor arrived and spoken with his client. Despite having had sandwiches Rosen realised he would miss his dinner, he usually had a curry on a Monday night at his local Indian but if the govenor wanted him in on the interview instead of Merry or one of the others, then such was life.

'Is this all really necessary?' Alima asked – immediately after the formalities of setting the tape running to record the interview and introducing the persons present – breaking her solicitor's injunction not to speak unless asked a question and then only to give the barest factual answer she could, preferably a simple yes or no. 'I've already told Matthew about my involvement with Jenny Cowan both as her therapist and originally as her friend, given the support role I have within the case I realise now I should have explained this earlier but I really didn't know it was important to do so. If I've broken any regulations it was unintentional.'

'I believe it is the case that you only told Inspector Merry of your history with Jenny Cowan after he asked you, following his investigations into her background. Is that correct?' Swift asked, still studying the notes he'd prepared beforehand.

'Yes,' Alima's face was fixed in a smile as she assumed her arrest, for perverting the course of justice, and interview a formality.

'You confirm that you have known Jenny Cowan since your early student days?'

'Yes, I had just completed my degree and was working on my Masters,' Alima explained.

'You bought drugs from her?'

'Yes, a little cannabis for my own recreational use,' Alima

glanced apologetically at the DCI. 'A rather stupid indiscretion of my youth, I'm afraid.'

'You travelled back with her from Mallaig to Fort William on the night she was attacked?'

Alima hesitated, the smile slipping, she had no idea the police knew that, she'd underestimated Matthew once again, though her smile was quick to return as she had her revenge lined up for him, 'I don't remember, it is possible.'

'We have a photofit of a woman who travelled with her,' Rosen placed the photofit on the table as Swift spoke, then gave the evidence number for the tape.

'No, that isn't me,' Alima was quick to deny, the picture was too generalised for it to stand as proof after all this time.

'Really?' Swift sounded genuinely surprised. 'Even when you compare it to a recent photo of yourself.' Again Rosen presented the evidence to the suspect and the tape.

'Where did you get this?' Alima knew the answer but was buying time to decide how to answer.

'You can see the resemblance, the headscarf is different, the current photo shows you wearing something I would describe as a hijab, but it is you in both pictures. You would agree?' Swift asked, as far as he was concerned it was a matter of fact.

'I don't remember wearing such a headscarf,' Alima stated.

'I'm surprised,' Swift pointed out. 'You seem to have worn such a headscarf or hijab on your frequent visits to the hair and nail bar in Burslem Street, near the Berner Centre.'

'I don't really remember,' Alima was thrown, this wasn't how she'd expected the interview to go. The solicitor at her side had turned to fix her with a stare, the signal they had agreed to remind her of his advice.

'We have dates of your visits recorded on CCTV,' Swift continued, pleased Hassan was on the back foot so soon, 'would you like me to read them out as it may help jog your memory?'

'I did go there once or twice,' Alima had decided the partial truth was better than an outright lie, 'I don't remember when exactly nor what I wore particularly.'

Swift read out the dates, times and evidence numbers of the various CCTV images, to which she agreed before he asked, 'So it is common practice for you to wear a headscarf or hijab, although you have said it isn't something memorable to you?' Alima smiled, shifting her position and broadening her smile, inwardly panic stricken as she realised that Swift's obsession with her headscarf was leading her down a path she didn't want to tread.

'I'm not particularly religious,' she stated, trying to sound as if the point was of minor importance. 'If pushed I would say I was Christian but I still occasionally wear a headscarf as a head covering. I used to own a hijab to wear as a courtesy if I travelled to Muslim countries or if I visit my father, even though my parents live in Shropshire.'

'So you own one currently?'

'No,' of that she was absolutely certain.

'So did you dispose of it after you were seen wearing one on Wednesday 10th May or was it after Friday 12th May?'

'I can't remember exactly when but before then, I decided after all these years as a non-believer it wasn't appropriate.'

'We have a witness who saw you, wearing a hijab, sunglasses in hand, a designer pair like the ones you are wearing in the previous CCTV shots...'

'Your witness is mistaken,' Alima interrupted, ignoring her solicitor's raised eyebrows.

'He picked you out from photos we showed him of you and other women,' Rosen put the photo sets on the table, again giving the evidence numbers, as Swift spoke, 'he not only picked you out wearing your hijab, but also recognised the sunglasses, nor did he hesitate in selecting your photo when you were not wearing a headscarf.' Alima made no comment as she hadn't been asked a question. 'So can you tell me where you were on Wednesday10th May between three and four pm?'

'That's when Lynsey Hensley was murdered,' Alima pointed out, looking shocked. 'I know because I read the summary file while helping you interview Jenny Cowan. As I was her therapist you've been very keen for me to help with the investigation as a consultant.' Alima was glad to get that fact on the tape.

'That was before this witness came forward to confirm you were at the scene during the time of Lynsey's killing. We also have CCTV showing a woman wearing a headscarf, who matches your general description, being in and around Swedenborg Gardens, prior to and after the attack. You have said the witness was mistaken so where were you?'

'At home, working, I was on my own but I did FaceTime my brother in America at about three,' Alima maintained her outward calm and confidence, it was her word against some black youth.

Swift continued with his questions, asking about the bogus research project at the local mental health centre, she repeated what she had told Merry but denied knowing or meeting Lynsey or Jody. She may have spoken to Madeline at the nail bar but she had little recollection of her. At one point it occurred to her to complain that Merry had forced her to have sex in exchange for keeping quiet about his findings. However, as they had now moved on beyond the concerns Merry had raised she thought it might seem like a malicious claim to divert Swift from his questions. Then all too suddenly Swift was taking a break, saying that sandwiches and coffee would be brought in, then he and the dour looking sergeant were gone.

'Now, Ms Cowan,' Merry started the interview, having gone through the usually formalities for the tape, 'you have already been arrested on suspicion of murder and interviewed by DCI Swift in the presence of your solicitor, then released on police bail, is that correct?'

'Yes, last week, but I'm not Jenny Cowan, my name is Leanne Solbury,' Leanne stated, she rather liked the inspector's quiet, calm tone and pleasing smile, so felt none of her usual panic when she found herself the centre of attention.

'I'm happy to use that name for the present moment,' Merry confirmed. 'Previously, when DCI Swift interviewed you, we had guidance from Doctor Hassan, acting as a consulting expert for the police, that your mental illness does not impair your ability to understand and answer questions. We still believe that to be the case, although we are no longer using Doctor Hassan, and, given that our police surgeon and your legal counsel agree, do you still agree that is the case?'

Cowan's solicitor nodded to her client before Leanne said yes, then Merry continued, 'As you are aware we found your fingerprints on a plastic bag at the scene of Lynsey Hensley's killing on Wednesday 10th May. Our forensic investigators can demonstrate that the bag was wrapped round a hammer, the head of the hammer created a sort of mould in the plastic when it struck and smashed Lynsey's skull.'

'I'm so sorry the girl is dead,' Leanne sympathised with a weak, ingratiating smile.

'We all are, Leanne, which is why we want to identify her killer so that Lynsey and her mother can have justice,' Merry said, nodding in recognition of Leanne's words. 'Your fingerprints, from the reconstruction undertaken by our forensics team, could only have been made in the way they were found if you'd held the hammer wrapped inside the bag. Can you explain how your fingerprints came to be on the bag?'

Merry paused, as Leanne looked decidedly downhearted, shrugged, then at a nod from her solicitor, remembered she should try to answer any questions truthfully but in as brief a way as possible. 'Yes,' she said, worriedly biting her lip.

'What do you mean by yes?' Merry asked after a further pause, Leanne, he remembered did not have an open and easy communicative manner like Jackie.

'Yes, I can explain how my fingerprints came to be on the

bag,' she said, with a helpful smile, 'Jenny would have held the hammer. Doctor Hassan has told me Jenny has been in trouble before for that sort of thing and I remember someone telling me a hammer was found at my flat, so it could have been that one.'

'By Jenny, you mean Jenny Cowan, which is your birth name, is that correct?'

Leanne hesitated, 'My name is Leanne Solbury,' she stated, sticking to the truth.

'Jenny Cowan is another personality completely separate from yourself, though physically you inhabit the same body, is that correct?' Merry noted Leanne's increasing unhappiness with the line of questioning but he wanted to establish who was who and how they were connected for the tape.

'That is how Doctor Hassan explained things to me,' Leanne conceded, breathing a sigh of relief as Merry smiled, nodded and moved on to another question.

'Do you remember where you were the afternoon of Wednesday 10th May?'

'No.'

'What about the night of Friday 12th May around midnight?'

'No, though I'm usually in bed by ten at night.'

'Or for the afternoon of Friday 14th April? You should be aware that a man, Mr William Craig, had claimed to be with you on that afternoon.'

'Not that I remember.'

'Which would be the truth as he has since retracted his statement, so you don't have an alibi for any of the three dates?'

'No, not that I can think of,' she sounded untroubled by the fact but, then, there were always gaps in her life she couldn't account for.

'Do you know Mr William Craig, he's usually called Billy, he claims to have had a brief relationship with you.'

'No, I don't know any men,' Leanne answered without hesitation.

'Yet we have a video of you speaking with him in the

Hungerford Arms public house last Friday, you were handing him a roll of money?'

Leanne looked confused, her head dropping down onto her chest.

'A video?' the solicitor queried, she wanted to see exactly what the police had before her client answered.

'Yes, taken by an officer on the surveillance team who was watching Leanne after her release on police bail,' Merry nodded to Lukula who was ready to show the video on her iPad.

'Not Leanne,' Jenny stated, her voice low and hard.

'What?' Merry asked, not catching the comment.

'Not fucking Leanne, you idiot!' Jenny erupted, standing up, sending her chair flying backwards and banging her hands on the table. 'Not her, not her!'

'Now...' Merry began as Lukula dropped her iPad and Cowan's solicitor leaned away from her client in sudden fear.

'Fuck you, you stupid shit, you fucking wanker...' Jenny launched herself across the table at Merry, who was getting to his feet, he caught her in his arms and the pair fell back onto the floor. Lukula hit the wall alarm as Cowan's solicitor slid beneath the table, terrified at the sudden violent eruption. It took two uniformed officers plus Lukula to pull Jenny Cowan off Merry and restrain her. Matthew had managed to stop her from biting his face but she had managed to knee him in the balls and pummel him with her fists.

# 22

'I half expected you to phone in sick today,' Swift told Matthew as he hobbled into the incident room. 'That's a nasty bruise you have on your face.'

'I'll live,' Merry said, his injuries were hardly life threatening, his pride being the part most hurt. 'Besides I'll not give Julie the satisfaction, she couldn't stop grinning yesterday.'

'You can hardly blame her,' Swift was less than sympathetic, 'given what you got up to with her girlfriend she probably thought you deserved a swift kick to the nuts.'

'Anything from forensics,' Merry changed the topic, knowing his indiscretion could well come out in court so Julie's displeasure with him was the least of his concerns.

'Yes, their preliminary findings are all in a file on your desk,' Swift explained. 'Both suspects have spent the night in the cells, they are back now and Doctor Hassan and her solicitor are waiting for us to resume. Hopefully I'll get something closer to the truth from her today. Cowan is still being seen by a psychiatrist, I don't think her mental health issues should cause us any worries but another opinion wouldn't hurt. To be honest I don't think this DID thing is an issue, Jenny Cowan might be unstable and may have DID but basically she is simply a nasty piece of work.'

'You won't get any argument from me,' Merry readily agreed with a frown as he eased his aching body into a chair.

'You can start to reinterview her once they are ready but her solicitor wants a uniformed officer present, she was really shaken by yesterday's assault,' Swift left Merry to feel sorry for himself and to read through the forensic team's initial findings; as always the SOCOs were thorough and had turned up some golden nuggets.

'My client would like to clarify some of the statements she made yesterday,' Hassan's solicitor began as soon as they were all ready, no doubt he had been giving her some strong advice before the start of the interview. 'Understandably she has been very shaken and confused at her arrest, given the assistance she has been giving the police, and realises she has been very naive in her approach. She believes this has led to a misunderstanding as to her actions.'

'Thank you,' Swift smiled, noticing that Doctor Hassan looked somewhat worse for a night in the cells but was still smiling, her demeanour still confident. For some reason this made Swift doubt her even more, it was his experience that innocent people became more despairing and hunted looking the longer they were held, only the guilty had nothing to lose by bravado. 'Perhaps we can restart with where you were when Lynsey Hensley was killed?'

'I barely knew Lynsey,' Alima began, determined to retain some control of the direction the questioning took, 'but I had spoken to her at the supermarket and discovered she was going to university to study Psychology. Naturally, I took an interest in this and wanted to help her.'

'That isn't what I asked you Doctor Hassan,' Swift persisted, his fixed stare giving no hint he was going to be deflected from his question. 'Where were you when she was killed?'

'I've already explained...'

'No,' Swift stated forcefully, 'you haven't. Our technicians have checked your laptop, your brief FaceTime with your brother ended at two, there was no other activity on your computer until twelve minutes past six. Ample time for you to get to Swedenborg Gardens and back and for our witness to have seen you.'

'You don't understand how scared I've been, how confused,' Alima switched to a pleading tone, holding her hand to her face as if holding back tears.

'Were you at Swedenborg Gardens at the time Lynsey Hensley was killed?' Swift demanded, his voice calm but intense. 'If I don't get the truth from you I will be charging you for her murder.' He tapped the folder of as yet undisclosed new forensic evidence on the table.

Alima still hesitated, not knowing exactly what the police had found made any decision on how much she should reveal to them difficult. Then, with a deep breath she took a gamble.

'I was there, I tried to stop Jenny but she was too quick for me,' Alima paused, lifting herself upright and squaring her shoulders as if some great weight had been lifted from her. 'Everything since then has been a nightmare of terror and confusion for me.'

Swift paused, studying the doctor, he still wasn't convinced, the performance he thought was just a little too perfect, a touch too contrived, 'Perhaps you can explain in your own words?'

Alima hesitated again, glancing at her solicitor who nodded as if to say it was now her chance to explain her part in things though of course he also meant for her to be truthful. 'As I told you I had worked with Jenny, as her therapist, for some years. I was confident of the diagnosis of DID but Jenny also presented other symptoms. I was able to document Jackie, John and two children and, to an extent, Leanne as being completely separate personalities. However Jenny's case wasn't straightforward, the abuse she must have suffered in her earliest childhood has shattered her, producing different personalities, different coping strategies within her. However, she also grew up learning to use the rage within her. I believe she was intuitively aware of the other personalities and would use her violent rages and *craziness* to intimidate and manipulate others. I would describe Jenny, specifically, as presenting Antisocial Personality Disorder, she is what you might call a sociopath.'

Alima paused to take a sip of water, more confident now she could present her story in her own way. 'During our time in Edinburgh she used every opportunity to find out about how her other personalities functioned. What's more I believe she occasionally tried to imitate them so as to further hide herself and use them as cover. I could usually spot this but, particularly with Leanne, on a number of occasions I believe I was fooled. Leanne is the antithesis of Jenny, a personality so featureless and mild that she is easily overlooked and ignored by everyone – the perfect cover for Jenny.'

'This is all very interesting,' Swift interrupted, feeling his time was being wasted, 'but what does it have to do with the killings?'

'When I first met Jenny, in Mallaig, we became lovers,' Alima's voice became smaller, softer as she increasingly touched on the truth, 'that love affair was rekindled in Edinburgh and again here in London. As her therapist it was, of course, beyond the pale and if it'd come out my career would have been over, my reputation ruined. But, she was an addiction I couldn't give up: the feral nature of her personality, the lack of boundaries, her wild and passionate violence, her very rage. It just sucked me in like a drug fuelled obsession.'

'So, you are saying, you helped her cover up for and murder three young women out of love?' Swift recognised the degree of truth he heard in Hassan's words but was still sceptical about her motive.

'To help her only in coming to terms with what she had done. Though increasingly I have been driven by fear of her. Her violent, jealous rages became more frequent and made me fear for my own life,' Alima stated her head down and shoulders slumped as if in despair. 'She told me she had killed Jody Grahame in a fit of rage, some argument over drugs. This was the day Lynsey was killed. Jenny was going on about Lynsey, how she wouldn't shut up about how terrible Jody's death was and how the man arrested deserved all he got. I said Lynsey was simply shocked by the killing of someone she had worked with, but Jenny just flew into another rage. My defending Lynsey had only made things worse as Jenny was already jealous of the interest I'd shown towards Lynsey and her studies. Eventually Jenny worked herself into a fury and stormed out saying she was going to have it out with her.'

'How did she know where to find her?' Swift wanted to know, looking for any points that didn't hold true.

'I don't know, perhaps she had been following her, but she headed directly for Swedenborg Gardens. I had fallen behind but I saw her climb over a fence and struggled to follow...'

'Wearing your headscarf, gloves and sunglasses?' Rosen asked, even less certain of Alima's tale than Swift.

'I had snatched them up out of habit. By the time I caught up with Jenny she had already attacked Lynsey,' Alima struggled to contain a sob before continuing, 'There was no one about, I was terrified, my mind numb, but I couldn't leave Lynsey where she lay crumpled up. I moved her into the shade of a tree and realised she was dead.'

'You didn't call for help? Phone for the police or an ambulance?' Swift asked, her failing to do so was evidence enough for him of her complicity.

'I'd left my phone behind and I was terrified of what Jenny might do next so I went after her, but couldn't see where she had gone. It must have been then your witness saw me by the gate. By the time I realised what had happened, there was a paramedic pulling up and I panicked. It was cowardice but I was terrified by what the police would think.'

'So you walked away?'

'Yes, as I said I already knew Lynsey was past help and the paramedic had arrived,' Alima admitted. 'And, yes I know I should have stayed but I didn't. I went to look for Jenny, I wanted to talk to her, to get her to give herself up.'

'But she didn't?'

'No,' Alima looked up, pale faced, but believing the worst of her confession was over. 'Instead she threatened me, scared me out of my wits, said if I told anyone she'd drag me down with her or, worse, that she'd kill me as well. She said she had nothing to lose.'

'What about Madeline Turner, how was she killed?' Swift asked, gauging he had about eighty per cent of the truth so far.

'Jenny must have been keeping an eye on me, she kept calling at my flat at odd hours. She must have seen Madeline leave, she had come to do my nails the day she was killed. Jenny must have followed her and killed her that night. I realised that Leanne must have been suspicious of what was going on and I'd tried talking to her about it, she was certainly terrified that Jenny would resurface and by retaking control, as it were, *kill* her. I guessed as much when she attempted suicide, a classic cry for help.'

'So you lied about Jenny's so-called confession?'

'Yes, I wanted you to focus on Jenny as the culprit. I knew I should have told you everything but I realised what the police would think. I thought that if I could help with the investigation I could ensure it was Jenny who was blamed and there would be some sort of plea for mercy to be shown to the others.'

'As well as keeping yourself out of it?'

'Yes, I didn't want to go to jail for loving Jenny but mainly I wanted to ensure that Leanne, Jackie and John got a fair hearing. A number of times I wanted to tell everything, to explain to you all, but I knew I wouldn't be believed and once I had started on that path I couldn't go back. I've lived in such fear, such confusion,' Alima finally broke down, crying into her handkerchief.

After a brief break Swift went through the forensic evidence they had so far. 'We have found Madeline Turner's finger print on the inside of your underwear draw, can you explain that?'

'She must have rummaged around when I was in the bathroom,' Alima looked annoyed at having trusted the girl.

'And, Lynsey's fingerprints in your car, under the passenger seat by the adjustment handle?'

'I did give her a lift part way home once,' Alima smiled, surely they had more than this she thought.

'We also have details of your bank account, money going out that corresponds with deposits made by both Lynsey and Madeline.'

'I liked them both. I wanted to help Lynsey with her studies, and Madeline had such grand designs for her life and was so enterprising, my tips were extremely generous.'

'We have also been able to match money you withdrew from various ATMs to the bank notes Mr William Craig was given by Jenny Cowan, in payment for his providing her with an alibi.'

Alima sighed, her face a study of remorse, this at least she had prepared for and she could be almost completely truthful in her answer. 'I was as shocked as everyone to hear about the alibi, I had no idea how it had come about but I knew with certainty it could not be true. As I told you at the time, I thought Jackie had gotten her boyfriend to lie for her. At first I thought you would disprove it in some way, but you all seemed to be convinced by it. You said the evidence you had against Jenny was slim and mainly circumstantial and the more I thought about it the more I thought Jenny might go free. I could not let that happen, not for my safety nor anyone else's, it was too likely she might kill again.'

Hassan glanced up, an almost imperceptible glance, she could not resist checking if Swift's expression showed he believed her. It was her most damning mistake. Swift was too experienced to let any emotion show on his face, unless he wanted it to, during an interview. And he was too perceptive to miss the glance, it told him all he needed to know.

'I knew you were having Jenny watched,' Alima continued, unaware of her mistake, 'I worked out how to avoid being seen and then it was simply a matter of getting Jenny to emerge. She has increasingly been the dominant personality so it did not take long, I gave her the money and told her Jackie had promised to pay the man for an alibi. She believed me and went to find him, using the information I had given her. I knew she'd be followed and you'd discover the alibi was a lie. I know it wasn't correct police procedure but I did it to assist the case, to help bring Jenny to justice.' Alima's tone was almost triumphant at the end. So wrong was she about the impact of her explanation on Swift that she half expected him to praise her in some small way.

It was not to be, his face remained inscrutable and his tone suspicious. 'And, finally, your sunglasses. Forensics have found blood on the hinge and inside the rim where the glass sits. Only microscopic droplets, not readily visible to the naked eye but enough for DNA analysis. It will take some time but I have no doubt the blood will be shown to be Lynsey Hensley's, can you explain how it got on your glasses?'

Alima just stared back at Swift. She had thrown all her clothes, gloves, headscarves and shoes that might incriminate her into the Thames and she'd wiped her sunglasses clean with a spray, they were expensive and such nice glasses, she thought it safe to keep them.

'You see, to get blood splatter on your glasses means you must have been very close to Lynsey at the moment of her death,' Swift explained, a satisfied smile breaking on his face, 'not approaching or running up after the fact but actually there as the blow was struck.'

'How are you today Jenny?' Merry asked, the bruise on his face showing livid, despite the rather murky, gloom of the old Leman Street interview room. 'Feeling rested I hope.'

'That's a hell of a shiner you have there,' Jenny gloated, though her smile seemed friendly and calm enough, 'I see you have reinforcements at the ready today,' she nodded over her shoulder at the constable standing behind her in the corner.

'I'm afraid I can't protect you from Doctor Hassan though,' Merry stated in best policeman tone, 'she has told us you are responsible for killing Jody Grahame, Lynsey Hensley and Madeline Turner, that she tried to stop you killing Lynsey and, afterwards, you threatened to kill her and falsely implicate her in the murders. As a result she has been too terrified to come forward until now.'

'Terrified, her! That's rich,' Jenny stated with resigned sarcasm, she knew Alima well enough not to be surprised, if she'd been able to remain focused long enough herself she would probably have spoken first and gotten her side on record before the lying bitch had opened her mouth.

'Let us pick up from yesterday. Do you know a William or Billy Craig?' Merry asked, wanting to clear up who knew and did what in bribing him for an alibi.

'Not as such,' Jenny began, she'd always thought that approaching Billy wasn't a wise move, 'Alima said she had heard about him from Jackie and he would give me an alibi for the time Jody was killed, if he was paid. She gave me the money and told me where I might find him. It didn't prove that difficult.'

'Doctor Hassan says you killed Jody Grahame over some argument about drugs, is that true?

'I went to threaten her. Alima said I'd find her at St George's, that she hung out around there. Alima had been paying her in return for a few drugs and a tumble but the girl was getting greedy.' Lukula stiffened as Jenny spoke, something that both Jenny and the inspector noticed. This wasn't going to be easy for Julie, Merry thought. 'Jody didn't take what I said well and got in my face, in the end I lost it. She saw it coming and had turned to run but I got her good. She stumbled a few steps, fell, got up and collapsed in the bushes. I'd hit her harder than I'd meant to, when I checked I saw she was a goner and simply walked away.'

'You just happened to have a hammer on you?' Lukula asked, her face hard and unforgiving, but exactly what it was that she didn't forgive Cowan for, Cowan wasn't certain.

'Always had something for protection on me, a hammer in a

shopping bag can be explained away as having been bought for DIY,' Jenny gave Lukula a knowing wink to the wise, 'having a knife on your person can lead to your being arrested. Ain't that right constable?' Jenny asked over her shoulder but received no response. 'Alima was pissed, but when some bloke got arrested she was happy enough. Then things went wrong with Hensley.'

'Wrong?' Merry asked. 'In what way?'

'Jody and Maddie were game enough, for a few quid, the four of us had some fun nights at my place but Alima really fancied Lynsey. A bright university girl, just like Alima and not at all like the rest of us. I didn't care, we all have our passing fancies,' Cowan looked Lukula directly in the eyes and smiled, even Cowan's solicitor noticed the exchange of looks and the sergeant's confusion but Jenny went on, 'but Alima got really worked up and tried it on with the girl and got a slap. She was pissed, really wound up and decided to have it out with Lynsey. She knew all about her runs, the parks she went to and the times, Alima spent the morning planning it all out, then had me go with her.' Jenny paused thoughtfully, then resumed, 'I don't know what she thought would happen, or even what she wanted. But I can tell you the doctor can't climb for shit, it was a struggle getting her over the fence, away from the CCTV, and I'm surprised we weren't seen. She swore blind she wasn't going back that way.'

'So what happened?' Merry asked as the pause grew, as Jenny reflected on the events, it meaning no more to her than trying to remember an evening spent in the pub. 'I thought perhaps she meant to surprise Lynsey, apologise, explain how she felt and expected that Lynsey would fall into her arms. But Hensley wasn't having it, tried pushing past, told Alima she was a disgusting perv and she'd report her if she didn't leave her alone. Then Alima hit her.'

'With what?' Lukula, asked, her voice no louder than a breath, not wanting to believe what she was hearing but unable to deny the conviction of truth in Jenny's matter-of-fact telling of how the killing occurred.

'My hammer, she'd pulled it from my bag just as the girl was pushing past her with a disgusted look on her face like Alima was a piece of shit on the path. Jesus did she fucking hit her. The girl went down with the fucking thing still sticking in the back of her head. I pulled it out and dragged the body under the trees, the plastic bag the hammer was in was still stuck to her but came off. Alima had already gone so I didn't hang round, some old biddy with a trolley was coming down the path, in a world of her own, but I wasn't risking being seen.'

Merry took two plastic glasses and poured water from a plastic bottle he'd brought into the interview room, handing one glass to Jenny, who stopped to drink it as he downed the other. There was something about the inspector that Jenny rather liked, a calmness, the fact he'd sat down opposite her this morning after she'd attacked him the evening before and made no fuss about it. It wasn't a sexual attraction, she had no interest in men, though she was happy to let them use her body if it brought her something in return. No, it was rather more like a longing that he could be her older brother, he'd make a good brother, not like that fucked up piece of shit she had the misfortune to be related to.

'Madeline Turner, why did you kill her?' Merry thought he already knew the answer but he had to ask for the tape, to hear Jenny say the words.

'She wasn't anyone's fool, happy to do anything for a few quid and a lot of fun in bed,' Jenny stated, almost with affection. 'Course she put two and two together, started dropping hints about wanting a business partner in her new shop, or maybe a paper would pay her for what she suspected. Alima might have gone for it but she was stony broke and, in the end, didn't like to be pushed around. She knew what Maddy got up to most Friday nights, if you knew what to look for in her blog it pretty well told you. We followed her and Alima kept lookout while I went after

Maddy. She started to run when she realised it was me coming up the path but I was too quick and easily caught her. I wasn't certain one whack had done the job, but I thought I saw someone, a shadow, further up the path so I legged it. Alima had caught up by then and checked her; she knew poor Maddy was a goner, like the other two.'

'What about your attempted suicide? Was that Leanne, or Jackie? I don't see you being the remorseful type,' Lukula asked, trying not to show disdain, Jenny had cooperated so far and she didn't want to set her off in any way.

'You're right, my lovely,' Jenny smiled and winked at the hard faced Lukula, 'but I don't really know. I wasn't there and I can't imagine it being Jackie, not her style from what I know and have heard of her. You'll have to ask Alima, she was there earlier talking to me until I went away, then sometime later I woke up in the ambulance. Wouldn't surprise me if that cold-hearted bitch talked Leanne into it, some devious plan she'd cooked up no doubt.

# 23

'Two women?' Maureen Turner, the mother of the deceased Madeline Turner, sat listening to the inspector's news about the investigation into her daughter's death with an increasingly perplexed expression on her face.

'Yes,' Merry repeated patiently, knowing from experience that informing the bereaved family that someone had been charged was only the first of many steps they would need to take to achieve closure. 'One of the women, the one who has confessed to actually striking the blow that killed your daughter, has mental health problems. Although it was her so-called therapist who we believe assisted her and actually drove her to do what she did.'

'For God's sake why?' Once again there was anger in Maureen's voice, fuelled by an understandable outrage at the lack of any logic as to why her daughter had died. 'Why would two women kill my daughter? I thought it would be a man? You are certain Alan had nothing to do with it?' Even though Maureen had alibied her husband she still couldn't believe he was completely innocent of her daughter's death.

'From what they have told us, it is likely that Madeline had said something that made them think she knew they had killed the other girls,' Merry thought it best to simplify Hassan's multifaceted motives: the doctor was a manipulative psychopath driven by greed, anger and desire for control over those around her.

'Why would they think that?' Maureen shook her head as if trying to clear the fog that seemed to cloud her thinking. 'If Madeline had suspected anything she'd have told me, told the police.'

'Madeline, knowing Lynsey from school, would naturally have talked about her death. It seems she did one of the women's nails,' again he wasn't about to go into Madeline's more lurid and enterprising sidelines, he suspected it wouldn't benefit either the prosecution or defence to mention that, so he hoped to save the mother a degree of pain, 'and they would have been on tenterhooks, almost paranoid, about killing Lynsey so it is likely they read too much into what was said.'

'You're telling me my daughter was killed for being too chatty?' Maureen's voice rose in anger and disbelief.

'No, Mrs Turner,' Merry explained, desperately striving for a sympathetic tone, 'your daughter died because she crossed the path of two disturbed and deeply unpleasant individuals. Nothing your daughter said or did, nor anything else anyone could have done, would have made a difference.'

Joanne Hensley, Lynsey's mum, sat in silence listening to Inspector Merry's news, she was so quiet and still that he wondered how much of what he said she actually took in and he was tending to say things twice as a result. He kept to what he had considered to be the facts and did not touch on the two differing explanations as to who had actually killed Lynsey or why, simply saying the pair responsible had taken a dislike to her daughter after she had stood up to them in a dispute. Nor did he make mention that the police and CPS both thought Alima Hassan to be the attacker, fuelled by anger and humiliation by Lynsey's refusal of and all too evident disgust at the doctor's advances. Eventually he fell silent and waited patiently for the mother to speak.

'I am getting Lynsey back, the coroner has released her. I want her to be cremated and her ashes scattered where she died, I've spoken to the council about having a memorial bench built nearby,' Joanne, for the first time since Merry had sat down, looked him directly in the eye. She had aged considerably in the short time since the inspector had first seen her to break the news of her daughter's death, but her eyes gleamed with an intensity he found discomfiting. 'She loved the green spaces around here, she had loved that park since she was little. I'll not have them take that away, not be robbed of those memories. I've even spoken to her school, to have some sort of memorial there and a small donation to their library in her name. What do you think?'

What could the inspector say, other than to agree it would be fitting and then go on to explain the next steps in the legal process. Whilst Joanne only listened to her own internal dialogue: outlining the funeral service, where the bench should be placed and how much she could afford and yet still be enough for a fitting donation.

'I wasn't expecting you back yet,' Swift stated, spotting Julie entering the office. 'You can have more time you know.'

'I couldn't put up with just moping around,' Lukula explained, glancing around to see Merry and Hayden starting towards her. The Leman Street incident room had been packed up and was now dormant, perhaps never to be used again if the building was to be sold off, and the team had returned to their main base in Barking. 'My step-brother is sorting out the house and the will, so I came back to get a few more things and then decided I'd be better off here. There isn't much I can do back in Manchester.'

'How are you?' Hayden stepped forward to give her a hug and, in motherly tone, commiserated, 'It's such a wrench, I know.'

'At least the end was quick,' Julie explained, it was she thought a blessing even if a strange one. 'They still don't know the exact cause, her heart just gave out on the operating table. The surgeon told me they did all they could but sometimes it just happens like that. He said the body is more than just electrical impulses and chemistry, that it has a will of its own to determine such outcomes. I think he meant it to be consoling but I didn't find it so.' The sight of Merry standing behind Swift and Hayden, looking uncertain what to do or say, tinged by embarrassment at a social situation he didn't quite comprehend almost reduced her to tears. She gathered her strength and took the initiative for him, moving forward for a hug.

'If there's anything… well you know, just ask,' he said, finally extricating himself from her grasp, noticing the look Swift and Hayden exchanged at his social ineptitude.

'Of course,' she said, 'I'll be expecting light duties and a sensitive approach at least for a couple of months, you know what a fading flower I am.'

'Certainly, for a day or so,' Merry confirmed, glad they had previously made their peace as they had wrapped up the case days before Julie phoned in to say she would be delayed coming back to London, as her mother had died in the middle of a routine operation.

'Ray is out, he's liaising with CPS to ensure they have everything they need,' Merry explained as they grabbed cups of coffee from the machine on the way to join Swift in his office at the far end of the otherwise open plan office area, shared by more staff than there were desks in the spirit of agile working. 'How are you?' he continued, feeling he should show more sympathy, 'What with the shock…'

'Fine,' Lukula cut in, not able to cope with his trying so hard to be sympathetic. 'How's your wife by the way? Has she heard about her redundancy?'

'Oh,' Merry was surprised she had remembered what was just a passing comment he'd made to her some while ago, 'she had her interview two days ago. Went off in the morning in the belief she didn't have a hope and had prepared a little speech to tell them what she thought of the structure, how they needed to put pupil needs first and be more enterprising about the budget. She had even prepared a list of ideas on how to save and generate more money. Apparently the chair of governors and LA representative loved it, even the head said she was thrilled at such an innovative approach.'

'You mean she got the job?' Lukula felt genuinely pleased for the woman she barely knew.

'Aced it apparently,' Merry smiled. 'You know, there are times when I think she is too good to be a mere copper's wife.'

'Certainly too good to be your wife,' Lukula muttered, though Merry diplomatically failed to hear her, no matter how much he agreed with her sentiment.

'We have the DNA report,' Swift explained, as Lukula and Merry seated themselves. 'It confirms the blood found on the doctor's sunglasses was Lynsey Hensley's but forensics have pointed out that the amount found is only from microscopic droplets. The problem is they believe that the splatter producing such droplets could occur from either version of events. It could have occurred from Hassan wielding the hammer or being a few feet away as Jenny struck the blow. The blow itself was struck with considerable force, but that also fits both stories. Nor is the height difference between the two women significant enough to rule one or the other out from delivering the blow. There are simply too many variables in the physical evidence we have.'

'I find it hard to believe that Jenny would lie, she has confessed to killing the other two girls, why lie about Lynsey?' Lukula stated.

'You won't get any disagreement from me,' Swift told her, 'nor CPS. In practice they don't think it matters and they are keeping the murder charges for both in place. The pair conspired and are equally guilty of the last two murders, Jenny will also be held responsible for Jody Grahame's killing. Hassan's story that she tried to stop Jenny and was too scared to go to the police doesn't hold water. She had ample opportunity when Cowan was in the psych ward or when subsequently detained by us. Hassan also spoke with me in private a number of times and was in a relationship with one of the officers working on the case. Although, personally I think she will perform well in court,' Swift added with a scowl. 'She's erudite, plausible and appealing, so I suspect the jury might be swayed to believe her and accept a not guilty plea.'

'Oh, that's for sure,' Julie couldn't help feeling downhearted at the thought of having to speak in court about her relationship with Alima. She felt deeply embarrassed and annoyed at herself for being taken in by the woman, 'she's a manipulative bitch and her testimony will be convincing.'

'No one blames you for being taken in by her,' Merry said, thinking of his own involvement with Alima, 'she manipulated everyone to get what she wanted, Jenny in particular. In practice she nearly got away with it, Alima was unlucky it all unravelled as it did.'

'True,' Swift confirmed, 'another session or two of Hassan directing Jenny's interview and I think we would have settled on just charging her. Our current psychiatric advisor for Jenny won't be drawn on a diagnosis but says that even if Cowan has multiple personalities he believes Hassan was acting to confuse them. Hassan had years of experience in manipulating Jenny and her various personalities when they were in Edinburgh. She would have gotten Jenny to confess then pushed her buttons to send her into a rage so she couldn't tell us of Hassan's involvement.'

'All so she could get a book deal,' Merry stated, half incredulously, though knowing that Hassan's motives had more to do with her humiliation over Lynsey's rejection. 'She's a real *chancer* and simply used the opportunity the killings gave her to develop another book. I suppose a second best seller would have confirmed her reputation and set her up for a long time, people have certainly killed for less.' Merry felt a sudden stirring inside him, sick at the thought of such a tawdry, mercenary motive for the deaths of such young women. A trade between so much grief and an easy life for the woman he'd been so attracted to, it turned his stomach. 'I can't help thinking she believes her own lies, so she'll almost certainly plead not guilty.'

'Her motives are likely to be more complex than financial gain,' Swift disagreed with Matthew, whom he thought tended to an Occam's razor approach when determining solutions, 'I don't think we'll ever fully understand the relationship between the two but their anti-social personalities seemed to gel and feed off each other, a mix of need and abuse.'

'Maybe,' Merry half-heartedly agreed, no one knew better than he Alima's need for approval but also her need to hurt and control others, attributes that typified her love making.

'The psychiatrist said their lives would have been very different if they'd never met, this all started in Mallaig,' Swift continued, though the more he thought about the pair's motives the less sympathetic he became. Anger, jealousy and greed he understood and could rationalise, but this, almost motiveless crime where the victims were collateral damage to the clash between two warped personalities, simply left him cold.

'What about Jenny?' Lukula asked, as the other two fell silent.

'Her defence will try for a diminished responsibility plea, but CPS are amassing counter opinions,' Swift told her. 'Seems that having DID doesn't mean she is incapable of stopping herself from acting as she did. Cowan's traumatic early childhood may have caused her other personalities to emerge but she was also a person full of rage, a sociopath, and often knowingly acted unlawfully. Whatever is determined in the end she will be under lock and key for a very long time. A least she will be spared having regular sessions with Hassan, doing her best to *unravel the mind of a killer.*' Swift sucked in his breath not finding his own words particularly amusing, he added, though without enmity, 'What a sick fuck that woman is.'

'In a perverse way,' Merry philosophised, 'that makes Jackie our fourth victim.'

'How's that?' Lukula wanted to know. 'She's still alive isn't she?'

'But incarcerated for a crime she didn't commit,' Merry explained, 'I suspect that won't bother the likes of John and Leanne, nor the others, but for Jackie who is social and likes to go out it will be hell.'

The other two pondered this for a moment before Julie asked what was still uppermost on her mind, 'I suppose I will have to explain my relationship with Alima in court?'

'Prosecution will want to use it to show she had ample opportunity to confide what she knew to the police, in your case someone she should have been able to implicitly trust. In other words, that she wilfully hid the truth,' Swift smiled reassuringly knowing Julie would worry as no one wanted their private life paraded in court, certainly not as part of a murder trial. 'I wouldn't worry, it will be Doctor Hassan being painted as the villain in this and CPS have no worries that your relationship in any way undermined the case. Fortunately for Matthew it doesn't look as if his brief liaison with Hassan will be used by either side, doesn't reflect well for the defence or prosecution,' he explained with a sarcastic smile, enjoying Merry's discomfort at his words. 'It's the chief who's in the shit on this one.'

'The chief superintendent's personal recommendation allowed Hassan access to the case,' Merry pointed out, 'given the doctor was involved in the murders it doesn't look too good.'

'Not exactly a commendation of her judgement,' Swift turned to Lukula, 'but the worst thing is that, as a result, all her initiatives are on indefinite hold. Which means we are stuck with Matthew as part of the team for a while longer.'

'Well that's pretty crap,' Julie stated, with as straight a face as she could muster.

# ACKNOWLEDGEMENTS

I would like to thank all those people I have worked with in the past: the many dedicated police officers, mental health care and support workers, teachers and head teachers whose stories and the work they do with vulnerable youngsters and adults have inspired this novel. The work of those in the public sector may not get the recognition it deserves in terms of monetary reward, despite the occasional cynical praise from politicians or the see-sawing commentary of the media as the under-resourced services teeter from one headline to the next. However, for those individuals they help and support these services are usually the only lifeline available. I thank them for their collective service.

I would also like to thank my wife, Susan, for her comments and suggestions on reading the draft versions of this book.

# NOTE

I have used Dissociative Identity Disorder, DID, as a plot device within a fictional setting, the reaction portrayed of those encountering this mental health condition is more realistic of the real world than the depiction of the illness itself. Diagnosis of the condition and its causes is highly controversial. I have, therefore, trodden a cautious line in detailing its causes in the character of Jenny Cowan and the role her therapist has played in further twisting Jenny's personalities.

If you would like to discover more about DID, including its more controversial aspects, there are innumerable books to be found, both academic and autobiographical works. However, as somewhere to start my own recommendations would be:-

*The Dissociative Identity Disorder Sourcebook* by Deborah Bray Haddock
Publisher: McGraw-Hill Education (16 Sept. 2001). ISBN-10: 0737303948
*All Of Me: My incredible true story of how I learned to live with the many personalities sharing my body* by Kim Noble & Jeff Hudson
Publisher: Piatkus (6 Oct. 2011). ISBN-10: 0749955902
*Recovery is my best revenge: my experience of trauma, abuse and dissociative identity disorder* (Collected Essays Volumes

1 & 2) by Carolyn Spring

Publisher: Carolyn Spring Publishing (1 Mar. 2016).
ISBN-10: 0992961939
*Sybil Exposed: The Extraordinary Story Behind the Famous Multiple Personality Case* by Debbie Nathan
Publisher: Simon & Schuster Export (12 Jun. 2012).
ISBN-10: 1439168288

If you enjoyed this
book, why not try
*The Hanging Women*,
also by John Mead.